Lying in Vengeance

Gary Corbin

This book is a work of fiction. Names, characters, businesses, incidents, and dialogue are either drawn from the author's imagination or are used fictitiously, and are not to be construed as real. Any resemblance to actual events or persons, living or dead, is entirely coincidental.

DEDICATION

To my brothers and sisters:

*Diana, Patsy, Donna, Judy,
Bill, Dawn, Linda, and Alan.*

*No one could ask for a
better group of friends.*

CONTENTS

Part One: Trapped   1

Part Two: The Planning Dance   87

Part Three: Framed   176

Part Four: Revelations   233

Acknowledgements   275

About the Author   277

Also by Gary Corbin   279

Excerpt from *In Search of Valor*   284

Part One

Trapped

Chapter One

Peter Robertson bolted upright in his darkened bedroom, awakened by Santana blasting "Black Magic Woman" on scratchy, poorly-amplified speakers. Why, he wondered in his melatonin-aided stupor, would an aging seventies band break into his ninety-year-old Portland bungalow and wake him at this hour? And why on such awful sound equipment?

Something lit his bedside table with a flickering glare. His stupid cell phone. That meant bad news. He rolled across the queen-size mattress, found the phone, and held it to his ear. "Christine?" he said. It kept playing music. Dammit! He pushed the answer button, and the music stopped.

"Well, good morning, Sunshine," she said, all chipper and happy. She sounded like she'd been up for hours, probably drinking double espressos and scheduling Twitter messages to promote her various clients' brands. "Have you missed me?"

"Do you know what time it is?" He propped two pillows up against the headboard and sagged into them. Closing his eyes didn't help. He only imagined every detail of her pretty face in front of him, from the thin, black eyebrows and long lashes to her brilliant smile, bright red lipstick and perfect sun-bronzed skin. He opened his eyes again and stared into the blackness. A faint glow seeped in through the edges of blackout curtains covering the window across the room. Beautiful or not, he did not welcome this call from her, regardless of the hour.

"It's breakfast time in New York," she said. "Which means it's mid-morning for you. About nine-fifteen, right?"

"Try three-fifteen." Peter rubbed his temples with his free

hand. "You got the time change backwards."

"Oh, silly me," she said. "I'm sorry." She didn't sound the slightest bit sorry. He even thought he heard her laugh. Typical Christine. She loved making his life miserable, in so many ways. Like making sleep next to impossible. She managed that even without three a.m. phone calls.

"Well, now that you're up, let's get that dinner planned that we talked about—what was it, a month ago now?"

"Two months."

"You're so right. Time does fly when we're busy, doesn't it?"

Peter scowled and turned onto his side. Monday morning was earning its awful reputation. "Christine, what do you want?"

"I just told you. I want you to buy me dinner."

"I'll mail you a gift certificate to Arby's tomorrow. Good night."

"Don't you dare hang up on me!"

Peter's finger paused an inch above the end call button. Even with the phone held a foot in front of his face, he heard her throaty warning with perfect, chilling clarity. He sighed and returned the phone to his ear. "I'm still here."

"Good." Amazing how her voice could transform from dark and dangerous to soft and sexy without missing a beat. "I thought we could go back to Pazzo's, for old times' sake. Remember our first date there? You were so nervous."

"It wasn't a date. We had lunch. And it wasn't our first anything. We'd had lunch together before." He adjusted the pillows behind him. Suddenly he couldn't get comfortable.

"Yes, but at Pazzo's, you paid, like a gentleman, courting the object of his desire."

"I was not—" He stopped himself. To be honest, he had been courting her—at the time. And he had to admit, he'd enjoyed her company. Maybe he was judging her too quickly. Maybe she really did want to date him after all. "How about someplace new?"

After a beat, she countered, "A place we've never been…? Say, perhaps, *Florentino's?*"

His blood froze in his veins. He'd known, deep down, as

soon as he gave her the opening, she'd remind him of the restaurant where, eight months before, he'd followed Marcia, now his ex-wife, and her lover. That foolish decision triggered events that changed—ruined!—his whole life. The scene of, if not the crime per se, at least where it all had been set in motion. The fancy restaurant where the victim of the crime worked, a man named Alvin Dark—a man whom Peter had never met before that terrible night. The victim whom Peter had later mistaken for his wife's secret lover. The man he'd confronted, beaten, and—

"S'matter? Cat got your tongue?"

He shook himself out of the foul memory. "No. Not there. Not Florentino's." His hoarse voice took him aback, increasing the chill spreading across his naked body despite the summer heat. "I'm never going back there."

"Fine. I tell you what. Surprise me. I'll be back in town later this week. Pick me up at my office Thursday at six."

"Thursday I have plans."

Her voice grew hard. "Make new plans."

She hung up without saying goodbye.

***

Christine Nielsen hung up the phone and smiled. Peter's buttons were so easily pushed.

But then again, so were hers.

She took a bite of the scrambled eggs on her plate, all runny and pale. Another hotel chain that served watered-down eggs from a carton to save money on top of their ridiculously inflated prices. If Leicester-Howe, LLC ever turned the corner on profitability, she'd insist on better accommodations on these hellish trips. She'd also remember, tomorrow, to order her eggs over easy. Even a runny yolk beat the pants off this goo.

Her phone chimed, a pleasant tone, soft and melodic. Caller ID showed the name. She hit ignore. It rang again. She pressed ignore a second time, and a third, when the caller persisted. Even three thousand miles away, she didn't want her day ruined by the man who had, for three awful years, abused her, physically, mentally, and emotionally—and then continued to badger her ever since. She made a mental note to ask the tech guy how to block calls on this phone, issued to her only days before she jumped on the red-eye to JFK. He'd offered twice, and she'd declined, knowing that what he really wanted was an excuse to hang out in her office and stare at her legs. That would lead to an unwelcome invitation to drinks after work, which she'd declined a dozen times before. As odd and unattractive as she found him, however, it might be worth it to be rid of Kyle and his harassment.

She charged the breakfast to her room and exited the hotel into the already oppressive heat and humidity of Manhattan in July. She needed to walk about six blocks to her client's office—long, New York blocks, rather than Portland's tiny two hundred foot squares. She might just melt away to nothing...which she might have preferred over meeting with this group. Obnoxious, greedy financial advisers, they prided themselves on cheating small investors, going low-bid on out-of-town ad firms like hers, and paying consultants late, if at all. But the market had tightened up in recent months, and she needed the work.

Her phone chimed again, and the display said "Caller ID Blocked." Probably the clients, wondering why she wasn't twenty minutes early. She answered in her chipper Clients-Are-King voice. "This is Christine Nielsen."

"Hello, baby."

She hung up. That rotten scumbag Kyle had called from a different phone, probably realizing she'd ignored his earlier calls.

Forget the tech. She needed to meet with Peter Robertson, soon.

***

That bitch! How dare she hang up like that, without so much as a hello. Rude, as usual. Kyle had no idea what he'd ever seen in her.

He glanced at the photo on his dresser, the two of them together in Hawaii. She looked pretty damned good in that bikini. Even better when it came off.

Oh, yeah. That's what he'd seen in her.

He hit redial. Like, really hit redial, literally smashing the phone with his fist. But the call went straight to voicemail. Again. And again.

She'd pay for that. God damn her.

He rolled off his bed, an iron-framed California king, one they'd used many times when they'd done the dirty deed. Truly dirty, too, the way he liked it: ropes, blindfolds, hot wax—she'd always preferred things a little rough. Or so she said whenever he asked, until she walked out on him. Then she was all, "Oh, honey, you hurt me." What crap.

He pulled on a pair of chinos, foregoing the boxers lying on the floor. They probably still had the scent of that useless, sobbing blonde bimbo he'd thrown out at two a.m. Like it was his fault she didn't enjoy their roll in the hay. In his experience, a woman's pleasure had nothing to do with what filled the space between her legs and everything to do with what filled the space between her ears. And that one had nothing.

He flipped a comb through his own blond curls and made a mental note to get on Gillian's schedule for a trim. Maybe a little touch-up on the roots, too. They showed a little of that mousy dark brown color that came on in his early 20's. He despised it. So very un-California. He envied his idiot brother Earl in this regard, two years younger and as blond as Kate Upton. Even his chest hair. Which he let grow, like a twerp. Kyle rubbed his free hand over his smooth, muscular chest and added a spa visit to his to do list. He hated stubble, or any sort of body hair. If he had religion, that was probably it.

That, and avoiding Earl. He'd succeeded at that for the last seventeen years, ever since Kyle left the foster home where they'd spent their teenage years. Earl had left him a message a year after Kyle left to tell him that their foster parents had died penniless—exactly what Kyle had wanted him to believe. The trust fund he'd convinced them to set up, naming then eighteen-year-old Kyle the trustee, had conveniently disappeared before Earl could come of age and squander it, like every other good opportunity he'd had in life. By contrast, Kyle had known exactly how to use the money, investing it in his personal training business and some passive-income funds. Make the money work for you, he'd always told his brother. But Earl just wanted to party. Cruise chicks. Get by in life the easy way.

Deplorable.

Kyle trudged downstairs, brewed a cup of chai and sat on the deck of his two-story condo overlooking the dark northern California coastline. The majestic beauty of the ocean, the moonlit beach, the mountains in the distance to the north—on a normal day this view had the power to calm his agitated soul. But today his frustration lingered. She had a way of getting under his skin, even when she'd flown a continent away from him.

Which he knew, because he always knew exactly where she was, who she was with, and what she was doing.

Every moment.

Every day.

Chapter Two

Peter arrived at work five minutes late after a fitful night of bad sleep. He'd lie awake for what seemed like hours, then doze off just long enough to have nightmares about being chased down dark alleys by freakishly large, mean bruisers, all named Alvin Dark. By the time his six a.m. alarm rang, he felt like he'd run a marathon.

Bad traffic exacerbated his sluggish pace. By the time he pulled into the employee parking lot adjacent to Stark's Lumber and Building Supply, he was ready to head straight back to bed.

Once he walked in the building's wide, swinging glass doors and saw who was sitting with Jessica, the firm's boisterous office manager, he wished he'd done exactly that.

"Petcy!" Jess waved an arm above her bright red hair, teased high in a retro '80s style she insisted was all the rage among the young set. She had a bad habit of believing whatever her fourteen-year-old daughter told her, no matter how outrageous. "Come in here!" she said. "Look who the cat dragged in!"

Peter forced a smile and waved back, pantomimed sipping from a mug, and headed to the coffee maker in Stark's cramped, windowless break room. He downed a cup of black crud in two swallows, then mixed gobs of cream and sugar into a refill of his UC Davis mug, stirring with no apparent haste. His brain churned. What was *he* doing in there?

"Dude! You trying to avoid me? Hey, mix me a cup of that too, would ya?" Frankie Kowalczyk, who moments before had been ogling Jessica's ample cleavage, limped in with the aid of a cane and slapped him on the back. "Man, I miss this place!"

"Frankie, what the hell are you doing here?" Peter grabbed a spare mug from the shelf and poured strong black coffee for his lifelong best friend. "I thought your severance agreement prohibited—"

"Yeah, screw that. That agreement ain't worth the paper it's printed on." Frankie took the cup Peter offered him and raised it in a toast. "In fact, I'm here to apply for a job."

"A job? Are you nuts? After your history here? I'm surprised you didn't get tossed straight out the door. And, what job? We don't have any full-time openings."

Frankie grinned and leaned his heavy, six foot two frame against the door jamb. He set down the cane, which he'd needed since recovering from drunkenly plowing his car into a guardrail a few months before. "My old job. Loading supervisor. Working for you again, buddy. Wouldn't that be awesome?"

Peter frowned and ran one hand through his thinning scalp of brown hair. "Putting aside the fact that I couldn't hire you back, even if I wanted, that job isn't available."

"A little birdie told me that it would be real soon." Frankie sipped from his mug and made a face. "Ugh. Did you guys let Gregg make the coffee again?"

"What little birdie? And why hasn't anyone told me? José—"

"Is quitting. Ask Jess."

"Jess told you? I don't believe it."

Frankie smirked. "I ain't saying who told me. I'm just saying, ask her."

"A birdie, huh? Sounds more like a magpie to me." He frowned into his coffee.

A diminutive, curvy brunette poked her head in the door and, after a furtive glance at Frankie, locked eyes with Peter. Donna, whose sexual harassment complaint against Frankie led to his resignation in May, scurried back out of the room, but not before her face betrayed a rash of guilt and shame.

"I think I found your magpie," Peter said. "You seeing her again? After all you two have been through?"

"Who?" Frankie looked over his shoulder. "I ain't talked to Don—er, anyone here in two months."

"Uh huh. Then why does Donna look like she wants to tear

your pants off with her teeth and eat you whole?" He grinned. With Frankie's boyish good looks and athletic build, he'd always enjoyed considerable success with women. With his roguish, playboy style, he'd also succeeded at staying single.

Frankie failed to suppress a guilty smile. "Was Donna just here? I need to say hi to her."

"Don't pull that crap. I've known you for twenty years. I know when you're lying, particularly about a woman. I take it she's no longer complaining about harassment."

Frankie shrugged. "She still insists I was out of line last spring. But, yeah, you could say things are better."

"Maybe because you're not her boss anymore." Peter stirred more sugar into his coffee. Gregg's worst pot ever. "Still, I don't believe it. Either thing—her, or José. Why didn't I hear it from him directly?"

As if on cue, José Nolasco, Stark's interim loading dock supervisor since Frankie's dismissal in May, appeared behind Frankie in the doorway. His neatly trimmed black hair and mustache, crisply-pressed shirt and tie, and shiny new shoes gave the impression of an office worker rather than a lumberyard supervisor. The nervous twitching of his lip and hands reinforced the impression of a man about to quit his job. Or one who already had, but hadn't told his immediate supervisor.

"Peter, can I see you in your office, please?" José asked.

Frankie's eyes widened. "I gotta go. Later, pal. Beers after work? I'm off the pain meds, so I can drink again." His lazy smile returned, and he picked up his cane.

Peter gave him a thumbs-up and followed José out of the break room. A white envelope protruded from José's back pocket. José held his head down as he walked, making his stout five foot eight inch frame seem even shorter and stockier. Five inches taller, Peter could see Jess in her office over José's head. She winced, then shrugged. Gregg, Stark's General Manager, stood beside her, his dark brown face wearing a deep scowl.

Everybody knew about José's leaving before Peter.

Peter closed the door to his office behind José and didn't wait to sit before jumping right in. "So, I hear you're leaving us.

Why?"

"I took another job," José said, his words coming rapid-fire. "A big promotion. With three kids now, I need more money."

Peter navigated the narrow space between his desk and a wall lined with crowded bookshelves, overflowing file cabinets, and stacks of product samples. He sat in his desk chair, flicked on his desktop computer, and swiveled toward José. "Is your mind made up, or can I counter their offer?"

José shook his head. "I doubt it. It's a big promotion, and I'll make almost twice what you're paying me." He sat up straight, and Peter swore he puffed out his chest.

"Okay, then." Peter sighed. "Well, good for you, and for them. They just stole a great employee. Who is it, anyhow?"

José looked away, saying nothing.

Peter's heart sank. "Not Home Depot?" José nodded, and stared at his feet. "Aw, man." A few moments of awkward silence passed. Peter sighed. "Well, what's done is done. Congratulations. When do you start?"

"Tomorrow."

"Seriously? What happened to two weeks' notice?"

José shrugged. "I'm sorry." Head down, he shuffled out of Peter's office and headed straight to Jessica's. Before the door closed, Gregg pushed it wide again and stepped inside. A cigarette, as always, lay perched atop one ear, and his black-framed glasses rested on the tip of his wide nose. "Got a minute?" He closed the office door and leaned back against it.

Peter's mood lightened. "My minutes are your minutes, Boss. Whatcha got?"

Gregg's expression grew grim. "Two things. First, we had another attempted break-in last night."

"Holy smokes. That's what, three times in three months?"

"Two months. Less. Luckily this time they didn't make off with anything, so far as I can tell. But we've got a busted window and a mountain of insurance paperwork to file."

"We?"

Gregg smiled. "Would I be bringing this up if I didn't need your help? Come on, Pete. You're good at this stuff. Help me out here."

"I would, but with José leaving…dammit. I wish he'd given us some sort of warning." Peter swigged his coffee and sat at his desk. "Losing a key guy like this during our busiest time…crap. I don't know what I'm going to do."

"I do," Gregg said. "You're going to work a ton of overtime."

"I guess I could promote someone on the crew, temporarily, and backfill—"

"Nope. Nothing doing." Gregg grabbed the cigarette off his ear and rolled it between his fingers, telegraphing that he had something on his mind. "I'm getting a lot of heat from upstairs about our hiring practices lately. Everything by the book. No quick-fills and asking forgiveness later. And…" He rolled the cigarette between the fingers of his other hand. "We gotta go with a diversity hire."

"We always try to consider that. You know it as well as I do. Hell, that was one reason I picked José."

"No, man. 'Consider' isn't good enough. If we don't hire someone with darker complexion than you, you'll be doing three times as much paperwork. And I mean *you*."

"I have no problem with that. But the full-on hiring process—that's gonna kill me. I'll be lucky to get somebody on before October." Peter finished his coffee. The cigarette continued to spin between Gregg's fingers. "But you're not done, are you?"

Gregg grimaced. "They're being very specific. I fill the African-American quota." He spat in disgust into Peter's recycling bin. "With José gone, we have zero Latinos in management slots. I'm counting on you to fix that. And not just someone with an Hispanic last name. We need someone who can speak Spanish. Preferably female. A disabled veteran would be a home run."

"Any other requirements?" Peter threw his hands into the air. "Parolees? Retired, piano-playing, left-handed Red Sox fans?"

Gregg grinned. "If you can do that, we'd fill all of our quotas for a year. Come on, Pete. You're my best manager in the store. Help me out here. Our government supply contracts are at risk if we don't show some progress on this. Now, get going on it. Oh, wait… we also have a half-dozen supply trucks rolling in this morning. With José gone—"

"I'd better get out there. I know, I know. Good thing I'm divorced now. Nobody's gonna get upset about me coming home late anymore."

Gregg winced. "I wish I could do something."

"You could. Go to bat for me with management. At least let me hire a temp or two. I promise, they'll all have brown skin and speak with a Mexican accent."

Gregg shook his head. "Like I said. I wish there was something I could do."

Peter frowned at his desk. When he looked up again, Gregg was gone.

Chapter Three

Peter worked past ten p.m. the next two nights, but managed to escape at a reasonable hour on Wednesday evening, despite the stack of unfinished paperwork—what should have been José's—awaiting completion on his desk. He justified leaving at 6:30 on two counts: one, that he was exhausted, and two, it was his regular night for visiting his ailing mother at Sunset Hospice and Convalescent Care Center. Having suffered a pair of strokes over the past year, she needed his attention even more than his suppliers, boss, and customers did. On this responsibility, above all others, he never reneged.

He wolfed down a couple of Snickers bars on the way, an upgrade over the dinners of microwaved buttered popcorn from the past two nights. So much for his recent resolution to eat better. Speaking of reneging on commitments, he also couldn't remember the last time he'd hit the gym. Two weeks, at least. He dared not hit the scale. Not if he wanted to pretend he still weighed less than two hundred. He loosened his belt another notch as he walked toward Sunset's welcoming front doors from the parking lot. There were no more notches left. Something had to change.

"Petey!" Thelma Robertson, sixty-five years young, remained glued to the TV when Peter entered her room minutes later. As usual, she had already changed into her pink silk pajamas, even though it was barely seven o'clock. Her bright smile shone as white as her hair, which she'd had done since he saw her on Sunday afternoon. He kissed the pale, wrinkled skin of her forehead and sat next to her bed, which she'd navigated into an upright, TV-watching position. Whatever other skills and memory she'd lost in recent years, she retained her mastery of her electric-powered hospital bed.

"I hope I haven't missed Jeopardy," he said with a smile. The smile was genuine, although his interest in her TV show was not. The fact that she'd called him by his own name, rather than his father's, brother's, or, as happened more than once, his sister's, gave him hope for a real conversation this time, an all-too-rare occurrence of late.

"It's just coming on," she said. "It's celebrity week. George Clooney is supposed to be on."

He cocked his head. "Really? I wonder if he's any good."

"He's super smart," she said. "You saw how he outsmarted those bad guys in that movie on Sunday."

Peter shook his head. "What movie? Oh, you mean Die Hard? That was Bruce Willis, I think."

"Don't be ridiculous. I know who George Clooney is, and he's going to be on Jeopardy tonight." She sniffed and picked up the TV remote, surfing channels rapid-fire.

"Okay, Mom. Whatever you say." He sighed. She'd skipped right past the station for her show and kept on going right through the sports channels, kids shows, and premium movies before cycling back to Channel Two again. When the Mariners game re-appeared on the screen, he reached for the remote.

"Get your hands off!" She slapped his hands away and held the remote on the far side of the bed. "I can do it."

He took a deep breath. "I know you can, but you've been through all the channels twice. Isn't it on Channel Twelve?"

"Of course not. Don't be stupid. It's never been on Channel Twelve." She surfed on, through young adult sitcoms with canned laughter and action movies replete with explosives and crashing cars. "You must think I'm stupid."

"No, I don't. I just...well, maybe they were on a commercial break. Let's check the guide." He indicated a plastic stand by her bed holding a laminated listing of channels. She glared at him and knocked the stand to the floor.

"You do think I'm stupid," she said under her breath. Sort of. "You're the one who's stupid." White foam dribbled from her lip. Peter picked up the channel listing and set it on the bedside table again, next to a framed photo of her with his father on vacation in Mexico. A smattering of other family photos and department store watercolors dotted the cream-colored walls of the ten-by-fifteen foot room. Tall windows filled most of the exterior wall, but she'd drawn the floor-length ivory curtains, as always, to reduce the glare on the TV.

Thelma continued to cycle through the channels until, finally, the familiar grid of topics and dollar values appeared on screen. A moment later, the screen displayed the night's three contestants—two women and a handsome, forty-something man with brown hair and bright blue eyes. The name scribbled on the stand in front of him read "Lester."

"You see?" she said. "George Clooney. So there, Mr. Smartypants." She smiled smugly and pressed the controls to adjust her bed.

Peter sank into his chair. So much for meaningful conversation.

***

Thursday evening he again left work at what was fast becoming "early," in Gregg's mind—in other words, well before dark. In fact, it was the middle of rush hour. After covering less than three miles in almost twenty-five minutes, he pulled his silver Ford Ranger pickup into the empty parking spot in front of Christine's office in Portland's trendy Pearl District. He ignored the "Loading Zone—No Parking" sign with its accompanying arrow pointed in his direction. He'd only be a minute, and he kept the motor running, anyway. He speed-dialed Christine, but his call went straight to voice-mail.

"Christine, Peter. It's five, no, make it four minutes before six. I'm parked out front. I hope you're hungry." He wished his own appetite would make an appearance. All day he'd fretted about his date with Christine, alternating between romantic fantasies filled with laughter and lustful passion…and paranoid visions of her holding a gun to his head. By lunchtime his stomach had tied itself in so many knots that the thought of food nauseated him. He worked straight through at his desk.

Besides, he had no time for food during the day anymore. He barely had time for coffee.

Someone tapped on his passenger side window. A fit, grey-haired man held a clipboard and some sort of electronic gadget in front of his chest. A chrome-plated badge, pinned to his light blue shirt, read "Parking Enforcement." Crap! He turned down the air conditioner, then lowered the curb-side window. "I'll be just a min—"

"This is a loading zone." The parking deputy pointed to the red-lettered sign. "No parking. Move along."

"I'm just picking someone—"

"Not here, you're not. Come on, clear the space." The deputy gestured with his device, ready to write the ticket.

"Please. Cut me a little slack, would you? I just need to–"

"You want a ticket, or are you going to move?"

"Oh, for God's sake." Peter exhaled with gale force onto the steering wheel. He shifted into reverse, checked his mirror, and was about to ease out of the spot when he heard a familiar female voice.

"Is there a problem, Officer?"

Christine appeared over the parking deputy's shoulder. The deputy turned toward her, and she grinned. "Adam! You nutty, handsome rascal. What are you doing here?" She threw both arms around his neck and smooched his forehead. "It's been ages. Have you met my driver for the night? Peter, this is my good friend and former neighbor, Adam." She released the deputy and opened the passenger door to the pickup. "Peter, darling. Was this big bad policeman giving you a hard time?" She laughed and pinched Adam's cheek like Peter's grandmother used to do to him.

"Hey, Christine," Adam said in an unsure tone of voice. "Long time."

"I know. You really need to call me. Isn't it your turn to cook me dinner?"

Adam stepped back, blushing, and Christine climbed into the truck. She tossed her purse and gym bag into the back of the truck's cab, winked at Peter, then smiled back at Adam.

"It seems it's always my turn," Adam said.

"And don't you forget it," Christine said. "Well, gotta run! Call me, okay, Sweetie?" She closed the door and rolled up the window. "All right, let's move it. I just ran three miles and I'm starved. Where are you taking me?"

Peter shook his head and grinned. "Somewhere that he won't come looking for me. That guy sure wanted to use me to fill his quota. You know everybody, don't you?"

"I try. Oh, and before I forget." She leaned across the narrow gap between them and kissed Peter on the cheek. A faint scent of honeysuckle wafted in with her—heavenly. "There, now. I wouldn't want you getting all jealous." She made a pouty face, then laughed and buckled her seat belt.

"How about that Pan-Asian place near the Park Blocks?" Peter eased the truck into traffic.

"I was hoping for something a little more private." Her long red fingernails traced the V-cut neckline of her bright yellow blouse. A short black skirt that landed well above the knee and a pair of black three-inch heels completed her ensemble. She wore no hose, but Peter, wearing khakis and a light blue short-sleeve button down shirt, felt underdressed.

"Like what?" he asked.

"There's a nice Italian place in John's Landing. Alessandro's, I think it's called." Her eyes narrowed to slits and her lips seemed to double in size. "It's very private."

"I know the place." He'd taken Marcia there once, for their fourth anniversary. She hadn't liked it as much as he did.

"You don't approve?"

"No, it's fine. I just…" Her hand crept up his thigh. He glanced down. Cleared his throat, took a deep breath, and let it shudder out of him.

She smiled, her face full of mischief. "Oh, sorry… is this bothering you?"

"It's, uh, kind of distracting." So was the amount of cleavage suddenly visible to his right. Warm pressure rose in his groin. He shifted in his seat to loosen things up. In response, she slid her hand up his leg to within an inch of his crotch and squeezed.

"Very distracting," he said.

"Too distracting?" She squeezed again.

"Uh, n-no, I g-guess not." He turned up the air conditioner. Sweat collected on his scalp just the same.

She smiled. "Oh, goodie." Her hand closed the gap, arriving at his zipper and holding. Literally, holding. He swerved, just missing a parked car.

"Maybe a little too—"

She unbuckled her seat belt, bent over, and kissed the hardness between his legs, right through the slacks. He moaned, nearly closed his eyes—not good. He slowed and pulled over. Leaving the engine running, he shifted into park and lifted her head off his lap.

"What the hell are you doing?" he asked.

She made a pouty face and slid her body toward him. The scent of her cologne filled his senses. She moved his hand to her own leg. "Peter," she said, "don't tell me you've been single so long that you've forgotten what a woman's advances look like." She smiled and ran her tongue across her perfect white teeth.

"No, I haven't forgotten. But this is all kind of sudden. Until a few days ago, I hadn't seen or heard from you in over two months. Now you can't wait sixty seconds to jump my bones. What gives?"

"You, I hope." She laughed and moved his hand up her leg, under her skirt, and kissed him full on the lips. His head swam. He'd dreamed of a moment like this, months ago, and again that afternoon. Like, all afternoon. But in his fantasy, he'd envisioned a more romantic setting.

He leaned away from her, against the driver's side door, and broke off the kiss. She pulled him back, laughing, and he pressed his hands against her shoulders. "Stop a second," he said.

"What's the matter?" Pouty again.

"I just...I don't get it. Why, after two months of radio silence, are you suddenly so hot for me?" He took a deep breath as she moved his hand further up her leg. "And don't tell me it's because I'm so incredibly good looking. And I'm not rich, so..."

"But Peter. You're wonderful. And very handsome. Don't

sell yourself short." She leaned closer and whispered into his ear. "And I've missed you so much these past few months." Her tongue flicked his ear, followed by a quick gentle grab of the lobe with her teeth. "Maybe we should just skip dinner and tend to our other appetites." Her lips moved down his neck, and her hand rubbed his chest. "Mmm. So strong. So muscular."

Peter chuckled. "That's something I haven't heard in a long time. You sure you're talking to me, and not your ex? What's his name? Kyle?"

She jerked away from him and crossed her arms over her chest. "Don't mention that name."

Peter's smile faded. "Sorry. It was just a joke."

"Nothing about that man is funny." She glared out the passenger side window.

"I know. Again, I'm sorry." He took her hand in his. "Has he been bugging you?"

She shrugged. "His very existence bothers me. But, yes. He called me the other day, shortly after you and I spoke."

"What did he say?"

"I didn't give him the chance to say anything. He's left me messages that…well, they sound innocent to the uninitiated. But I know what he means, and what he wants."

Peter waited for her to elaborate. When she didn't, and not knowing what to say, he coughed and pulled his truck back into traffic.

"Aren't you going to ask me?" Christine said.

"Uh, no. I can pretty much guess, based on what you've told me." He signaled and turned west on Burnside Street.

She stared at him for a long moment, then shook her head. "Okay. You're so smart. What does he want?"

Peter shrugged. "What any guy in his right mind would want. He wants to get back together with you."

"He wants to kill me!" She slammed an open palm onto his thigh and squeezed hard, digging in with her fingernails.

Peter winced. "Hey, ease up a bit, will ya? I'm still attached to that leg." She loosened her grip, but kept her hand on his thigh. He tried to ignore how close her little finger was to his testicles. "Aren't you being a little bit melodramatic?"

"No, I am not." She let go of his leg and stared out the passenger side window again. "He's made threats, and he's hit me a few times. I know what he's capable of."

"Wait. He hit you?"

"That's what I said, isn't it?"

"Why haven't you told me this before?"

"Before, I didn't know you as well. I didn't know if I could trust you with that information." She faced him again and leaned toward him again, in cleavage-display mode, her seat belt still unbuckled. "Before, I didn't... need you." Her hand returned to his leg, this time gently, and began traveling northbound. He stopped her by clamping his hand onto hers.

"You're making it very hard to drive."

She grinned wickedly. "I'm trying to make it hard."

"Yeah, you're succeeding at that, too." He stopped the truck a full car length behind a Volvo, waiting for traffic. She slid over next to him again, sliding an arm around his shoulders. She whispered, "I think we should start with dessert." She kissed his neck, and slid her free hand across his chest. He pulled her close, breathed in the honeysuckle scent, pressed his lips to hers—

Peter's eyes flew open—when had he closed them?—and he realized the truck was rolling. Just in time, he stepped on the brake, his truck's front bumper inches away from the Volvo. He still wasn't hungry—not for food, anyway, and for a different reason than at lunchtime. He held the steering wheel with rigid arms, breathing hard. "Whatever you want to do, Christine."

"Your place?"

"My place it is." His pulse quickened. He mentally inventoried the state of his house. While no neat freak, he usually kept the place in pretty good shape, by a guy's standards. He'd given the place a thorough cleaning the prior weekend after hosting a friendly poker game with the boys from work. A few coffee cups in the sink, perhaps, but he hadn't left anything embarrassing hanging around. No dirty underwear on the floor or anything.

Not yet, anyway.

"On second thought, I am a little bit hungry," she said. "Do you have any food at all at home?"

He thought a moment. "I have a pretty well-stocked pantry at the moment. We can figure something out when we get there." He managed to turn off the slow-moving shopping street and headed toward home.

"Really? So you're going to cook for me?"

"In more ways than one." He grinned, and she laughed. "I love to cook," he went on. "I'm pretty good at it, too. If I had to do it all over again, I'd be a chef."

"Really?" She smirked, an evil expression. "Of all the things in your life you'd do over, that's what you'd choose?"

Peter's throat tightened, and sweat flowed from every pore. Why did this woman have to inject double meanings into every word she spoke?

"I mean, after all," she continued, "I can think of a few things you might want a do-over on, just in the past eight months."

His heart pounded. "What do you mean?"

"Peter, don't treat me like a fool." Her voice grew sharp, and her eyes flared. "Think of what happened eight months ago. Say, oh, I don't know, pick a date. November 17. Anything in particular come to mind? Anything…traumatic?"

His breathing grew short and difficult. He gripped the steering wheel in both hands and hit the brake too hard to stop at a red light. "Way too many things come to mind."

"Yes. Well. I should think you could prioritize just a bit."

He shrugged, not looking at her.

"For starters," she went on, "your wife left you that night, if I recall."

He nodded. "I'm surprised you remember that detail." A lie. He'd feared she'd always remember it. Which, apparently, she did.

"And why did she leave?"

He coughed, tried to swallow, but his throat was too dry. "She hooked up with a new guy."

"David Simmons was his name, if I recall."

"You recall a lot." Too much. Disturbingly so. Better than

his memory of his own life.

"Yes, I do." She shifted in her seat. He stole a quick glance at her. Arms crossed, lips set in a line, determined. "Shall I tell you what else I recall?"

He shrugged, a miserable attempt at nonchalance. He eased up on the brake, accelerated through the intersection, and joined a long line of cars trudging their way through the Pearl District.

"I'll take that as a yes," she said. "I recall you stalked her that night."

"Followed her, to prove she was cheating on me."

"Then stalked her boyfriend—"

"Tried to follow them to their rendezvous point—"

"Yes, tried. And instead, followed the wrong man."

His blood froze. He'd never told her that part. How had she pieced it together?

"Then you deliberately crashed your car into his—"

"Not true!"

"Then beat the living crap out of him with a tire iron."

"You don't know that!"

"I do know that!" She stared at him, triumphant. "I know it like you know it. Deep in my bones. Right, Peter? Does it bother you at all that you killed a man? Practically with your bare hands? The wrong man—"

"Shut up!" He pointed a finger an inch from her face. "Shut the hell up, right now!"

A horn blared, and car tires screeched around him. He'd run a stop sign and nearly gotten T-boned by a Prius. He gunned it to escape the intersection before anyone else got a similar idea.

Christine laughed. "I see you still have the killer instinct."

"I said shut up!"

She laughed louder. "That's not a bad thing. On the contrary." She leaned toward him again, lips pursed as if to kiss him. "I find it very sexy."

"I don't know what you're talking about."

"Oh, cut the crap." Her sexy pout disappeared. "We both know you did it. Luckily, Raul Vasquez didn't go to prison for it. That poor man! But, neither did you. It doesn't quite seem that justice was served, but that's fixable. Let's see, what would be a suitable consequence for you?"

"You don't know what you're talking about. You're—you're crazy." His voice betrayed his lack of confidence.

"Don't I? Well, let's find out then, shall we?" She whipped out her cell phone and tapped it a few times. Not enough to dial a full phone number. One of the taps turned on the speaker, because Peter could hear the sound of a phone ringing on the other end.

"Who are you calling?"

A voice on the other end answered the question for him. "Portland Police Bureau. How may I direct your call?"

Chapter Four

Christine's eyes narrowed and she kept her focus on Peter as she spoke into the phone. "I have information relating to a crime that occurred several months ago that I'd like to report." Peter started to protest, but she shushed him and pointed to the phone.

"Yes, ma'am. What was the incident you'd like to report on?"

Peter reached out to grab the phone, but she yanked it away in time. He pulled over into a mini-mall parking lot.

"It was a homicide case," she said. "The victim was a Mr. Alvin Dark."

"Thank you," the dispatcher said, "please hold." A pre-recorded public service announcement about pedestrian safety replaced the dispatcher's voice.

"Hang up!" Peter reached for her phone. "You have no idea what you're getting into here."

She moved the phone to her opposite ear, evading his grab. "I know exactly what I'm getting into," she said, ice in her voice. "Do you?"

He fretted, drumming open-handed on the steering wheel. "Just what do you think you're going to tell them? What evidence do you have that I had anything to do with that...incident?"

"Listen and learn," she said.

The recording changed. "Your call is very important to us. Please continue to hold."

"You've got nothing," he said.

"Do you really want to risk that?" she said. "All I really need to do is give them your name. Their investigators will take care of the rest."

He sweated another moment. The recording stopped, replaced by a woman's voice. "Cold cases, Homicide. How can I help you?"

"All right!" Peter said, his voice hoarse. "You win. I'll…I'll help you."

"Excuse me?" said the policewoman on the phone.

"Promise?" Christine asked.

He nodded, a slow bob of his aching head. "I promise."

"Sorry, wrong number," Christine said into the phone, and turned it off.

Peter took several deep breaths and stared out the driver's side window. When he felt calm enough to speak, he turned toward her. "That was pretty screwed up."

"More screwed up than what you did last November?" She put on an innocent face.

He opened his mouth to speak, but no words came. He looked away again.

"Peter, listen. This doesn't have to be a bad—" Her phone buzzed. She smiled, a mischievous grin. "The police, calling back. Should I pick up?"

"Are you going to turn yourself in for blackmailing me?"

She laughed. "Good one." She brought the phone to her ear. "Hello? No, I'm sorry. That was my niece, playing a prank on me. She will never do it again, will you, Honey…? Thank you, Officer." She hung up. "At least, we can hope that my naughty, naughty niece never gets hold of my phone again. Can't we, Peter?" She laughed again.

Peter scowled. "I'm more concerned about her naughty, naughty aunt."

She lay a hand on his thigh again. "Oh, you have no idea how naughty Aunt Christine can be. But I hope you will." Her fingertips danced on his leg. "Soon."

He pushed her hand away, but she folded it into his, and he let her. Dammit. It felt good. "Yeah, I have a pretty good idea."

"Really? I'd love to hear your ideas." Her fingertips danced on his thigh again. He grabbed her hand and smothered it in his again.

"What do you want from me, Christine?"

She smiled sweetly and caressed his face with her free hand. "How about we discuss it over a nice bottle of pinot noir? I recall you saying once that you have a nice stash in your basement."

He shook his head, moving his face away from her hand. "I don't think that's a good idea."

Her eyes narrowed, then relaxed. She drew his hand close to her body, peeled open his fingers, and pressed his palm against her breast. Despite his apprehension, his body reacted. She thrust her other hand between his legs and squeezed. He moaned, closed his eyes. "Don't."

She pressed closer, moved his hand inside her blouse. "How long has it been for you, Peter, since you've been with a woman? Weeks? Months? A year?"

He fought the urge to even consider her question, but his mind betrayed him. Marcia had left him in mid-November. They hadn't been intimate for a good two or three months before that. It had been too long. But—

"And how long since you've been with a woman like me?" Her hand slipped inside his suddenly unzipped slacks. He sucked in a deep breath, then felt her lips cover his. He put up no resistance. Her tongue danced inside his mouth.

How long had it been?

Never. He'd never been with a woman like Christine.

He wrapped his arms around her and pulled her close.

Chapter Five

Christine sat against a stack of pillows piled up against the headboard of Peter's queen-sized bed. A sheet covered her to the waist. One of Peter's UC Davis T-shirts covered the rest. She didn't really need it in the heat, particularly since Peter's ancient bungalow didn't have air conditioning, but if he woke up with naked boobs staring him in the face, he'd probably get all horny again. And if that happened, she'd have to play along, or risk raising his suspicions anew.

Not that having sex with him a second time would be a bad thing. She'd gone almost as long as he had without it. He had turned out to be a fairly passionate and attentive lover, considerate of her needs, without going all beast mode like Kyle used to do. And, bless him, he'd satisfied her. That was a pleasant surprise.

But she had to remain focused on her goal, and that meant not letting emotions get in the way. It would require taking great care to keep her messages consistent, and to keep him believing that she'd fallen for him—without actually succumbing to the urge. At least not until she accomplished her objective. After that, she'd make new plans—for him, and for her.

She rubbed the tension out of her neck, closed her eyes, and ran down the list of her recent and next moves. She'd accomplished what she'd intended, for the time being. Much more to do, and soon, but first she needed to sleep. More important, she needed him to sleep.

His breathing got heavier next to her. "Please, God, don't snore," she whispered. She'd never sleep if he started that. Kyle had been a bad snorer, loud and obnoxious, like the rest of him.

And, true to form, when she asked him to roll over that one time, he blamed her ("Don't let me drink so much!") and threatened to kick her out of the house—her own house!—if she woke him again.

But if that had been his worst side, she may never have left him. Instead, being a boorish, inconsiderate rube probably ranked among his most likeable traits. Mean, violent, selfish, and vain, on a good day he left her feeling worthless and humiliated. He criticized her every move, made fun of her to their friends, and ignored her when she needed him most. And on the bad days, he made her wish for the simple mistreatment of those "good" days. On bad days, he frightened her with threats, controlling behavior, angry outbursts, unreasonable demands, constant suspicion, and jealousy.

And then there were the really bad days. Days when it didn't stop at threats. Days when he lost control. When makeup couldn't hide the bruises, and it hurt to even try.

Peter stirred next to her and reached one arm across her legs. "Time is it?" he said, barely a murmur.

"Shh." She caressed his shoulder with two fingertips. "Go back to sleep. It's the middle of the night."

He snuggled closer to her, pressing her legs against his side. She held her breath and counted to ten. She loathed snuggling, particularly after first-time sex. It implied an emotional closeness she didn't share, and felt controlling. Dominating. Suffocating. *You are mine,* it said, when she most definitely was not. Not his, not anyone's. Not yet.

But. The Objective.

She drew her legs in, bending the knees, hoping to nudge his head off of her so she could slide away a few inches. Instead, his arm slid toward her waist, and his hand flopped against her breast. She wondered if she'd woken him, and if he was feigning sleep to cop a quick feel. But his hand flopped away, and she chastised herself for being overly distrustful.

"I'm glad you're here," he said out of the blue. Plain as day, no mumbling about it. Dammit, he was awake. So much for good, decent men.

She regretted that thought as soon as it came to her. Peter was a good, decent man. He didn't take advantage of women, or overpower them, or use them like property. He treated people with respect—men and women. Stood by his friends. Cared for his aging, ailing mom.

Yet, he had killed a man. Of that she was certain. They'd served on a jury together, the Alvin Dark murder trial, and he had too many connections to the case. Personal connections. Like, his wife's actual lover testifying as a witness. Peter knew the area of the crime scene so well. Drove a virtual copy of the defendant's vehicle, and knew things only the killer would know. He'd had a motive to kill—not the actual victim, perhaps, but another man who somehow gave him the slip, setting up Alvin Dark as the unfortunate casualty.

Yes, he was a good, decent, loyal man—and a killer. That's what made him so perfect.

"Of course I'm still here," she said. "I wouldn't leave without telling you." Unlike Kyle, who once left her stranded in a motel in rural Arizona.

"You're wonderful," he said. "So good…" His breathing became regular and heavy again. She lay still, hoping—

"I can't sleep," he said, sitting up. "You?"

"I'm okay," she said. "Do you want me to get you something to help you sleep?"

"No, no." He lay an arm around her shoulder and nudged closer again. Outside, a dog barked, then quieted. "Gypsy," he said. "Always barking."

"The bitch." She waited a moment and Peter rewarded her with a tired chuckle.

He ran his fingers through the hair behind her ear. The pace of their breathing fell into sync, the deep inhalations of tired people late at night. He turned his face toward her, and she responded in kind. Their lips stayed an inch apart for several moments. She wondered if he was waiting for her. She brushed her lips against his, and he pressed his onto hers, a sweet, gentle kiss. The kiss of new lovers.

Blah.

"We need to talk," she said. "If you're awake enough."

He sat up in bed next to her and flicked on the bedside lamp. The bulb cast a dim light onto the curtains and dark shadows on the bed between them. "Is this the Are-we-in-a-relationship-or-is-this-just-physical discussion? Already?" He smiled, but a heavy weight of seriousness underlay his tone.

"Not unless you want it to be. I mean, I'm a one-man-woman type of girl, if that's what you're getting at." With no other prospects, except a violent stalker. She kissed him again.

"Me too. I mean—you know what I mean."

She nodded. "I figured as much. And Peter, you know how I adore you." She nibbled on his ear, nipped at his lobe with her teeth.

He squeezed her shoulder. "So, what do we need to discuss?"

She pulled away so she could see his face. "You know about my situation with Kyle."

Peter nodded. "Has he threatened you?" He shifted in the bed so he could face her.

"Indirectly. He's never overt—not when he thinks he's being watched, or if there's the potential of being traced or recorded. On my cell phone, he'd have to believe that's possible."

"I thought you'd gotten a restraining order."

She scoffed. "Like he cares. He'd love it if I tried to bring him to court. Anything to put us in the same city, much less the same room."

Peter sighed. "What a creep."

"He's beyond creepy. He's sadistic. He knows how this affects me—scares me. Intimidates me." She leaned against him, arms around his back, holding him close. "It's working, too."

"Is that what's keeping you awake?"

She nodded, and traced a finger through the sparse patch of hair on his chest.

"There's got to be something you can do," he said. "The police—"

"Are useless," she said. "No, I need a more direct approach. Something more permanent." She looked into his eyes. "I need you to do something for me."

***

Across the street, a black Ford GT500 coupe occupied the space along the curb in front of a 1920s English Tudor. In the driver's seat sat a man with brown, shaggy hair that hung about an inch above his collar. Sweat slicked the stubble on his face, still scarred from a horrible bout of teenage acne. The extra fifteen pounds he carried exacerbated his sweating problem, but he'd become far too attached to beer, pizza and nachos to do much about it. Like working out, for example, which his boss did to obsession. Like everything he did, really.

Some sort of cattle dog barked in the house next to the bungalow he'd been watching. Not from in the bungalow itself, but even neighbor dogs could be a nuisance. Somebody yelled at the dog to shut up. Like that would help. Sure enough, the dog kept barking.

The man lowered his binoculars and let them hang by the thin black canvas strap onto his chest. He couldn't see inside the darkened bungalow anyway. Even before the lights had gone out, he couldn't make out much beyond shapes and shadows.

Too bad. The woman was a looker, and those shadows moved in the unmistakable motions of two bodies joined in passion, oblivious to all around them.

Which worked to the shaggy-haired man's advantage. When following someone, the more oblivious they were, the better.

She'd made it more complicated by making the man drive. He'd loaded her car with tracking devices, including some she'd probably find, and others she wouldn't. The strange car meant tracking her on other devices, like her new high-tech smart phone, which had been a bitch to get bugged. The mole helping him inside her ad firm had started to get cold feet. Or at least he pretended to, milking it for even more money than the ridiculous amount he'd already been paid. It might be time to look for a new source.

He picked up the digital camera from the seat next to him and perused the digital images on the camera's viewer. Mostly he'd taken shots of the woman getting into and out of the man's pickup truck, and going into the man's house. Who the guy was, he still had to research. But that wouldn't take long, thanks to the Internet.

Still. He needed more, if he expected to get paid. His employer, ensconced down in northern California somewhere, had a nasty temper, a short fuse, and a fighter's physique to back it up. He'd landed a punch once, right on the kisser. It bled for two days, and he lost two teeth, now replaced at great expense with excellent-looking falsies. Best to keep the man happy, even at a distance.

But the information wasn't going to volunteer itself. He needed to take some risks.

He made sure he'd turned off the dome light in the GT, removed the keys from the ignition, grabbed his gear sack, and opened the driver's side door. Luckily it faced away from the bungalow. He stayed low, stepped to the curb in a bent-over position, and eased the door shut.

Still crouched, he made his way to the driveway side of the house, then walked upright to the detached one-car garage. The garage door was locked, as was the side entry door, but he found the entry keypad right where he expected it. Judging by the faded plastic and the make and model of the device, the keypad had been in place for some time. Decades, perhaps. That made his job easier. He shone the dim light of his cell phone onto the keypad. Sure enough, four of the numbers showed greater wear. Tiny bits of the black digits had flecked away, and the center of the buttons shined with a brighter sheen than the edges. Same for the Enter key on the bottom.

That simplified things even further. A four-digit combination yielded twenty-four unique combinations, assuming no duplicates. Unless a security professional had chosen the combination, it was almost certainly a date. That reduced the list of options even further.

He guessed it on the third try.

The door slid upward. Well-maintained, or at least well-lubricated, it made very little noise. When the bottom of the door reached knee height, he re-entered the combination, halting its progress. He slid under the door, dragging his gear behind him, and stood in the tight space left by the man's silver truck. A Ford pickup. Excellent. Very familiar to him, and very predictable.

Also predictable: with his garage safely locked, the owner had left the truck unlocked. He slid open the driver's side door, popped the hood, felt inside for a secure spot, and slid the magnetic side of the tracking device onto the truck body. He placed another one inside the rear bumper, and one on the frame underneath. All easily accomplished, even in the dark.

He opened his smart phone app, activated all of the devices, and tested them. All working. He slid out under the garage door and entered the combination on the keypad again.

Clunk! This time, the door sounded like a hammer smashing steel as it began its downward path, advertising the door's descent. A moment before the base of the door touched concrete, a light came on inside the house on the second floor.

He froze in place, huddled close to the door. Shadows appeared in the window. A feminine shape. Very feminine. He bit his lip. The owner of the bungalow was a very lucky man.

He pressed against the wall, still as a rock, afraid to breathe. The shadow in the window fidgeted a bit. Another shadow joined it, which he guessed to be the man's. Still just shadows, though—no bodies. Quiet reigned over the yard. The next door neighbors must have brought their yappy little mutt inside. Thank God. He'd almost forgotten about that idiot dog, somehow, even though it had barked nonstop for the first hour of his surveillance. He resumed breathing, steadied it. That sort of mistake could prove fatal in this business. He'd lucked out this time.

The shadows disappeared from the window, and moments later, the lights went out.

He couldn't risk going inside the house, not yet. That would require a return trip. But with their attentions focused on each other indoors, he could risk installing a little outdoor surveillance. He slid into the back yard and made his way to a back corner, where the neighbor's wire fence joined one running across the back made of tall cedar planks. He checked out the line of sight. Nothing blocked the view of the house. Perfect. He removed a tiny camera, motion detector, and solar power pack from his satchel and examined the wooden fence to select the ideal spot—and discovered a problem.

Mounted in the ideal spot was a camera very similar to the one he had intended to install. Someone had already beaten him to it!

He crab-crawled at top speed out of the back yard, speed-walked along the edge of the house to the front, then crouched for the final sprint to his car. He slipped inside and lay down on the front seat, breathing hard. Calmed himself, and gave them time to get to sleep before disturbing the quiet with engine noise.

He swore under his breath. The camera in the corner spooked him, but maybe he'd overreacted. He could think of two possibilities. One, the owner might have installed security cameras on his own. Which was bad, but not horrible. If the owner checked them—and he'd only do that if he had a good reason—he'd see a shaggy-haired man crawling around his back yard in the middle of the night. So what.

The second possibility: someone else was monitoring this guy. But who? He had no idea. And, he decided, it wasn't his problem.

After fifteen minutes or so, he sat up. All quiet. Lights still out, he started the car. He kept the car tuned to perfection, so the engine, despite its size and power, made a minimum of noise. More of a purr than a roar when it started. He kept his lights off, waited.

Nothing stirred inside the bungalow. Nor the Tudor. The quiet little neighborhood stayed quiet.

He put the GT in gear and slid the car away from the curb, lights still off for a few blocks. Only when the main collector street came into view did he turn on his lights and breathe a sigh of relief.

Chapter Six

Peter coughed, but the tightness gripping his throat wouldn't go away. A clunking noise sounded outside, but no dogs responded, and with bigger issues sitting just inches away from him, he ignored it. "D-do s-something for you?"

"Yes. You said earlier tonight you'd help me. Didn't you mean it?" Her eyes moistened and her head dipped, her face forming a sweet little pout.

Peter cleared his throat, but the pressure remained. "If the police and the courts can't keep him from bothering you—"

"The police and the courts don't really care what happens to me." She turned onto her side and lay her head on his chest. "You're really the only one who cares." She craned her neck to look at his face. "You do care about me, don't you, Peter?"

"Of course, of course." He put his arm around her and held her close.

"And you know that he won't ever stop, as long as he and I are both alive."

"Eventually he will. He just—"

"Eventually?" She jerked her body upright in the bed. "That's your answer? 'Just wait twenty or forty years, Christine. Eventually, after your whole life is ruined, he might stop.' Does that sound like a life worth living to you?"

"It's just that—well, I'm not really a fighter, you know? And Kyle—"

"Not a fighter?" She smiled, shook her head, and lay against him again. "Of course you are. In fact, one might say you have the killer instinct." She twirled a few hairs together below his belly button.

"Christine, you know, that whole thing back in November? That's not...me. Not the real me. I'm—"

"Peter." She sat up in the bed and turned her body to face him. "I'm not saying what you did was wrong. Others might. The police and courts, say? But not me. You did what you had to do. A man stole your wife away from you. Stole your whole life, really."

"Alvin Dark didn't—"

"Alvin was an unfortunate bystander. Not an innocent one, though. He did the same thing to another man—to Raul Vasquez. He deserved to die." Her words hung in the air like dark clouds about to burst into a storm. Peter's mouth hung open, wordless. She leaned closer to him. "Yes, I said it. He deserved to die. Just like Kyle."

"Kyle?"

"Kyle. The man who torments me. Stalks me. Threatens my very existence, every day. He's a dangerous man, Peter." Something caught in her voice, but she continued, her voice raspy, yet at the same time, growing stronger. "Have I told you how he abused me? How he forced me to have sex with him? Overpowered me?" Her voice dropped to a hoarse whisper. "Hit me...hurt me?"

Peter held his arms out and drew her in. "No. No, you didn't tell me all of that. I didn't know. He...he raped you?"

She nodded. Her body shook in his arms, and tears wet Peter's shoulder. She clung to him, squeezing him hard, crushing the air out of his lungs. "Yes," she said. "Raped me, hit me, choked me if I resisted. Then he was so rough with me...hurting...so much..." She burst into sobs again. This time she cried for several minutes. He held her, rocking her body side to side, soothing her, kissing her hair, mumbling reassurances.

Finally she lifted her head and put her face inches from his. "I thought I'd told you."

"It's all right. You're telling me now."

She nodded and slid into his arms again. He held her a long time, until what seemed like hours later, she fell asleep.

***

Peter slid out of bed well before his 6 a.m. alarm, careful not to wake Christine, still slumbering beside him. Gazing on her lithe form in the dim light, he appreciated her stillness. For the first time since he'd met her, she seemed at peace.

He envied her for that. He hadn't had such a moment in over a year.

Shaking himself out his reverie, he shrugged on a robe and slippers and padded down to the kitchen. He had coffee made and a breakfast of eggs, bacon, and toast well underway when Christine yawned in the doorway, wearing one of his dress shirts, buttoned at the navel and strategically hiding everything of interest except her toned, tan legs.

"Why do you get up so early?" She stifled another yawn. "Even the birds are still asleep."

"I usually start work by seven." He smiled, tore his eyes away from her, and stirred scrambled eggs in the pan with a rubber spatula. "And I'm never the first one there."

"Everything smells wonderful." She pressed her body against his back and wrapped her arms around his chest. "Especially the coffee." She sniffed, then giggled. "You, not so much."

"I figured you'd like the coffee. It's your favorite, if I recall—Javatown." He poured her a mug. "As for how I smell, I figured we could take care of that after breakfast…together."

She laughed, stepped back, and patted his butt. "Sounds fun, but can you risk being late for work?" She opened the fridge and grabbed a carton of half-and-half, mixed a glop into her coffee with a scoop of sugar, and snuggled up against him again. "After all, I like long showers…especially if I have company."

"I'll take that risk." He reached behind him to draw her closer, squeezed her firm rump, then returned both hands to the task of serving breakfast. "I hope you're hungry."

"Starved. You never did give me any dinner last night. You wild man!" She snatched both mugs of coffee and followed him into the dining room.

Eating took only moments, amorous tension rising again between them. When Peter dropped their dirty plates into the sink, she whipped him around and planted a long, deep kiss on his lips and ground her pelvis against his. After several enjoyable moments, she leaned her head back, her lips pursed, eyes squinting as if in doubt. "So, are we good with our plan, then?"

"Sure. Long shower, then I'll drive you—"

"Not that plan, silly. Of course we're good with that plan. I mean the other plan. The one we talked about last night. You know…the plan for Kyle?"

He shook his head, his blood chilling. "We-we talked about how he bothers you, and—"

"Bothers? Ha! Harasses, you mean. Stalks. Intimidates. Completely ruins my life. It goes way beyond bothers." She gripped his upper arms, hard, her fingernails biting into his skin.

"Right." He nodded. "But I don't recall coming up with anything I'd call a plan." He flexed his triceps, hoping she'd let up a little, but it had no effect.

"We agreed it needed to stop."

"Of course."

"And that you'll help me."

"I will. Exactly what I can do, I don't—"

"You know exactly what you can do. What needs to be done." Finally she loosened her claw-like grasp of his flesh and slid her arms behind his back. She pressed her chest against his, her lips an inch from his chin. "Only you can do this for me, Peter. You're the only one who's shown he has the guts to protect his woman the way she needs to be protected."

He encircled her back with his arms in what he hoped would feel like a reassuring hug. "I'll try to protect you, but, Christine, I don't even know the man. I've never even met him."

"Which is why you're perfect. Just like last time."

"L-last time?" He leaned away from her, but she clutched his body close. Tight. Too tight.

"You know. With Alvin Dark."

He froze in an awkward position, his head suspended over her shoulder. Not this again. She'd hinted at this after the trial, but when she'd disappeared from his life for the next two months, he'd passed it off as a sick joke. He still wanted to believe that. She couldn't be serious…could she?

She continued on. "You didn't know Alvin, but you killed him. Ah—don't protest. This charade of innocence is getting tiresome. We both know you did it. We do, and no one else. Right?" She leaned back, her eyes on his, as if analyzing him. He stared blankly at her.

She ground against him some more. "And you want to keep it that way, right?"

Slowly, he nodded.

"And we both know that the only way to do that is to stop Kyle from hurting me." A cold, wicked smile curled her lips. "Because, good Lord, what if he did hurt me, and I was in the hospital, all medicated. And those medications, I've heard they're like truth serums. People start talking without knowing what they're saying, without any sort of…control." She locked eyes with him on the final word.

Peter just stared. She leaned closer and whispered. "And the only way to stop Kyle is to do the same thing to him that you did to Alvin Dark."

"Christine." His voice registered just above a whisper, hoarse and rough. "There must be another way."

"There is no other way! Damn you!" She pushed him away and stomped to the opposite wall, then whirled to face him. "The police can't stop him. The courts can't stop him. I can't stop him. He can't be stopped—as long as he's alive." Her eyes blazed, fixed on his, her chest swelling with every ragged breath. "As long as he lives, he is a threat to me. He has said as much—shown as much. Do I need to show you the scars?"

Peter shook his head, but she paid no attention. She thrust one foot onto the edge of the counter, her leg at a sharp angle to her body, and pointed to a white line running down her shin. "See this? That's where I had to have surgery to remove bone chips—from him kicking me." She planted her foot on the floor, spun away from him, and lifted up her shirt. She pointed to another white line on her lower back. "See this one? Back surgery. Slipped disc from being pushed down two flights of stairs." She took two backward steps toward him and lifted her hair to expose her neck. A small circle of rough red skin interrupted the bottom of her hairline. "Cigarette burn, while I was tied up in his bed, during what began as consensual sex." She spun around, stepped away, and lifted the shirt up again. Another scar ran from her mons pubis upward several inches. "Here's the scar from the hysterectomy I had to have after that little night of fun. Shall I go on?"

Numbed by her invective, Peter shook his head again.

She covered herself again and closed the distance between them. "That doesn't even include the cuts and bruises that healed without leaving a mark—and the psychological traumas that never show up on the skin. Now, do you think he can be stopped by ordinary, civil means? Do you think he'll stop hurting me just because someone in a black robe or blue uniform tells him to? Do you?"

He shook his head again.

"Good. I'm glad you're finally convinced." She exhaled and ran a finger down his chest, letting it rest at his waistline. "So. Are you going to help me, or not?"

He stared blankly at her. Words would not form.

"Or...do I need to talk to the police again about what happened in November?" She leaned closer. "Because, while Kyle can't be stopped by the police and the courts, you can. Right, Peter?"

He closed his eyes, his body swaying. His head weighed a thousand pounds. He could not feel his feet. His heartbeat pounded in his ears. This couldn't be happening. It just couldn't be.

"Christine, I...I can't kill a guy in cold blood."

"Of course you can. You already have."

"No!" His eyes sprang open and he latched onto the counter behind him with a white-knuckle grip. "It wasn't like that. It–it was an accident."

"An accident? How? You beat him to death with a tire iron. That doesn't happen by accident."

"He attacked me first. I fought back—"

"You followed him and crashed into his car. That's practically the definition of premeditation."

"I didn't mean to! I mean, I meant to follow someone else. The crash was an accident. Then things just got out of hand."

She laughed, a wicked, cunning cackle. "Got out of hand? You beat him a hundred times with an iron bar. Cracked his skull. Pulverized his hands and fingers. Crushed his damned testicles. You meant to kill him!"

"No!" He lunged at her, grabbed her arms. "I didn't even know him!"

Her face went white, then relaxed again. "Of course. It was all a mistake." A sneering smile drifted across her face. "You meant to kill the other guy."

He stared at her, still holding her arms another long moment, then another. Then, against his will, his head bobbed up, then down. "Yes," he said in a low voice. "I suppose I did." He let go and turned away from her.

She surprised him by pressing her body against his from behind, her lips behind his ear. "And, my dear Peter," she said, "you will do it again."

"I—"

"Or," she said in a whisper, "you can take your chances with the police. See if they like your story of what happened that night."

His head swam. She had him, right where she wanted him. All exits blocked. If he resisted, or if he ran, she'd turn him in. His life would be over. His mother's care would be in the hands of his crazy brother and sister, who believed they could cure her life-threatening strokes through prayer. Thelma would never understand. Everything he'd lived for would be wiped out. He would die in prison.

There had to be another way. But he couldn't see one.

Chapter Seven

"Dude," Frankie said, finishing his pale ale off with a giant gulp, "we got slaughtered last night in the darts tourney without you. Skip couldn't hit the broad side of a brewery, much less a bull's-eye." He motioned to the waitress for a second round, then pointed to Peter's mug, still two-thirds full of a dark, chocolaty porter. "Drink up, man. You're already a pint behind me."

"Maybe you could slow down a little," Peter said. "I can't guzzle this stuff. Besides, it's meant to be savored."

"Cut the crap and drink. Where the hell were you last night, anyway? And don't tell me it was a woman, or I'll—"

"It was. I had a date."

Frankie's jaw dropped. "No way. You? With who? That new blonde gal, what's her name, in Accounting?"

"Get out of here. She's old enough to be my mother." Peter cracked open a pistachio from the bowl on the table and tossed the tender meat into his mouth.

"When's that ever mattered to you? Your taste in women has always been, what should I call it, a mystery?" The beers arrived and Frankie drained a third of his in one swig. "Speaking of your mother. How's she holding up?"

Peter grimaced. "Physically the same. Holding steady. No strokes since the one in May. But the dementia is getting pretty scary. The doctors say if she has another bad stroke, even if she survives it physically, she could end up..." His voice trailed off. He couldn't bring himself to say it.

Frankie clapped a hand on his arm and gave it a reassuring shake. "At least you got her in the right place. They take good care of her at Sunset."

Peter frowned and drank a giant gulp of beer. "Tell that to my brother Jimmy. He's making noise about moving her again. Some new fundamentalist, evangelical facility near him, down in Oakland, with no in-house medical staff."

"That bozo. What's wrong with him? He knows damn well he can't take care of her like you do." Frankie took a long sip and grabbed a handful of nuts from the bowl, crushing them in his fist.

They sat in silence for a long moment, drinking beer and munching pistachios. Peter imagined life for Thelma in Oakland with Jimmy and their volatile sister Libby. Jimmy's plans would fall apart like so many of his empty promises in the past, starting with his broken commitments to contribute more money to pay her escalating bills. Her ongoing therapy, essential for her recovery, far exceeded the amount Medicare would pay, but at least Sunset could provide it in-house. It would cost double if it had to be provided by a separate caregiver—if Jimmy or Libby even allowed it, given their religious objections to all things scientific. Her health would decline faster than the bank accounts of Jimmy's enthusiastic parishioners.

Frankie interrupted his reverie. "So, okay, who was she?"

Peter, startled, nearly spilled his beer. "Who?"

"Who? The woman, man. Your date last night. Anyone I know?"

Peter shook his head, swallowing a small sip of porter. "Gal I met on the jury a couple of months ago. Christine."

"The hottie?"

Peter smiled and ducked his head. "She's pretty, yeah."

Frankie raised his glass in salute. "Well, good for you. It's about time you moved on. I mean, Marcia's practically married already, ain't she?"

"Engaged, so I'm told. Whatever. That's her business. And not mine, anymore." He sipped his porter again, got it down below half full. The second pint sat sweating on the table. "Anyway, thanks. I think."

"So, how'd it go? You, ah, get any?" Frankie's eyebrows widened on his forehead, and he leaned in conspiratorially.

"You know I don't kiss and tell."

"Oh, so she stiffed you."

"I didn't say that."

"So you stiffed her?" He guffawed. "Get it? You stiffed her?" He smacked Peter's arm, causing porter to splash onto the table.

"Yeah, I get it. Dork." Peter wiped up the mess and took another long hit on his beer.

"Okay, so you were a perfect gentleman. Where'd you go? A nice dinner somewhere? Paley's, The Huntsman, what?" Frankie drummed on the table with flat palms. "Come on, spill. It's the least you can do, since it cost us a hundred bucks each in lost prize money."

"We, ah, hung out at my place."

"Wha…? Oh, you *dog,* you!" Frankie laughed and clapped him on the shoulder. "You did get some sugar—and on the first date. Man! I'm impressed." He toasted Peter with his pint glass and sipped from it. "Damn. So, tell me. What's she like? She go for anything kinky, or—"

"Forget it, I'm not talking. Never have, never will."

"Not true. You told me all about that red-haired gal, freshman year of college. What was her name? Gertrude?"

"Gwen. Lordy. You had to remind me of her? I still have bite marks on my neck from her." Peter laughed and rubbed the spot of the ancient injury. "I thought I'd need garlic and a cross to get rid of her."

"See? There's precedent. Now, spill."

"No."

"Come on, man."

Peter finished his first beer, sipped from the second. "So, how did you shoot last night?"

"Dude. You're killing me here."

"We should move, so we can see the TV. The Mariners game is coming on."

"Peter." Frankie shook his head in disgust, then shrugged. "So, you think she's a keeper?"

Peter's turn to shrug. "She seems interested."

"What'd you guys talk about?"

Peter's mouth went dry. A long sip of porter didn't cure it. He sipped again anyway. "Ah, well. You know. The case we were on. Ourselves. Stuff like that."

"She rebounding too?"

Peter's brow moistened with sweat. "Kind of. She had a guy a while back, didn't treat her too well. She's still kind of afraid of him." He swallowed a lump forming in this throat. It remained, making it hard to breathe.

"That sucks. Maybe you should give her some space, let her work it out with him first."

"Why, so you can ask her out? Screw that, buddy." Peter laughed, and Frankie joined in after a moment's pause.

"No, seriously. If she's got a bad dude hanging around, she might be more trouble than she's worth." Frankie slammed the rest of his beer and wiped foam off his lip. "Take it from me. I've got more experience than you on this."

"Yeah, well. The thought crossed my mind." Peter chewed another pistachio, then washed it down with beer. Everyone had more experience than he did.

"But…" Frankie drummed on the table again.

"But what?"

"But you already have another date with her set up, don't you?"

Peter spread his arms wide, opened his mouth to protest, then closed it and nodded. She'd insisted on getting together again over the weekend, to start "planning," as she put it. The very idea sent chills down his spine. It did again, sitting in the pub with his friend.

"Dude. She has you wrapped. Or should I say, whipped?"

"Huh? Did you say wrapped, or trapped?"

"Which should I have said?"

"I–I don't know. God, I'm a mess."

Concern spread over Frankie's face. He leaned closer and lowered his voice. "Dude, what's wrong? You don't seem real happy about this. From the way you've described her, I'd have thought you'd be ecstatic."

Peter sighed and shook his head. "I should be. But…" He

looked all around them and leaned forward also. In a low voice, he said, "She knows."

"What do you mean, she knows?" Frankie's voice stayed low and even, but filled with trepidation.

"Remember I told you about that guy I beat up last fall? After the car crash?"

"Marcia's dude? Yeah. Except it turned out not to be her dude, right? So, who the hell was it?" Shock replaced concern on Frankie's face. "Dude. She knew him?"

"No, no. But…she knows about it, somehow. And she's holding it over me, like a, you know. A threat, or something."

Frankie sat back, puzzled, and poured some of Peter's beer into his empty glass. "I don't get it. How could she do that? I mean, who cares? You got into a fight, right? So what? What's he gonna do, sue you or something? Dude, what is the matter?"

Peter gripped his beer glass with both hands and took quick, shallow breaths. He glanced up at Frankie, then back to the table. He shook his head.

"Dude? If that's not what—wait. Peter. What happened to the guy?"

Peter stared into his beer, unmoving.

"Did he…go into the hospital?"

Peter shook his head.

"Did he come looking for you or something?"

Again, a shake of the head.

Frankie stared at him, the dawn of recognition sweeping over his face. "Can he come looking for you?"

A third, very slow, shake of Peter's head sank Frankie back in his chair. The lump in Peter's throat doubled in size.

"Peter." Frankie's voice dropped to a hoarse whisper. "Did the guy survive?"

A fourth, and final, glacial shake of Peter's head. His vision blurred. The lump in his throat expanded to the size of a basketball.

"Oh. My. God." Frankie collapsed forward onto the table, all air rushing out of him. "How in the hell…why in the hell did I not know about this, all this time?"

Peter fought to remain in control, taking deep, slow breaths. He failed. Moisture leaked from each eye, and he wiped it away with the back of his hand. "It just…I didn't know for a long time, and then you got in your car crash, and…I didn't want to bug you with it."

"Bug me? Jesus, Peter. Of all things. God." Frankie sat up and rubbed his face with his palms. "How did she find out? Christine, I mean?"

Peter gestured palm-up with one hand. "You're not going to believe this."

"Try me."

He sighed and bit his lip. "The jury I was on? The victim? That was my guy. My freaking guy."

"Holy shit." Frankie's mouth hung open. "I can't even imagine."

"Yeah."

"And she, like, figured it out?"

Peter nodded.

"Holy mother of tacos. That is some screwed up shit, boy-o."

Peter's eyes widened, but he said nothing.

"And so…you said she's threatening you with it. How? What's she gonna do?"

"She wants me to…" He swallowed, but the lump in his throat refused to budge. "To do it again."

"What?"

"To her ex. Or else she'll turn me in." Peter sucked down every last drop of beer in his glass.

"That's insane! You'd be better off knocking her off." Frankie laughed. "Hey, maybe that's not the worst idea."

"No way. That's…that's just as crazy." Peter's face felt warm. For a brief moment, he could envision being free of her, stopping her threats, wrapping his hands around her throat…He shook himself, trying to rid his mind of the horror he'd imagined.

Frankie squinted at him. "Dude, I was only kidding. So, anyway, how'd she react?"

"To what?"

"To you telling her no." Frankie waited. "Dude. You did tell her no…?"

Peter bowed his head, unable to look at his friend.

"You're not seriously considering it?" Frankie's voice reached a screeching pitch, far too loud. Peter shushed him.

"Of course not. But I had to play along. What the hell else am I gonna do?"

"You're gonna get the hell away from her, that's what!" Frankie stood and gripped both Peter's shoulders. "Dude. Get. The. Hell. Out. Now!"

"I can't. I'll go to prison."

"So what? Instead you're gonna kill a guy?" His voice got even louder and screechier, but he ignored Peter's attempts to shush him. He rose to his feet and leaned over the table, breathing in Peter's face. "Dude. Listen to me. Get away from this bitch before she gets you killed!"

Peter covered Frankie's mouth with a firm hand. "Shut up, you idiot! You're making a scene!"

Frankie smacked Peter's hand away, pulled cash from his wallet, and slapped it on the table. "Fine, then. You want to screw up your life and be a stubborn idiot, you can do it without me." He spun on his heel and stomped out the door.

Peter slunk into his seat. Frankie was right, of course. Part of him wanted to break it off with Christine, sooner rather than later. But another part of him knew he could not. Not, anyway, until he came up with a way to escape her trap.

And on that front, he had nothing.

Chapter Eight

Peter pulled into Sunset Hospice's parking lot at ten minutes before eleven on Sunday morning, giving him plenty of time to make it to his mother's room before she returned from her knitting group, an all-female club of seniors that the members referred to as the "Stitch and Bitch" club. Thelma rarely made any progress on her knitting since her last stroke—she'd been working on the same scarf since April—but being around the other elderly women at Sunset stimulated her mind, a must for any patient battling senility. As such, Peter always took care to arrive after the session ended.

He arrived at her room two minutes early, and, to his surprise, found her door open. A short, brown-haired woman in nurse's scrubs bustled around the room with her back to him. He cleared his throat and knocked on the open door. The nurse turned toward him, providing his second surprise of the morning.

"Angela Wegman? What are you doing here?"

The nurse, a buxom woman of about thirty, smiled in recognition. "Peter Robertson! How nice to see you!" She extended her arms and closed the gap between them, enveloping him in a warm hug. He stiffened, then forced himself to relax a bit, and patted her shoulders.

"H-have you left OHSU?" he asked. Angela had been the nurse on duty at Oregon Health Sciences University hospital the night of his mother's first stroke. He'd never seen her at Sunset before.

The embrace continued another uncomfortable moment. Every microsecond reminded him of his secret, murderous connection to her friend, Alvin Dark. Just when he thought she would let go, she enveloped him in an even tighter, vice-like grip. His chest constricted. Breathing became impossible. Her arms surrounded him, engulfed him like his own guilt, like Christine's threats to expose him, like the trap in which she'd ensnared him—

Angela squeezed him again, then stepped back. "No, not at all," she said, busying herself with Thelma's room again. "OHSU is still my nine-to-five, but an old nursing school classmate on staff here needed someone to pick up her shift. They're short-handed, I had a day free, so I figured, why not? Besides, I'm saving up for a trip to Europe next year. I could use the extra cash." She glanced back at him and smiled. "When I saw Thelma's name on the door, I hoped you might come to visit."

"Twice a week, without fail." He glanced at the empty bed. "Where is she?"

"Visiting her friend Zoe, who's not feeling well. Your mom is a sweetie. I see where you get your compassionate side." She flashed him a big, flirty smile, and arranged some electronic instruments on a tray near Thelma's bed.

"It looks like you're preparing for some sort of procedure, or something. Anything I should know about?"

"Just a check on her vitals and responsiveness. For repeat stroke victims, we like to do those at least once per quarter. Normally we'd bring her to OHSU for that, but since I'm here, I'm taking care of it." She fluffed the pillow on Thelma's bed but kept her eyes on him. "So, how have you been?" She blinked a few times and flashed her pretty smile again. Her big brown eyes glowed.

Warmth rose in Peter's face. "Good, good. Uh, so, why Europe? Are you researching your ancestors, or just for fun?"

"More the latter," she said, wrapping her arms around herself. "Well, actually, I need something to lift my spirits. I've been so depressed, ever since my friend Alvin died. Especially since they let his killer off on some technicality a couple of months ago—did you hear about that?"

"I, uh…" Damn it! He searched for a way to answer her.

Something other than the fact that he'd served on the jury and convinced all of the others that Raul was innocent, because Peter had actually committed the crime—

"Donald?" Thelma's voice drifted in from down the hallway. Relieved, Peter turned to greet her. A nurse guided her into the room, nodded at Angela, and exited without a word.

"Hi, Mom. It's Peter." He kissed her forehead and helped her to the bed. "This is Nurse Wegman. You may remember her from—"

"Of course I remember her. I'm not stupid." Thelma pushed Peter's hand away and scurried to the bathroom. Before pulling the door shut, she pointed at Peter, then at Angela. "Don't try to come in here. I'm locking the door."

Angela waited for the door to close before asking in a low voice, "Is she often like this?"

Peter nodded. "If anything, she's been getting worse lately."

"I see." Angela drew closer to Peter and lowered her voice even further. "Depending on what we find in her examination this morning, we may want to bring her in for a more extensive evaluation. I'm sure the doctor will want to see her."

Peter sighed and chewed the inside of his lip. "I was afraid you might say something like that. What can you do to help her?"

Angela placed a warm hand on Peter's shoulder. She stood close to him...so close. He noticed a faint and pleasant scent of lilac emanating from her. "It depends on what we find. There are some experimental new approaches we could try."

"Whoa." Peter held up his hand, shaking his head. "My brother and sister are already none too keen on—well, pretty much anything that smacks of modern medicine, really. I doubt they'd sign off on anything experimental."

"Don't you have power of attorney?" she asked.

He shook his head. "Only for emergency situations. For everything else, I need to negotiate strategies with my siblings. And their attitudes are, well, pretty firmly entrenched."

She frowned, and her large brown eyes reflected his own sadness and frustration. "I see. That's too bad. Well," she said, brightening, "maybe we could work this out as part of a new study we have going on. It's a cooperative program with Sunset, a behavioral approach to stimulating the centers of the brain that—"

The bathroom door flew open, and Thelma shuffled out, drying her hands on a towel. Her feet could only move six inches at a time, though, bound, as they were, by the white cotton underwear cuffing her feet.

"Mom, pull up your underpants, please."

Thelma looked at her feet, snorted, stepped out of the undies, and dropped the towel on top of them. "No," she said. "I need new ones. Those have holes in them." She shuffled to her dresser and pulled open the top drawer.

Peter turned to Angela. "I should give her some privacy. Could you, er, help her?"

Angela smiled and pushed Peter toward the door. "Of course. Give us a few minutes. And, Peter?" He stopped outside the door, and she leaned closer to him. "Why don't you call me sometime? We can, uh, talk about that study. Maybe over a glass of wine somewhere?"

Before he could stop himself, he nodded. She widened her eyes and her smile, then waved good-bye and closed the door.

***

Peter arrived at Stark's at 6 a.m. on Monday morning to prepare for another grueling day. He'd spent the weekend catching up on paperwork to clear his schedule for the first round of interviews to fill the loading dock supervisor position. Four one-hour interviews, back-to-back, starting at 8 a.m., lay ahead of him. Jess had done a terrific job screening resumés and scheduling candidates, and he owed her big time. After a half hour of clearing his inbox and returning emails, he approached her office with her thank-you gift in hand: a two-pound box of salted caramel truffles from Moonstruck Chocolate.

"Petey!" She stood when he entered, waving a well-manicured hand in the air in her trademark gesture, indicating pure excitement. In her other hand she clutched a sheaf of papers in two-inch-long fingernails, painted purple and gold in solidarity with her daughter's high school lacrosse team. "I'm so glad you're here early. We got a change of schedule. A new candidate interview. Hispanic guy. Gregg says we gotta squeeze him in." She shook the papers at him until he took them out of her hands. "What's that you got there?"

He held the chocolates out to her, exchanging them for the resumés. "This is for you. Thanks for all your extra help on this, Jess. You're a lifesaver."

"Oh, you're so sweet!" She bounced around her desk and crushed him in a tight hug. Dressed in her usual low-cut blouse and skimpy short skirt, her embraces often gave men—and sometimes women—the wrong idea.

"Easy, girl, before one of us gets busted for harassment," he said with a laugh.

She ripped open the box, stuffed a truffle into her mouth, and scampered back to her seat. "So," she said, still chewing, "I got this Raul guy set up at seven-thirty. I pushed all the others back, and shortened each interview ten minutes, so we should still finish close to noon. Just you, Gregg, and Manuel doing the interviews, so it should be okay." She swallowed and picked out another truffle.

"Okay. Who's Raul?" His ears tingled at the mention of the name. Coincidentally, the defendant in the Alvin Dark murder trial had been named Raul. But, he reasoned, a lot of Latino families name their sons Raul. A common enough name, he reassured himself.

Then he looked at the resumé in his hand, and the blood drained from his face.

Chapter Nine

"You're kidding me, right?" Peter staggered backwards, steadying himself against the wall of Jessica's office.

"I know! Look how perfect he is. Experienced, Latino, business degree, double-majored in English, all while working two jobs." Jess took a huge gulp of coffee, then somehow, miraculously, snapped a pink bubble of chocolate-streaked chewing gum. "Why Lumber City would ever let him get away is beyond me."

"He's only been there six weeks." He supported his head with his free hand. Still, it felt like it might wobble off his neck any second. "Jess, we can't interview this guy, much less hire him."

"Wrongsy-dongsy, my friend. Gregg says he's must-do. Top choice, in his book. The only Hispanic who applied, although we also got a woman and a black guy. What's the matter?"

Peter glanced around, closed her office door, and slumped into a chair. "I know this guy. Well, kind of. I mean, we've, er, crossed paths, so to speak."

"Cool! What's he like? Hey, you don't look so hot. Like you're gonna puke. Gawd, please don't be sick. Rescheduling all these interviews again would be murder."

"I–I'm fine. This guy…Jess, you remember that jury I served on in May?"

Jess snapped her gum again. "Do I ever. You nearly killed us, being out that long. Right when Frankie got hurt, too. Was this Raul guy on the jury too?"

Peter shook his head. "Not the jury. Jess, he was the defendant. The guy accused of committing the murder."

Jess's mouth gaped open. "Whoa! Did he do it? Wait a second, that can't be right. He'd be in jail. Hey! He didn't put any of that on his application." She snatched it back from him and flipped through the pages.

"No. We found him not guilty."

"Okay, so what's the problem? Hey, I get it. Was he really innocent, or did he get off on a technicality? Gawd, I hate when lawyers pull that crap. It's a wonder they can sleep at night."

"No, no. He really didn't do it. He's innocent."

"Really? Or do you just gotta say that since you were on the jury that let him go?" She snapped her gum again, eyes gleaming. Peter guessed at how much delicious gossip she'd get out of this tidbit.

"No. He's really, really innocent."

"You sure?"

He swallowed, hard. "I'm sure." Boy, was he ever.

"How do you know? Some of these guys are pretty clever."

"I just do, okay?" He regretted the sharp tone as soon as the words left his mouth.

Nonplussed, Jessica shrugged and chomped her gum. "Okay. So, what's the big whoop? Why can't we interview him?"

Peter sighed. He couldn't explain, so… "I guess we can, then." He shuddered. He'd have his work cut out for him. But at least they had four other candidates. Surely at least one of them would be more qualified than the man who'd haunted his dreams for two of the worst weeks of his life.

***

Frankie approached the metal-framed glass reception desk in Cascade Legal's office in northwest Portland and waited for the young man who occupied it to notice him. The man spoke in hushed tones into a wireless black headset that carved a deep ridge into his sandy-colored, overly-moussed hair. The guy dressed like a freaking Californian, with a bright orange tie over a white button-down shirt. Nobody in Portland wore ties. This was a stupid idea. Or at least, the wrong lawyer. Frankie turned to leave.

"Mr. Kowalczyk?" The young man extended a delicate, blue-veined hand. "I'm Aiden, Ms. Pullen's assistant. Can I get you some coffee?"

Well, free coffee sounded good. "Sure," Frankie said. "Cream and sugar if you got it." The man scurried over to a coffee pot across the room. Frankie took in his surroundings. Very Californian. "Quite the place you got here," he said. "Man, you guys got a lot of weird art."

Aiden made a face, as if disapproving, and seemed to consider a reply. He brightened. "French press okay?"

Frankie blinked. "Uh, sure. Whatever."

Aiden scooped coffee beans into some sort of grinder and pressed a button. The machine whirred, and Aiden turned back to Frankie. "It'll just be a few moments. Ms. Pullen will be out in—oh, would you look at that. There she is now."

Through a solid wooden door behind Aiden's desk emerged a blonde woman, about five foot five, mid-thirties, Frankie guessed. Despite her doll-like face and perfect figure, he first noticed her bright blue eyes—the kind that could make a sailor give up the sea. The rest of her made quite the case for staying home too.

Definitely the right lawyer.

"Hi, I'm Samantha Pullen," she said. "You must be Frankie."

He stepped toward her, hand extended. ""Ms. Pullen, thanks for meeting with me. I hear you're the best."

"Please, call me Sam." She guided him into the confines of her office and they sat in comfortable leather chairs around a low coffee table. Moments later, Aiden set down matching mugs of coffee. Well, almost matching. Sam drank hers black. "How can I help you today?"

"Well, when I first made the appointment, I wanted to see if you could sue my former employer for me," he said. "I got a lousy deal on a severance package on a bum rap for sexual harassment a few months ago. You see, I was dating this gal Donna, and we got caught doing the you-know-what at work, so—"

"Did Donna bring charges?"

Frankie nodded. "They kind of made her—the company

threatened to fire her, too. So she—"

"Was Donna your employee? By that I mean, did you supervise her?" Her tone took on a more accusatory tone.

Frankie's heart sank a little. "Um…technically, yeah. But I always thought of her more as my co-worker." He cringed when he saw Sam's frown. "That's bad, huh?"

"Do you have a copy of the agreement?" she said.

"Right here." He sat forward and pulled a folded stack of stapled pages out of his back pocket. "It says I can't go anywhere near Stark's—that's the company—but I'd really like to get my job back."

"Mr. Kowalczyk, I'll look over the agreement, but unless something is very awry—and sometimes they are—a civil contract like this doesn't usually give the former employee much wiggle room to sue." She took the agreement from him and scanned it. "Now, you said there was another matter? What was that?"

Frankie sipped his coffee. "Damn, that's good stuff," he said.

Sam grinned. "Aiden's very proud of his coffee. He roasts it himself at home. Now, that other matter…?"

Frankie sipped more coffee. He'd known exactly how he wanted to raise this issue with her, but all of a sudden it didn't seem so easy. "I have this…friend," he said. "He might do something bad…like, real bad." Another sip. "Because he's being, kind of, blackmailed."

"Kind of blackmailed?" She cocked her head.

"Well, definitely blackmailed," Frankie said. "And nobody else knows it, except me. And the blackmailer, of course."

"And you're wondering if you should turn him in?" She sipped her coffee and jotted something down on a legal pad on the table.

"No, no, I'd never do that," he said. "I'm just wondering—well, let's say he does this thing. Because of the blackmail. Is he still…you know…guilty?"

"We're all responsible for our own actions," she said. "Perhaps your friend needs to seek legal advice directly, rather than through you?"

"You don't believe me," he said, heat rising in his face. "I swear, it's not me. It's—it's someone I've known a long time, and he'd never—well, I used to think he'd never, but—"

"He's thinking about it?" She set the coffee down, along with her pen. No more notes. Just talking and listening.

Frankie nodded. "So, even though he's being blackmailed—"

"Has your friend talked to the police?"

Frankie shook his head. "And he won't. Because what she's got on him...well, it's just as bad."

Sam pursed her lips. "Thinking about doing something is one thing. Doing it's a whole different story. And knowing in advance that it could happen puts you in a tricky position. If your, uh, *friend* is serious and looks like he might follow through on this, I hope you'll come talk to me immediately. Whatever happens to him, I want to make sure that you do the right thing here. Okay?"

Frankie's heart fell into his gut. He lowered his head, which weighed a million tons. "I hear ya," he said. But he wished he hadn't.

***

Peter sat between Gregg and Manuel, his hard-working lumber sales specialist, at the round mahogany table in Gregg's office. This allowed him to face the job applicant head-on during the interview, his preferred vantage point under normal circumstances. That provided the best perspective for observing a candidate's body language, a key factor in assessing their candor and confidence. It also established him as the candidate's principal audience, and, subconsciously, as a straight shooter.

But these were not normal circumstances.

Gregg and Manuel made small talk in the minutes leading up to the first interview, but Peter remained quiet. He attempted to study the resumes stacked in front of him, but his eyes refused to focus on the pages.

His mind raced. How did Raul end up here? It could not be pure coincidence. Plus, Raul's background prior to the trial didn't mesh well with this position: farm work, dishwasher, odd jobs here and there. He had some supervisory experience, but only six weeks in building supply retail. What had led him to apply for the job at Stark's?

"He's here," Manuel said. He stood and greeted the man smiling in the open doorway, escorted by Jessica, whose height, heels, and retro 1980s hairdo made her a towering figure over the compact, five foot eight inch frame of Raul Vasquez. He wore a cheap blue suit over a crisp white shirt and inoffensive red tie, held in place by an old-fashioned shiny brass tie clip. A sheen of sweat glistened on the light brown skin of his face, plastered with a genuine, if nervous, toothy smile.

Raul shook Manuel's hand, then Gregg's, and then extended a hand to Peter. After a moment, Peter shook it with a firm grip, returned double-fold by the stocky, black-haired job candidate. Their eyes locked on each other for a silent moment, recognition flickering in the shorter man's dark brown eyes.

"Have we met?" Raul said in slightly accented English.

Peter admired the man's chutzpah. Did he really want to relive his ordeal as a falsely accused murderer during a job interview?

Time to find out.

"Not formally," Peter said. "I'm Peter Robertson. I was a juror on the Alvin Dark murder trial."

Raul nodded, seemingly unsurprised, and a sly smile creased his face. "Ah. So, perhaps we should begin the conversation there." He spoke formally, but haltingly, like translators Peter had experienced when traveling. "At the very least," Raul went on, "it would allow me to explain to your colleagues about the gap in my work experience. May I sit down?" He gestured to the open chair.

Peter opened his mouth to respond, but Gregg spoke up first. "Please, sit," he said, and waited a moment for Raul to get comfortable. "I wondered about that gap. Fired from that restaurant, what's it called again?" He flipped through his copy of Raul's resumé on the table in front of him.

"Florentino's," Peter muttered. A gleam of satisfaction twinkled in Raul's eyes.

"That's it," Gregg said. "Nice place, I've heard. Peter, you've been there, haven't you?"

Raul stared at Peter, one eyebrow raised. Peter coughed into his fist and shook his head. "My ex-wife has been there," he said. "She liked it."

Raul smiled, lips together, waiting.

Gregg set down the papers. "So that all happened last November. Then it looks like you were out of work until June. Can you explain all that? It's really the only big question mark I have about you."

"I have others," Peter said.

"Let him explain this first," Gregg said. "Go on, Raul."

Raul met the eyes of each of his three interviewers in turn, lingering on Peter's an extra moment. "I was falsely accused of a serious crime—the murder of a co-worker," he said. "I spent six months in jail awaiting trial. I was acquitted, as I was completely innocent, and all charges were expur—expo— expunged from my record. But after all that time, and all that had happened, I could not return to work at Florentino's."

Peter cringed again at the mention of the ill-fated restaurant's name, but kept silent while Raul continued.

"Lumber City was kind enough to give me a second chance on their loading dock. But opportunities for promotion there are slim to none, as they say. When I heard of the opportunity here, I had to apply."

"And how did you hear of this opportunity?" Peter asked. Gregg's raised eyebrows indicated that Peter had failed to keep the suspicion out of his voice.

"A friend told me." Raul locked his eyes on Peter's.

"Somebody here, at Stark's?" Manuel asked.

"No," Raul answered, still staring at Peter. "A friend of someone who does."

"Who?" Peter asked, his voice hoarse.

"I believe you know this person," Raul said, smiling. "Her name is Christine Nielsen."

Chapter Ten

One hundred ninety-seven.

Kyle grunted, lowering his upper body back to the floor. With ten pound weights in each outstretched hand, completing the back end of a sit-up strained his muscular arms and shoulders as much as his rock-hard abs. Strain that verged on pain.

One ninety-eight.

But oh, the payoff. Most guys worked hard to lose ten of the extra twenty pounds lining their beer bellies. Elite athletes worked harder to burn decent six-pack abs. Kyle's looked more like a dozen bottles of wine laid neck-to-boot in a row across his abdomen. Muscles rippled over muscles with not an ounce of fat between them.

One ninety-nine. One more.

His ab muscles tightened. He lifted his hands from the floor, the weights straining his forearms, biceps, and shoulders. His torso peeled off the mat, fire burning in his gut, every muscle screaming for relief.

Still his body arched upwards. His torso straightened at thirty degrees, a straight line from hips to the base of his skull, and climbed like the needle on a pressure gauge. Forty-five degrees. Sixty.

And, ninety. He exhaled, a whoosh of breath cooling his sweaty, smooth chest.

But he wasn't done. A sit-up had two parts: ascent and descent. Each required perfect execution to achieve maximum impact, with no rest between. He inhaled a deep gulp of air and resumed his downward descent with only the slightest pause.

The slow, steady path back to the mat required the same precision, the same discipline, as the arc upward: back straight, arms wide, holding the weights even with the back of his head, for maximum muscular stress.

Seventy-five degrees. Sixty. Almost there. Forty-five—

A shrill ringing of bells split the silence. Damn that phone! He'd forgotten to turn it off before beginning his workout. How was that possible? Damn it all. He was slipping in his old age. Turning thirty-five a month before had signaled the beginning of the end.

He fought to maintain focus, keep his body straight and the motion smooth. Just another few seconds—

It rang again, jarring his concentration. His body collapsed to the floor, the weights bouncing on the mat and out of his hands. One of them rolled to within an inch of his head.

He rolled to his side, seething. How frustrating. So close! Just inches from finishing the intense workout. But he couldn't take credit for a full workout. When he marked his journal, he'd write 199, not 200. He hadn't earned it.

He climbed to his feet and crossed to the phone, which rang a third time. Whoever it was, it'd better be good.

He wiped his hands on a towel before picking up the phone. He tapped Answer, then Speaker, and set the phone back on its stand on the table. "Yeah?"

"I've got an answer for you," the voice said.

Kyle wiped his face and neck with the towel, then draped it across his shoulders. "Good news, I hope."

"Call it a mix."

Crap. A mix meant mostly bad. "Anything I need to write down?"

The man on the other end of the line cleared his throat. "Nope. I'm sending you some numbers by courier. They should arrive tomorrow. Nothing too surprising, except…"

Kyle waited a beat, gritted his teeth, exhaled as loudly as he could. "Well?"

Rustling noises emerged from his phone's speaker, the sound of papers being shuffled. "She opened a new bank account.

About ten grand. Haven't been able to track down where the cash came from."

"Seriously?"

A pause. "Do I ever kid around with you?"

"Damn straight you don't. What's the money for?"

"Not sure," the man said. "Still sussing that out. But she's been checking airline prices to various places—Europe, South America, Australia. Seems like she's making some plans."

"Do they involve the new guy?" The skin on Kyle's scalp tightened. She'd traveled abroad before, but rarely alone. Still, one could hope.

"Her searches have all been for a solo ticket. We don't have his computer tracked yet. I should say, computers, plural. Work, home, phone. Waiting on the green light from you."

Kyle leaned over the phone, hands flat on the table. "Do it. Add it to your scope. He's to be scouted as closely as her."

"Got it. Although that'll overlap our work on her a fair amount, if trends continue."

Kyle swore. "How often does she see him?"

"Calm down." The man chuckled. "They've only spent the night together one time, at his place. But that's about to change. She's got him all over her online calendar in the coming month—more and more each week. This morning she packed an overnight bag before leaving for work, and they have a date tonight."

Kyle took a long, deep, calming breath. "Be there. And set him up for sound, too. I want them recorded in stereo."

"Will do, boss. Enjoy the rest of your workout."

"How did you know that I—"

The line went dead. Kyle swore again. So the asshole did interrupt him on purpose.

***

"Unbelievable!" Gregg stomped around his office, crashing into chairs, lamps, and even the heavy mahogany meeting table at which Peter and Manuel had been sitting since early morning. "Don't these people want jobs? How can we possibly have so many no-shows?"

Peter shook his head in disgust. After Raul's interview—one of the longest, most grueling hours of Peter's life—the next four candidates for the vacant loading supervisor position had all either canceled or simply failed to show up for their scheduled appointments. One said that she'd accepted another job. Another called in sick, and refused to reschedule without explanation. The other two never even tried to get in touch, nor did they answer their phones, despite Jess's repeated attempts to reach them. When the noon hour arrived, Raul stood alone as the only candidate vying for the position.

"Should we run another recruitment?" Manuel asked.

"No way!" Gregg grabbed the back of the empty chair Raul had occupied earlier. "Peter needs someone ASAP. I busted my balls to get these people in so he doesn't have to keep working twelve hour days. Even that was too slow for him."

"I never said that," Peter said. "It's more important that we get a qualified candidate than to fill it fast with the wrong person."

"That's not what you said last week when José quit." Gregg pointed a blunt finger at him. "You wanted a temp, remember?"

Peter frowned. He never thought those words would come back to haunt him. "Yeah, but someone with experience. And just as a temp. Look at this." He held up Raul's resumé. "He has less than two months in the business."

"But he is qualified to do the job," Manuel said. "He's worked in retail, he's been a supervisor, he's worked in shipping and receiving—and, he's a minority candidate. You did say you preferred a diversity hire, didn't you, Gregg?"

"I did," Gregg said. "Well, what about it, Peter? Why don't you think he's qualified?"

"As I said, his experience is awfully thin."

"We knew that might be the case when we decided to go with a minority hire," Gregg said. "The best minority candidates get snapped up quickly in this market. Hell, I had less experience when I started than he does. People of color don't always get the opportunities extended to white dudes."

"How else does a guy get experience, other than getting jobs like this?" Manuel asked. "How did you get experience as a supervisor, Peter?"

Peter sighed. "Through promotion, of course." Exhaustion crept over him like a heavy blanket. He hadn't slept well since that phone call from Christine, and not at all since their date the week before. The long days at work had started to catch up to him as well. "I get that whole unequal opportunity thing, and I support the diversity goal. But—"

"There's always a 'but,'" Gregg said with a snort.

"Let me finish," Peter said. "I don't think hiring him solves our problem. I'll be working just as late training him as I am now doing both jobs."

"Short-term," Gregg said. "In a week or two, you'll be back to normal."

"I'm not so sure. And what about his time in jail? Doesn't that concern you?"

"You're the one who acquitted him," Gregg said. "You and your eleven fellow jurors. If you were convinced he didn't do it, how can I possibly argue?"

"It's not his fault that he was falsely accused," Manuel said with a hostile stare. Or so it seemed to Peter. "And they wouldn't even set bail for him. What was he supposed to do—break out of jail so he can keep his job? Do you think a white dude would get the same treatment?"

Peter looked at each of them in turn, out of arguments. He shook his head again. "I don't know. He just doesn't seem to be a good fit."

"That's what white hiring managers always say," Gregg said. "Too often, anyway. No real reason, just 'It's not a good fit.' That's the B.S. upper management wants stopped—and I do, too. So, unless you have a good, specific reason not to hire him, I say we go with Raul."

Peter hung his head. "At least let me check his references."

Manuel chuckled. "Isn't his chief reference a friend of yours? That Christine something-or-other? That should be a slam dunk."

Peter glared at him in silence. It would be a slam dunk, all right. But not for the reasons his colleagues expected.

Chapter Eleven

Christine signaled the waiter and held up her empty porcelain mug, nodding when he mouthed, "More coffee?" She smiled at him, exposing her perfect white teeth, and hoped he didn't take it as flirting. Too many men thought the slightest display of friendliness meant a woman wanted to bear his children. There might exist such a man, but not a waiter in a pretentious sidewalk café. Even one located, literally, on the sidewalk.

She spotted Peter parallel parking his silver Ford Ranger across the street and waved. He smiled at her, but kept both hands on the wheel, and centered the vehicle in the available spot on the first try. So conscientious. So competent. So…boring.

But so essential to her plans.

He walked toward her with a determined, confident stride. The man had his good points. Good-looking, outside of the receding hairline. Fit, too: he'd trimmed down over the summer, built up some muscle. Smart. Very much in control of his emotions—up to a point. Beyond that point, he could explode with passion, even violence. She'd seen it in brief flashes during the trial. She hoped she'd see it again, at the right moment.

The moment of her choosing, of course.

She stood and greeted him with a soft kiss, the way lovers do, and held her arms around his back for a second longer than a mere friend would have. His body pressed against hers, firm and strong. A hint of cologne overcame the expected smell of sweat on such a warm day. "It's so nice to see you in the middle of the day," she said into his ear. "What a pleasant surprise it was to get your call."

He surprised her again by stiffening and breaking the embrace. He did not smile, and in fact, his mouth remained set in a line, his eyes afire. "We need to talk," he said, and sat in the chair opposite her, like mere acquaintances do. Not the one perpendicular to her, the way couples do.

"Something specific?" She sat, alarm bells ringing. Her face flushed with warmth, and not from the summer heat.

"Raul Vasquez." He glared at her, drumming two fingers on the table.

"Yes," she said, putting on a big smile, her heart beat racing. "How is he doing?"

"You tell me." He leaned forward. "He said you referred him to us. I just finished interviewing him this morning."

"How wonderful!" She tapped her hands together in a tiny golf clap. "Did he do well?"

Peter sneered and sipped some water. "Let's put it this way. He did better than all of the other candidates."

She smiled to prevent the tension from showing. "I'm so glad to hear it. He's had such a difficult—"

"Because the others didn't show up!" Peter's voice rose, drowning out the ambient street noise around them. The waiter, busy taking another table's order, excused himself and hustled over.

"Can I get you something?" He placed a cardboard coaster emblazoned with the JavaTown Café logo on the table in front of him.

"I highly recommend the hazelnut lattés," Christine said, sipping from her own mug.

"Coffee, cream and sugar. And a BLT. Thanks." He never took his blazing brown eyes off of Christine.

"I guess we're ready to order food." Christine's hands shook as she picked up the menu. "I'll have the teriyaki salad." She smiled at the waiter, grateful for any excuse to avoid Peter's hot glare. Her fake smile muscles were getting a serious workout.

The waiter thanked them and returned to his other table. Peter poked his index finger onto his folded cloth napkin. "I understand how you got Raul in. When I told you about this job opening the other day, I should have known you'd exploit that information somehow. Well, you did. But what I don't get is, how did you get to the others?"

Her heart pounded. Her ears were on fire. "Others?" She sipped her coffee, buying time.

"The other candidates for the damned job!" His voice rose again, and he glanced around the half-dozen or so tables on the sidewalk. The patrons each broke their surprised stares and looked away. "I want to know how four otherwise disconnected people suddenly lost interest in a well-paying job with benefits and potential for advancement."

"I don't know what you're talking about." Christine set her coffee down with a clatter, spilling a quarter of it onto the table top. Damn. She'd thought she'd covered her tracks better than this. Maybe he was just guessing.

"Bullshit. You got to them, somehow." His voice dropped to a stage whisper and he leaned far over the table. "So now I'm in the position of having to hire a guy who will, every day, remind me of the worst damn day of my life. As if I needed a reminder!" He slammed his open palms on the table and pushed his chair back so that he no longer faced her head-on.

Christine steadied her coffee cup, minimizing further spillage. "I should think that a reminder of your lowest moment would do some good for a man of faith such as yourself. What do they say? Repentance is good for the soul?"

Peter gritted his teeth and spat out his response. "I am not a man of faith. In fact, I..." He leaned back in his chair and wiped his brow, calmer. "I don't know what the hell I am anymore."

She laid her arm across the table, palm-up, and wiggled her finger, a "come-hither" gesture. He glanced at it, met her eyes, blinked a few times. She dipped her head a touch, gestured once more. Come on, boy. Meet me halfway.

He let it linger a moment longer, then slid his hand onto hers. She closed her fingers around his hand and stroked the side of his palm with one finger. "I know what you are," she said.

He shrugged. Such a lost little boy. "What? What am I, Christine?" His voice came out ragged, broken.

"You're a good man," she said in a soft voice. "A passionate man." She gave him a knowing smile, and the corners of his lips turned up, even as his eyes remained sad. "A dutiful son, who takes care of his ailing mother. A great friend. Loyal. Reliable. A man his loved ones can depend on."

His mouth opened, closed again a moment. "I try to be."

"You succeed." She squeezed his hand and covered it with both of hers. "And I love the confidence it gives you."

"Confidence?" He coughed out a bitter laugh. "Are you talking about me?"

"I am." Light caresses continued on his forearm. "Sure, you have vulnerable moments. We all do. But those moments of vulnerability—like now—only make you more attractive. More...desirable." She narrowed her eyes, parted her bright red lips, danced her tongue across her teeth.

His breathing grew heavier, deeper. He put his hand onto hers, arresting the caresses on his arm. Blinked. Set his mouth in a line, exhaled through his nose. "You confuse me," he said. "I don't really know what you're about."

"I'm not so mysterious," she said. "Just a simple girl who's been hurt a few times, that's all." The words caught in her throat. She needed a sip of water, but that would mean letting go of his hands, breaking their connection. She cleared her throat instead.

"I just can't help but feel that you want something from me." He lowered his gaze. "Something other than a little T.L.C."

She laughed. How delightful he could be when he tried. "Of course I do, silly. I want much more than that." She pulled his hands closer, squeezed them again. "I want everything from you."

"Everything." He frowned, blinked his eyes. "I guess I keep getting the feeling that you want something specific."

She shook her head. "I've never made a secret of what I want from you. What I need from you." She lifted his hands to her lips, kissed them. "Do you want me to tell you again?"

He caressed her cheek, then tilted his head forward and back again in a slow nod.

"I want what every girl wants from her man," she said.

"Strength. Safety. Protection."

He pulled his hands away. "Yeah. That's what I mean. Protection. From—"

"Are you two ready to eat?" The waiter materialized at the side of their table, plates in hand. "A BLT for the lady—"

"Actually, that's mine," Peter said. "The teriyaki salad is hers."

"Of course! I'm so sorry." He swapped the plates and refilled their water glasses. "Can I get you anything else?"

They waved him off. Christine poked her fork into her salad. "I think we may need to discuss this later. It's sort of, I don't know, a little too public here, don't you think?"

He nodded, bit into his BLT, chewed, and swallowed. "Let's talk about Raul, then."

"Yes, let's." She chewed on a piece of stringy, tough chicken, drowning in a spicy brown sauce. "He seems like a dependable sort."

"How in God's name did you come up with the idea of recommending him for a job at Stark's? Working for me?" He set his sandwich down on his plate without taking a second bite.

"Actually," she said, "you gave me the idea. You said you needed a diversity hire." She cocked her head, tried to keep her voice light. "Plus, I knew that a fair-minded person like you would be able to overlook his recent trauma. Such a shame that he was so unjustly accused, don't you think?"

The muscles in his neck grew taut, his voice strained. "Didn't it occur to you to check with me first?"

"Now, how awkward would that have been? I bumped into him, quite by chance at Lumber City," and her face warmed again with the lie. "I asked how he was doing, and suddenly I remembered you mentioning the job opening. Did I do bad?" She gave him her sweetest, most charming smile. It didn't work.

"Dammit, Christine!" He banged a fist on the table, sending silverware flying. A white-aproned café employee scooped it up and scurried off to find replacements. Peter paused a moment, either calming himself or collecting his thoughts, or both. "You know why he's a problem for me."

"Yes, of course."

"If you know, then why—"

"Because you need to overcome this problem. I want to help you."

"What are you talking about?"

She fixed him with a level stare. "The problem is, you don't know what your problem is. You men, especially white men, think the world is your oyster—"

"This is not about white male privilege!" He stabbed his napkin with his new, unused fork, poking holes in the white fabric.

She chuckled. "Of course it is. Think about it. Why was he accused of murder in the first place? A murder committed, as we now know, buy a middle-class white male? Why did most of the jury believe him guilty in the first place?"

"Including you, I might add."

"True."

"And not me!"

She set her elbows on the table, arms upright, and rested her chin in her open palms. She allowed herself a tiny, triumphant smile. "Only because you had a special reason for knowing he was innocent. Am I right, Peter?"

He stared at her, taking fast, shallow breaths, and, almost imperceptibly, nodded.

"Good," she said. She paused. She needed to take this slowly. Play it just right. Reel him in.

"Justice was served," he said, his voice hoarse.

"Some might argue otherwise. Raul, for instance. He spent six months in jail awaiting trial. Because of...who, Peter?"

"I never accused him. I helped acquit him. I—"

"You committed the crime he was accused of. I'd say you're at least partially responsible."

He glared at her, taking deep breaths, followed by loud exhalations. "So, hiring him is my retribution, then? I pay him back on Stark's dime?"

"You make it sound like charity. It's not. They need someone. He's a hard worker. Give him a chance. You owe him that much, don't you?" She kept her voice soft, the voice of empathy for a man wronged by the system…she hoped.

Peter stared at her a long time, picked up his sandwich, set it back on his plate. He tapped the table with his thumb, pursing his lips. Then he leaned back and crossed his arms. "Does he know?"

"About you? No. I've told him nothing." Kept a poker face. She hoped.

"You're certain? This isn't some sort of setup, his revenge—"

"Don't be ridiculous. How would that help me get rid of Kyle?"

He stared at her a few moments longer, thinking. Weighing alternatives in his mind. Or his doubts. Or—

He stood, grabbed his sandwich, and threw some cash on the table. "I think I understand, Christine." He spun on his heel and returned to his truck.

"What?" Christine said under her breath with a devilish smile. "No kiss goodbye?"

Chapter Twelve

"Dude, I'm telling you again," Frankie said, seated on Peter's sofa and draining a brown bottle of India Pale Ale. "Get away from this woman. And I mean yesterday."

Peter shook his head and sighed. "I wish I could. It's not so easy."

"What are you talking about? A year ago you couldn't hold on to the only woman who ever treated you right. Now you can't get rid of this crazy bitch who treats you like crap. Why the hell not?" Frankie stood and grabbed both of their empties off the coffee table. He gestured to Peter with them, tipping them back as if sipping from them.

"No more for me," Peter said. "I have to get to work early tomorrow."

"Yeah, must be nice to have a job and all." Frankie's voice rang with bitterness. "I can't believe you guys wouldn't even let me interview."

"Frankie. You were tossed out on your butt for sexual harassment. What makes you think you'd have the slightest chance at that job?"

"Officially, I got medical disability." Frankie grabbed his cane and limped toward the kitchen with the empties, shouting back to Peter as he went. "I even asked Donna. She's totally cool with me going back there."

"Yeah, well, Gregg isn't. Honestly, I think it's for the best, too." He sat back in his chair and rubbed the steel cables in his neck.

"You're against me now, too?" Frankie called from the kitchen. A bottle cap bounced on the tile floor, then kerplunked into Peter's trash can. Frankie returned with an open bottle of IPA, already a third gone.

"I'm not against you. I told you I'll help you find work, as soon as you're healthy." Peter eyed Frankie's beer, reconsidering his choice to stop drinking for the night.

Frankie, noticing Peter's interest, handed him the bottle, then eased himself onto the sofa. "Yeah, well, fat lot of good that's gonna do me. Doc says I may never walk without a cane again. What the hell am I gonna do? I can't work in an office. They'd lock me up in the loony bin in under a week."

Peter laughed, snorting IPA out of his nose. That got Frankie laughing, too, and he grabbed his beer back.

"So, anyway, back to this Christine chick. You have got to get away from her."

"I can't just walk away from her. She's got me in a bad spot." Peter stood and stared out the picture window of his bungalow. The streetlight in front of his neighbor's house flickered off, plunging the surrounding homes into blackness. It was after ten o'clock, and most of his neighbors had already put their young children, and themselves, to bed. He should do the same. But there'd be no point if he, once again, couldn't sleep.

"A really bad spot," Frankie said. "She's trouble. And believe me, I know trouble when I see it."

Peter nodded and smiled. Too true. Except that more often than not, Frankie brought the trouble, not the woman. "Frankie, she's not going to go away. I told you what she wants me to do. I've been trying to string her along, hoping I can find some graceful exit, but I don't see a way out. I can't do what she asks. But if I don't…Frankie, what in the hell am I going to do?"

"I'll tell you what you're going to do. You're going to call her bluff. She'll never turn you in."

"But what if she does?"

Frankie grabbed him and shook him by the shoulders. "She won't. She can't. Listen, if she's known all this time, and hasn't told anyone, she's guilty, too. Withholding evidence, right? She'll go to jail just as fast as you will."

"Unless she cuts a deal."

Frankie opened his mouth to object, but no words came out. Instead, he nodded. "Yeah, she probably would do that, wouldn't she?"

Peter nodded too. "So, what do I do?"

Frankie drained his beer, rubbed his chin, then snapped his fingers. "I have an idea. She doesn't know me, right? I follow her, I get her alone somewhere—"

"And what? You take her out? How is that better than what she's asking me to do?" Peter shuddered. Once again, the idea had far too much appeal—and it scared him.

"She ain't exactly asking you," Frankie said. "But no, I won't freaking kill her, dude. I'd just, you know, scare her off."

"Like you did with Donna—" Peter stopped himself and covered his mouth. "I didn't mean to say that."

"But you thought it." Frankie pushed himself off the couch to his feet, fists clenched. "You asshole. All right, you want to play it that way? Fine. If you don't back away from this bitch, and I mean right now, I'll go to the cops—on both of you."

"Frankie, don't—"

"Don't what? Don't try to be your friend by helping you? Don't try to keep you from doing another stupid, awful thing? Dude, you are so screwed up right now, you don't even know who your real friends are." He grabbed his cane and stomped toward the door.

"Look, man, I'm sorry. I didn't mean it." Peter grabbed his friend's shoulder from behind, and Frankie stopped. "Yes, I thought it, but I don't really feel that way. You said you didn't interfere with the harassment investigation, and I believe you. Sometimes I say things before I think. This was one of those times. Haven't you ever done that? Come on, man." He held on to Frankie's shoulder, but his friend made no real attempt to pull away.

Instead, Frankie turned and glared at him, inhaling and exhaling deep breaths, one hand still holding the doorknob. Finally, he let his hand drop. "Peter. I can't let you do this. This, this thing. With her. I just can't."

Peter spread his hands. "Give me some time to figure things

out. I'll come up with a way out. I promise."

Frankie stared, doubt and anger still clouding his face. "All right. I'll give you a week. You come back to me with a better plan. If you don't, then I go to the cops."

"The cops won't believe you. Besides, you don't know anything, really. Just what I've told you, and I'll tell them you're a lying drunk. Which you are. Well, a drunk, anyway." He chuckled. "Just like me."

Frankie didn't smile. "Fine. Maybe the cops won't believe me. But I know who will. Your brother Jimmy. And if he gets hold of this, you can bet your unsaved soul that Pastor Jimmy will bust your ass faster than you can say 'Hell and Damnation.' And then who takes care of your mother? What happens to Thelma then, huh?"

Peter's knees grew weak. He'd spent the last five years fighting his brother's attempts to block the medical treatments that had repeatedly saved his mother's life. Prayer, Pastor Jimmy railed, was all her good soul needed, not the "abomination" known as medical science. "Frankie. You wouldn't."

"In a heartbeat."

"That'd kill her."

Frankie scoffed, almost a laugh. "Looks like no matter what you do, somebody dies. Except one thing: the right thing." He stepped closer and jabbed a finger into Peter's chest. "You tell this broad No Effing Way. And you do it now. Otherwise…"

He let the words hang, nodded once, and shuffled out the front door.

Chapter Thirteen

"Peter, come quickly!"

The whispered voice, with its familiar northern California lilt and dangerous intensity, shook Peter out of his groggy half-sleep far more than the phone's scratchy chiming of "Black Magic Woman" had moments before.

"Christine? What's wrong?"

"It's him. He's here. Outside my house. Peter, I'm so afraid!"

"Who? Kyle?"

"Sh! Don't say his name!"

Peter shot out of bed, pulling on pants one-handed. Never mind that Kyle almost certainly couldn't hear anything Peter said. Christine's panic was palpable and contagious. He shoved the phone between his chin and shoulder to free his hands for zipping and buckling. "He can't hear—"

"Oh my God. Something just broke—it sounds like he just kicked in my front door. I think he's coming inside!"

Peter pulled on a shirt he picked up off the floor, leaving it unbuttoned, and slipped into a pair of sandals. "I'm on my way. Lock yourself into your bathroom. Do you have a knife or anything?"

"I have a pistol in my closet. But I've never shot it at anything, other than paper targets. And honestly, I'm a terrible shot. Oh, crap! I think he's inside!" Her breathing grew fast and ragged, and a door slammed in the background. "Okay. I'm locked into the bathroom. How long will it take you to get here?"

"About ten minutes, this time of night." He ran out the front door to his house, not bothering to lock it. The grass glistened with late-night dew, reflecting the glare of the street light. Gypsy, the neighbor's border collie, barked at the twisted-wire fence.

"Can't you get here any faster?" Another crash sounded in the background. "Please hurry! Oh my God. Oh my God!"

"Call 9-1-1!" Peter burned rubber down his sleepy little side street and around the corner. Times like these he regretted living in the maze of the narrow streets of Ladd's Addition, built in a time when few people owned cars, much less parked them on the street. But he'd learned to drive on Portland's skinny neighborhood streets, and had raced to Sunset Hospice more than once late at night to respond to distress calls about this mother. Navigating through tight spaces didn't faze him.

He'd already run several red lights southbound on McLoughlin Boulevard, the four-lane highway that ran in rough parallel to the winding Willamette River that divided Portland's east and west sides, when his phone sang the Santana tune to him again. He put it on speaker. "Are you okay? Is he still there?"

"He's banging on my bathroom door," Christine said, fear wrapped around her every word. "I think he's trying to kick it in. It's not going to last…it's already starting to break. Hurry!"

"I'm hurrying," he said. "Did you call the police?"

"I did. They said they're on their way. But—oh, my God. I think the door is breaking! He could be inside any second!"

Peter groaned, recalling the old saying: When seconds count, the police are only minutes away. "Do you have your pistol with you?"

"Yes. But I don't know if I can shoot at him. I'm scared, Peter!"

"Getting close. Stay calm." Peter slowed to make a right turn into Christine's neighborhood. The faint whine of a siren sounded outside his car window.

"How close are you?" Her voice dropped to a whisper, almost inaudible over the noise of Peter's truck engine and the approaching siren.

Peter drove as fast as he dared, but the cars parked on either side of the narrow residential streets kept him below forty. His tires squealed around a corner, then the next, and a third quick turn put him on her street, two short blocks away. "Almost there. Are you—"

"Shush!" she said in the same low whisper.

He nodded, finally understanding. She didn't want him to hear even the buzzing noise that a cell phone might produce in the quiet house. He raced the remaining 400 feet down the street and slammed on his brakes in front of her house, not even bothering to pull over to the curb. He grabbed the tire iron behind the passenger's seat, pushing out of his mind the image of the last man who'd fallen victim to this weapon, before jumping out of the truck and racing to her front door. Sure enough, the door hung ajar, the lock broken. Screaming at the top of his lungs, he dashed into the house, tire iron held over his head, ready to do damage.

Something moved to his right. A man, athletically built with short blond hair, ducked down a hallway. Peter chased after him. A bedroom door slammed shut in his face. Peter tried the handle. Locked.

A noise from inside the room caught his attention. Something sliding, then clicking. Something metallic rattled to the floor. A gun? A knife? No. Not the right sound. A clattering instead of a thump or clunk. Then grunting, followed by something brittle crashing to the floor. He tried the handle again. No dice. He stepped back, lifted his foot to kick the handle.

"Peter?" Christine's muffled voice emanated from somewhere behind him. From inside the locked bedroom, another grunt, a muted thump, and then, silence.

"Peter? Are you out there?"

He spun around, ran the short distance down the hall to another locked door. He listened and heard some shuffling inside. Then, breaking glass.

"Oh, my God. Peter, he's trying to come in the bathroom window!"

The door flew open and Christine ran out, dressed in a plain white camisole and panties. She hid behind him, clutching his shoulders. A breeze blew in from a broken window on the far wall, and shards of glass littered the floor. A baseball bat retreated from view outside the window.

Peter shook Christine off and crossed the bathroom in two quick strides. The swinging bat reappeared, and he met it with a jab of the tire iron. The vibrating bar stung his hands, but the bat fell away. From the sounds that ensued outside, he guessed that it clattered down the side of Christine's house and landed painfully on the intruder's head. Swearing followed, a man's voice. Fast footsteps followed, growing quieter with every thud on the sunbaked yard. Peter looked out the window and caught a glimpse of a man running across the street and into the neighbor's back yard. Dogs barked their complaints, and sirens blared closer and louder.

Christine wrapped her arms around him again from behind. "Is he gone?"

Peter nodded and rotated inside of her embrace, folding her into his own arms. "He's gone." He patted her back, and she sobbed into his chest.

The sirens screamed at peak pitch, and moments later, blue and white lights reflected off the nearby homes. Loud footsteps thumped outside the house. Then a man's voice shouted. "Police! Nobody move!"

"We're in here!" Peter called out to them. "We're all right."

A bright light blinded him. "Hands where I can see them!" A uniformed man pointed a flashlight into his eyes. Peter raised his hands above his head.

"Lady. Get your hands up!" More footsteps thudded into the hallway.

"It's okay," Peter said. "This is Christine Nielsen. She's the one who called you. The intruder's gone."

The cop lowered the flashlight. Christine turned her head toward the policeman, and he nodded. "That your truck in the middle of the street?"

Peter nodded.

"Go move it," the cop said. "Then get back in here. Miss Nielsen, we have a lot to discuss."

***

"He's gone," the shaggy-haired man said into the phone. "And wherever he's going, he's in a pretty big hurry."

"Probably got a booty call," his boss said. "Take advantage."

"I'm all over it," the shaggy-haired man said. "After tonight, he won't be able to take a dump without us seeing it, hearing it, and smelling it if you want to."

The man on the other end of the line emitted a deep sigh, and the shaggy-haired man broke the connection, laughing.

***

Patrolman Tennyson Howard, or "Tens" as his fellow uniformed officers called him, scowled at the pretty brunette and her balding boyfriend in the woman's living room. The two victims sat across from him on a spare, Danish-style wood-frame sofa. Tens occupied a matching chair, stylish and uncomfortable. He turned the chair to face them and ignored the woman's disapproving glare. Miss Nielsen had changed out of her skimpy nightclothes into jeans and a loose-fitting button-down blouse since he'd first arrived. The man next to her, who said he'd driven over from a few miles away, wore jeans, sandals, and a half-buttoned, completely wrinkled dress shirt. He looked even more tense than she did, shifting in his seat and rubbing his hands together in his lap.

"Did either of you get a good look at the intruder?" he asked, looking at each of them in turn.

"I know who it was," the woman said in a rush of air. "The same man who's been stalking me since—"

"But did you see his face?" Tens asked. The woman opened her mouth again, then closed it and shrugged. "From the front, no. Not this time. I heard him trying to get in, and, on Peter's advice, I locked myself in the bathroom."

"You're Peter? Er, Peter Robertson?" Tens asked the boyfriend. Peter nodded. Tens checked his notes. "You said you saw the man from behind, correct?"

Peter nodded. "I caught a side view of his face, but it was dark. I could tell he had blond hair, was clean-shaven, and had a pretty athletic build. I got a general idea of his height, a little over six feet, but I couldn't pick him out of a lineup, if that's what you're asking."

Tens frowned. "That's unfortunate. Well, we'll dust the bedroom you saw him go into, and I'm sure we'll need prints from each of you to eliminate the ones that aren't his. If the intruder touched anything and has a criminal record, we should be able to track him down."

"Kyle's been here dozens of times," Christine said, "We used to be a couple."

Tens frowned. "I see. Well, that complicates matters, but we should probably go ahead with it anyway, for future reference."

"Why don't you go search for him?" Christine crossed her arms and tossed her head to one side. "He couldn't have gotten very far."

"We have patrol cars circling the area, but he could be anywhere by now," Tens said. "Look, I understand your frustration, and we want to catch him as much as you do—"

"I doubt that!"

Tens bit back a smart-assed retort and took a deep breath. "Okay. Maybe not quite as much. But we'll keep on looking, and I'll pass by a few extra times on my rounds for the next few days. Will you be staying here tonight, Mr. Robertson?"

The couple exchanged a long glance. So, this boyfriend must be a new thing for her. The woman took his hand in both of hers. "Would you?" she asked him.

"Of course," the man said. Lucky bastard.

"All right, then." Tens stood, and caught the eye of his partner, who'd just reentered the room. "Tell forensics to ink these two, and let's get out of here." His partner escorted the couple into the kitchen where forensics had set up temporary shop.

Something about this situation bothered Tens. Approaching the end of his second decade on the force—his second set of "tens"—he'd developed a nose for situations that didn't add up. This was one of those. On the surface it looked like a straightforward breaking-and-entering, maybe with intent to do more. But from what they'd told him, it seemed that the guy should have had time to get to whatever he'd been after—if he was, in fact, after something. And the bad guys were always after something.

Nope. Things didn't add up here. He couldn't put his finger on it, but he knew something just wasn't right.

Part Two

The Planning Dance

Chapter Fourteen

"Now do you understand?" Christine sat on the sofa, wrapped in a pillowy patchwork quilt to stave off the late-night chill. Peter, next to her, rested one hand on her knee. It felt...good. Warm. Protective.

"I never denied that you were at risk," he said. "I just think there are other ways of dealing with it, other than—than—" He paused, and after a moment, closed his mouth and shook his head.

"It's the only way to stop him." The steely edge in Christine's voice surprised even her. "Until he's gone, he'll never stop coming after me." She stared at him. "Never."

He fidgeted in his seat. "The courts can order him to—"

"Do you know how many court orders he already ignores?" She sprang forward, placing her face inches from his, and gripped the hand on her knee, digging her nails in. He winced. Good. He needed to feel some of this pain. "The courts can't do anything to stop him. What happened tonight proves it."

"They could put him in jail."

"And then what? I've been over this with the lawyers. They can only hold him for twenty-four hours, maybe forty-eight. After that, he'd be back on the street—Portland streets, mind you. They don't view him as a threat. Do you know what one prosecutor told me?"

Peter shook his head, as if numb.

"He said, 'There's no room in the jails for him anyway. They're overwhelmed with pimps, prostitutes, and teenagers busted for drug possession. We don't have room for trespassers.' Trespassers! They called him a God damned trespasser!" She gripped his arm even harder. He winced, then pried her fingers loose and zippered his fingers into hers.

"Christine, I'm sorry. I want to help you. I will help you. But what you're asking, I just—I can't—"

"You can." She leaned closer, her lips an inch from his. "You have. Like last November, with Alvin Dark."

He shook his head. "That was different. He attacked me. I defended myself."

"Self-defense? Hah! You followed him and crashed into his car, then beat him to death."

"I know how it looks, but—"

"And how is this any different? You're defending me. From a stalker. A violent, angry man. Don't I deserve protection, the same as you?"

"If I saw him attacking you, then, yes, it could be considered a defensive act, but—"

"You did see him attack me. Tonight!" She wanted to add: And that's the whole point. But she needed him to see that for himself.

"He broke in. That's diff—"

"In order to kill me!"

Peter sat back, as if pushed, and took a deep breath. "We can't prove that."

Heat rose in Christine's face. How could he be so thick-headed? "He's threatened me. So. Many. Times. What do we have to do, catch him in the act? Stop him while the bullet's in the air, or while his fists are flying?"

Peter's shoulders drooped. "Unfortunately, the law is on his side. Until we witness an actual attack—"

"I have witnessed an actual attack. On me!"

"But it was your word against his. Look, I believe you. But until we can, yes, catch him in the act, the burden of proof is on us."

"Until it's too late, you mean." She shifted her tone from angry to pouty. Maybe that would reach him.

He swallowed, nodded. "I won't let anything happen to you."

She smiled. That's what she needed to hear. She wrapped

both arms around his neck. The blanket fell away, and she leaned into him, her body pressing into his. "That's all I want," she whispered. She kissed his face, then nibbled on his ear. "Now, tell me. What do you want?"

***

Peter awoke in a strange bed, rested and comfortable, but alone.

He sat up, shook out the cobwebs, and took in the space. Girly, soft, and tasteful. Pillowy mattress and comforter, all pastels with modern Danish-style furniture. A make-up table with a large mirror. Bright white drapes, drawn shut, allowed morning light to seep through around the edges. An open door revealed a walk-in closet. A closed door, he guessed, led to a bathroom. He slid out of the bed and padded over to it, confirmed his theory, and closed the door again behind him. He relieved his bladder's ache, washed his hands, frowned at his unshaven reflection in the mirror. Tried to remember what day it was. Tuesday? Wednesday? He'd lost track. A workday, though. Speaking of which, he needed to get there.

He exited the bathroom and searched for a clock. None. He wondered how she ever managed to arrive anywhere on time.

The door to the hallway opened, and Christine entered, holding two large mugs of steaming, aromatic bliss. "I hope you like Sulawesi Peaberry dark roast," she said, handing him one. "Cream and sugar, if I remember correctly."

"You always do." He took a sip. Hints of caramel, toffee, and sweet citrus danced within the dark, chocolaty roast. Pure heaven. He kissed her. "You make a damn fine cuppa Joe, m'lady."

She laughed at his horrible attempt at an Irish brogue. "I'm glad you like it. Making great coffee is one of my superpowers." She glanced at the unmade bed and winked. "One of many."

He tried, and failed, to ignore the stirring warmth rising in his loins, and surrendered a nervous laugh. "Unfortunately, I'll have to forbear enjoying your other great superpower for a bit. I need to get to work." He set the coffee on an end table, sat on the bed, and pulled on his pants. She sat next to him and stopped the pants' progress mid-thigh.

"So early? Pity." She ran her hand up his thigh to his boxers. "I was hoping you could, maybe, take the day off. Don't you need a sick and tired day?"

She continued to caress him, and he moaned, both in pleasure and, when he stopped her, in pain. "I can't. I'm buried at work. Until I get that loading supervisor on board—"

"Raul." Her hand resumed its caresses. He blocked it again, removed it from his body.

"Whoever we choose. It's not final."

"It's Raul. We both know it. You have no one else, remember?"

He turned to face her. She was all business now, no sensual allure remaining. He stood and pulled the jeans up the rest of the way. "Yeah. Well. There is that."

"I think you'll find him useful." She smiled, a Cheshire cat grin.

"Useful? How about qualified, or experienced? That's what I need."

"He's very qualified and experienced at what we need him for." Her grin widened, in a twisted sort of way.

Peter's chest tightened. "We?"

"You and me, darling. For our task ahead."

"Our task." He shrugged on his shirt and started buttoning.

"Yes. Solving the problem that brought you here last night. Or have you already forgotten?" She sipped her coffee and her eyes narrowed over the rim.

He froze. "Wait. You set all that up so that Stark's could hire a—a—co-conspirator?"

She laughed. "Call it whatever you like, darling. Just keep in mind that he is comfortable getting his hands dirty, if need be. And after last night, I hope the need for dirty work is as obvious to you as it is to me."

As much as he wanted to deny it, he could not.

***

Peter parked his pickup in Stark's employee lot on the side of the building, much farther from the door than usual—one of the many penalties for being a half-hour late. He'd left Christine's place only after watching her drive off in her Miata, top down, hair blowing in the wind in an illusion of carefree safety. With Kyle now physically present in the area, she was neither carefree nor safe. That worried him, almost as much as it did her.

Walking toward the front entrance of the store, he passed a familiar-looking truck, one that bore a striking resemblance to his own Ford Ranger, albeit older and a bit more beaten up. A silver early model Mazda B-series pickup with a dented hood and damaged grille. One he'd seen photos of during Alvin Dark's murder trial.

Raul Vasquez's vehicle.

He hustled inside and made a beeline for Jessica's office. She sat at her desk, concentrating on some paperwork. Gregg stood beside her, bent over her shoulder, his trademark cigarette tucked into the gap between his ear and his tight graying curls. They looked up when he entered.

"I wondered if you were going to show up today," Gregg said. "What happened? Car trouble?"

"Where is he?" Peter planted his feet should width apart in her office, hands on his hips. "And more important, why is he here?"

"Who?" Gregg glanced at Jessica. She shook her head, confused.

"Don't play dumb with me. Raul's truck is parked outside. Why?"

Gregg shook his head. "You already know what kind of truck he drives? How?"

"Don't change the subject. He hasn't even been officially hired. Hell, I haven't even made a decision yet, much less an offer, and he's already putting down roots. What the hell is going on?"

"Petey, I'm sorry," Jess said. "That's my fault. When Gregg told me that all of the other job applicants dropped out, I asked Raul to come in and fill out the paperwork. I assumed—"

"You assumed wrong."

"Well, he was the only candidate," Gregg said. "And he's qualified. And a diversity—"

"Aren't we even going to pretend this is my choice to make? At least a little bit?" Peter stomped back to her doorway, then spun back to face them. "So, where the hell is he?"

"I figured you'd want to brief him," Jess said, "so I put him in your office for now." She looked to Gregg for support, who grimaced. Peter glared at them for a moment, then darted down the broad aisles toward his office.

Raul, as Jess predicted, was filling out paperwork when Peter burst into his office, head down, studious and focused. Which should have reduced Peter's frustration and assuaged his suspicions. But one little detail blew all of that out of the water: where Raul had chosen to sit to fill out said paperwork.

At Peter's desk. In. His. Chair.

"Get the hell out of my damned chair," he said before the door had even swung all the way open.

Raul jumped, dropped his pen on the floor, then stood, panic written all over his face—proving, to Peter, that he was at least part human. "I am sorry," he said, clutching the papers in front of his chest. "Miss Jessica told me to—"

"She didn't tell you to take over my office. Go on, get out of there. Wait outside for me." Peter set his keys on his desk and glared at the shorter man, scooting out of Peter's way so he could scoot by.

"Now hold on." Gregg's large frame blocked Raul's exit. "Peter, calm down. This isn't his fault."

Raul paused next to Gregg, glanced up at him, then turned back to face Peter. "My apologies for sitting at your desk. I—I needed a pen, and—"

"And you thought, what the hell, I'll just move in, right?" Peter shoved some paperwork into a folder, confidential stuff that a non-employee shouldn't see, and bent over to power up his computer. "This doesn't bode well for your tenure here. You haven't even started, and already you've pissed me off."

"Again, I am sorry."

"Peter, chill out," Gregg said. "Now."

Peter removed another folder from a drawer and slapped it onto his desk. "I'll chill when I'm damn well good and ready. This stinks." He swept an arm wide, across his body. "This whole situation stinks, big time. First I'm told who I can and can't hire, then I—"

"Peter!" Gregg strode forward, glaring at him. "Raul," he said in a calmer voice without turning to look at him, "would you mind finishing up in Jessica's office? We'll come get you in a few minutes." Raul nodded and slipped out of the room. Gregg, still glaring, exhaled with a flourish. "What the hell is wrong with you?"

"Wrong with me? What the hell's wrong with this place?" Peter collapsed into his chair and stared at the computer screen, still showing his machine's boot-up sequence. "I thought it was my decision of whom to hire on my staff. Now I don't even get to choose who to interview."

"You can't blame me for all those people not showing up." Gregg sat in the guest chair facing Peter. "And you're the one who wanted this to happen fast. So, we did that. And he's a good man, Pete. Really. We got a good one."

"I should think we'd at least want to check his other references."

"Jess did that yesterday, like she always does. He checks out. She emailed you about that."

Peter's computer finished its boot sequence and he opened his email application. Sure enough, Jessica's email sat on top of the list in his inbox, flagged "Urgent." He clicked on it and scanned its contents. "So, he already quit his job at Lumber City? What happened to giving two weeks' notice?"

"Apparently he'd already given notice before applying here. They were very sorry to see him go. They love him there, said he was the hardest-working employee in the store. Diligent, punctual, reliable—"

"Yeah, he's a real boy scout. Did you call Florentino's?"

Gregg sighed. "We did. Their manager refused to talk to us. Blamed it on their lawyers."

"And that didn't raise any red flags?"

"He told us about that in the interview, remember? Hell, you were on the jury when his boss testified. What more could we ask?"

Peter tapped a pencil on his desk for a few seconds. Maybe he was overreacting. Christine had somehow manipulated this outcome. She hadn't explained how. As for why, her reason still rang in his ears. It made him uneasy, to say the least.

But if he hoped to see Christine, or share her bed, anytime soon, he needed to shorten his twelve-hour workdays. That meant hiring someone, soon.

And that meant hiring Raul.

Maybe he could turn this to his own advantage. Right now, Raul probably felt he owed Christine for this opportunity. If he owed Peter instead…

"Send him in." Peter smiled. "Let's get him trained on how to run Stark's loading dock."

Gregg stood, grinned, and extended a beefy handshake. "That's my boy."

Chapter Fifteen

Peter gave Raul a tour of Stark's entire physical plant, focused on the parts with which he'd need the most familiarity: the loading and receiving dock, the warehouse, and the retail floor, where he'd spend time helping customers between shipments. Back in his office, he gave Raul a quick run-through of their inventory and timekeeping system. "But you'll get formal classroom training on those," he said, "as soon as Jessica can set that up for you."

"Muchas gracias," Raul said. "I mean, thank you."

Peter grinned, the first time he'd relaxed all day. "You don't have to translate that. I remember that much of my high school Spanish. And on the floor, we hope to exploit your bilingual skills. We're getting a lot more Hispanic customers these days."

Raul nodded and cleared his throat. "If you don't mind me teaching you something, señor…?"

Peter shrugged. "Sure. What ya got?"

"The term 'Hispanic' refers to a person who speaks primarily Spanish," Raul said. "While it is not technically incorrect, people from South and Central America prefer to be referred to as 'Latino' and 'Latina'—although that is not a universal preference."

"Good to know," Peter said. "I appreciate you setting me straight on that."

"It is my pleasure."

Peter paused a moment. "There's something else I want you to set me straight on, if you don't mind."

"Of course," Raul said. "Anything."

Peter leaned in and set Raul with a level gaze. "What's your relationship with Christine Nielsen?"

Raul blanched and froze in his seat. "We, uh...we are friends."

"How did you become friends?"

Raul cleared his throat and lowered his gaze. "We happened to meet at Lumber City about six weeks ago, just after I started working there. She recognized me and asked me about a siding product we carry." His vocal cadence seemed steady.

Too steady. As in, rehearsed.

"Which product was that?"

"A composite material from Carolina Lumber," he said. "I don't think you carry it here at Stark's."

"We."

"We?"

"*We* don't carry it at Stark's. You work for us now."

Raul smothered a sheepish grin. "Of course. I am sorry."

Peter chuckled, hoping to convey more mirth than he felt. "No worries. You're new. You'll get used to it. So, how did it work out?"

Raul's eyebrows curled in puzzlement. "How did what work out?"

"The siding. For Christine."

"Oh." His face blanked again. "She said she was not ready to buy. I do not think she ever followed up." He sounded unsure.

"Interesting," Peter said, "that she went to Lumber City when she knew I could get her a better deal."

Raul set his lips in a firm line and glanced away.

"And I've been to her house. The siding appears to be several years old, but in perfect condition." Peter waited for a reaction, and again got none, other than a general reddening of Raul's face and neck. "Well, I suppose she must have changed her mind, then."

"As I said, she never followed up about that."

"But she did follow up with you. Socially, I mean. Did you two date?"

"No!" Raul swiveled in his seat, his body taking a more aggressive posture. "Mr. Robertson, I do not know why Ms.

Nielsen took an interest in me. But I did appreciate her help in finding this opportunity. At least, I thought so before this conversation."

Peter suppressed a smile. "If you're having second thoughts…"

Raul's eyes widened. Peter had the impression he was thinking about it. Then Raul shook his head. "No. I am excited to be here." His pitch, though, rose a notch. Nerves, perhaps.

Peter studied him a moment. Opportunity lost. Gregg would blow a gasket if Peter pushed Raul away, but if he'd walked out on his own, Gregg could hardly blame Peter. On the other hand, he couldn't say for sure that Christine had planted him here to spy on him. Maybe she really did just want to do both of them a favor.

"Okay. I'm satisfied with your explanation. I won't bring it up again." He grabbed a thick binder from his bookshelf and handed it across the desk to Raul. "Here's our Employee Handbook. Give it a read-through, especially the guidelines for supervisors and the section on harassment. We've had some issues with that lately. Jess will set you up with a login to our computer system, and links to our standard operating procedures. Get up to speed on all that and be ready to unload some trucks at seven a.m. tomorrow."

Raul accepted the notebook and stood. "I will do that. Thank you for your time this morning, and for the opportunity to work at Stark's. I won't let you down."

Peter shook his hand. "I know you won't. And you're welcome."

When Raul had gone, Peter checked his messages. He'd missed a text from Angela Wegman, checking to make sure he had her number. He replied: "Thanks. Will call soon." Saved her number, deleted the message. He had a girlfriend…or at least, a woman interested in him. A committed monogamist, he'd never dated more than one woman at a time. And at that moment, he needed to call that one woman. For so many reasons.

He dialed her number, got voice mail, left a quick "call me back" and fired up his email. Ten minutes later, "Black Magic

Woman" played from his cell.

"You've been a bad boy," Christine said, her voice playful.

"I've been bad?" He stared at the phone, incredulous. "Remind me, which one of us interfered with—no, make that completely manipulated—the other's hiring process? If I didn't know better, I'd say you sent Raul here to spy on me."

Christine laughed. "Do you know better?"

Peter's voice caught in his throat. "Wait," he choked out, "are you saying he *is* here to spy on me?"

"Spy is such a nasty word," she said, still playful. "But isn't it convenient, having him in a position where he owes us both? A man who, shall we say, has some relevant experience?"

"Relevant? To what?"

She laughed again. "I think he could be very helpful in our plan to take care of Kyle. Don't you?"

"What plan? We don't have a plan."

Peter's office door opened, and Jessica appeared in the doorway. Raul Vasquez stood behind her, a faint smile on his face. His eyes bore straight into Peter. Jessica waved a fistful of papers in the air. "Petey, hon, we need your signature—"

He held up a hand to shush her, then pointed to his desk. Jessica slapped the forms down and leaned back against the door frame, arms crossed. In his ear, Christine continued, "You're right. We need to put a plan together, you and I, and soon. How about this evening? Your place? I'd rather not go home right now. I'm sure you understand."

"Sure, I understand." Peter scanned the forms in front of him, but none of the words on the page registered. He held up an open palm and gave Jessica a questioning look. "That would be fine. What time?"

Jessica pressed a bright purple fingernail next to a "sign here" sticky tab on the top form and held out a pen, clacking her gum in a rapid rhythm. Peter grabbed the pen and once again tried, but failed, to comprehend the meaning of what she had asked him to sign.

"Seven. I'll bring wine, you cook," Christine said. "Oh, and think about how you'll want to use Raul."

"Raul?" Too late, the name escaped his lips. Raul reacted by stepping into the open doorway, a foot behind Jessica.

"Yes?" Raul said. "You have some questions for me?"

"Is he there?" Christine asked. "Right now?"

"Uh, huh," Peter said. He still needed a cover for his verbal slip, so he held up the form in the air, print-side facing Raul. "Is this all correct?"

Raul squinted at the form and shrugged. Jessica blew a hurricane-force burst of air between her lips. "How the heck would Raul know if his network login authorization form is filled out right? Jeez Louise, Peter, you're such a dodo sometimes." She smacked the page back onto his desk and pointed at the "Sign here" tab. "Just sign it, all right? It's all perfect. Sign 'em all."

"Who's that?" Christine asked.

"Hold on." Peter scanned the top form, signed it, and handed the stack to Jessica. She glared at the ceiling, then set all but the top form back onto his desk.

"Sign all of them, birdbrain. Here—his tracking authorization." Another painted fingernail indicated the signature block. He scribbled something indecipherable on the empty black line. "His uniform and supplies requisition." Another scribble. "Phone and office info." Again. "Pay and benefits." Scratch, scratch. "And his authorization to access confidential crap we got here. Raul, you're about to learn all of our deepest, darkest secrets." She laughed and pointed another fingernail.

Christine laughed. "Not all of our secrets. Right, Peter?"

Peter, about to sign, found he could no longer move his hand.

Chapter Sixteen

"So," Frankie said, setting fresh pints in front of Peter and his own empty chair in the back of a dusty neighborhood pub, "How'd you break it to her?"

Peter slid the beer closer and lifted it to his lips, careful not to slosh any on his last clean pair of trousers. Nearly a dozen others lay in a pile in his laundry room next to a mountain of underwear, socks, and beer-logo-imprinted T-shirts. He took a deep swallow of the bitter, amber brew, Lucky Dog Altbier, his summer favorite. He averted his gaze from Frankie, who remained standing across the table from him. No answer—no truthful answer—would satisfy his friend. Nor himself, for that matter. Maybe if he took another sip or two or three, Frankie might forget what he'd asked.

No such luck. "Well? What'd you tell her?" Frankie leaned against the wobbly table, splashing IPA out of his own mug.

"I'll get a napkin." Peter rose from his chair.

Frankie laid his beefy paws on his friend's shoulders and forced him back into his chair. "Never mind the napkin. What did you tell her?"

Peter sloshed the spilled beer to the floor and pretended to be preoccupied with the inch-thick layer of peanut shells absorbing the pale froth.

"Dude." Frankie twisted his body back to full height and ran the fingers of both hands through his blond, curly mop. "Tell me you told her no to killing—"

"Shh!" Peter tamped at the air with both hands, palms down, and waited for Frankie to sit. Once his friend had eased his bulky frame into his chair and taken a sip of beer, Peter leaned forward. "I haven't, yet. It's not a good time."

"Not a good time?" Frankie's voice carried over the hubbub of the half-filled, cavernous pub. Several heads turned to stare and a few conversations quieted. Frankie lowered his voice, but tension still streaked through every word. "Dude, you've got to tell her before you get, you know, addicted to her. You get what I mean?"

Peter averted his eyes again and shrugged. Frankie pinched the edges of the table and pressed his face close to Peter's. "It's already too late for that, isn't it? You're hooked. Aren't you?"

Peter said nothing and stared at the soggy mess on the floor.

"Oh, jeez." Frankie grabbed his beer, sucked half of it down in one quick gulp, and wiped foam off of his upper lip. "Peter, you're in trouble, man. Don't you see? You've got to get out."

"Out of what?"

"Out. Just out, man. Out of here, out of her clutches, out of this situation. You're getting in too deep, man. Why don't you— hell, why don't we get out of town for a while? Let's take a road trip!"

"You're suggesting that I run?" Peter shook his head and twirled his half-full beer glass around on its base. "I don't think that'd work."

"It's the only thing that'd work. Unless you want me talking to your brother."

"Of course not!"

"Then come on. You're long overdue for a vacation anyway." Frankie stood and threw some bills on the table. "Come on, let's go pack."

Peter waved him off. "Not gonna happen. It's midsummer, the busiest time of the year. Gregg would never give me time off now. Plus, I've got Raul to train."

"You're not going to ask Gregg." Frankie pulled on his arm.

"What do you suggest I do? Call him from the road?"

"Not a bad idea. Come on." Frankie lifted Peter up from his chair by the shoulders. "I'll carry you if I have to."

Peter resisted at first, then laughed. "Okay, okay, I'll go. But not like this, out of the blue, with no warning to anyone."

"Awesome! Okay. This weekend, then."

Peter shook his head. "Not this weekend. Maybe next. Give me one week to train Raul and get my life in order."

Frankie eyed him with suspicion. "You're not going to tell her, are you?"

"What could I tell her? I don't even know where we're going. And," he held up a hand to stifle Frankie's protest, "I don't want you to tell me. Deal?"

"You promise not to tell her anything?"

"Just that I won't be available for a couple of days."

"Weeks."

Peter crossed his arms, cocked his head. "Frankie, come on. I can't take more than a week right now."

"Okay. Two weekends. But you take all of next Friday off."

Peter grinned. "You drive a hard bargain."

"This is gonna be great!" Frankie pumped the air with his fist, then grabbed his cane and led Peter toward the exit. He pushed open the door—

And stumbled down the steps, landing hard on the gravel of the parking lot. Peter rushed to him and helped him up. "Frankie! You all right, man? Are you hurt?"

"I'm fine. Just a scratch. Where's my walking stick?" He found it, pushed himself off the ground, and dusted himself off. His hand came away bloody, courtesy of scraped knees poking through freshly-ripped jeans. "Crap. These were my favorite Levi's." He stumbled backwards and landed on his backside on the steps. "Ow! Damn."

"Frankie, let me drive you."

"No, dude, I'm fine. I'll be fine." He pushed himself back to his feet.

"Frankie. You're barely out of rehab from the last time you drove drunk."

"Technically, I'm still in rehab. Physical therapy, too. Ouch! Damn. That knee hurts."

"Come on. My truck. No arguments."

"I'm fine, I tell you."

"Look, man, if you expect me to drop everything and take a road trip with you at a moment's notice, the least you can do is let me keep you alive long enough to take the trip with me."

Frankie laughed. "All right. It'll let us start planning the trip, right?"

"That's my man." Peter helped him into the truck, and moments later, they were on the road home.

***

"He's in his car," the shaggy-haired man said. "His friend is with him."

"Male or female?" his employer asked.

"Male. The big Polish guy."

"Okay. Follow them and listen in. But stay invisible."

"Of course. I know what I'm doing." For good measure, he stuck his middle finger out at the phone, resting in his cup holder on the center console.

"That's what you said before. I'm not impressed."

The shaggy-haired man snarled and ended the call. Damned micro-managers.

***

"I'm thinking Santa Fe," Frankie said. "Camping. Completely off-grid."

"I hate the desert." Peter slowed for a yellow light changing to red a half-block ahead. "If we're going to camp, let's do it close-by. Mt. Hood, maybe, or the Snoqualmie Pass. Someplace with water I can trust."

"Too close," Frankie said. "Dude, you could have made that light."

"If we're going to take a road trip, rule number one is, no bitching about my driving."

"No. Rule number one is, I drive."

"No way. Deal's off."

"Come on!"

"There's a reason you walk with a limp, and it ain't football." The light changed and Peter eased his way through the intersection. "Your private little NASCAR imitation turned into a demolition derby."

"Rule number two," Frankie said. "No cheap shots."

Peter cringed. "Okay. Sorry. I deserved that."

"Rule number three. No cell phones."

"No way. I'm on call twenty-four-seven with Sunset Hospice. Which is why I need to be closer than New Mexico."

Frankie sighed. "Okay. But no outbound calls, and no inbound from anyone who isn't family."

"Agreed." Peter high-fived him. "Man, this is gonna be fun."

"Yeah it is! Say, I know where we should go. A buddy of mine has a cabin in Madras. He said I could use it anytime."

"Is he there?"

"Not this time of year. He works summers at the coast, cleaning houses."

"At the coast is where we ought to be instead of the high desert in August. Besides, what's there to do in Madras?" Peter stopped for another red light.

"Nothing. That's the point."

Peter rolled his eyes. "You and I have very different ideas as to what constitutes a good road trip. At least at the coast we could surf and swim and gorge on seafood."

Frankie considered this. "The coast is too expensive this time of year. But I like the idea of being near water. How about near a lake instead? The company my buddy works for has places near C'oeur D'Alene."

"I love it! It's a plan!" Peter blasted the horn, causing Frankie to jump out of his seat. But then he laughed, and Peter joined him.

"Okay, dude," Frankie said. "You're on."

"Call me when it's all set up. I'll give Gregg the bad news."

"Cool. And, Peter?"

"Yeah?"

Frankie wagged a long finger at him and narrowed his eyes. "Remember: no telling Christine."

After a long moment, Peter nodded.

Chapter Seventeen

Peter studied the figures on his computer screen, a complex array of totals, percentages, and averages, summed up in an equally complex set of graphics to one side. A difficult decision loomed before him: switch lumber suppliers, or continue the current contract? A close call, based on the numbers. At this point it came down to a gut feeling. Prices from the current supplier, Cal-Tex Lumber, had crept up above the competition, but they'd never missed an on-time delivery. Instinct told him to remain loyal and renew. But a few of his crew members had complained about mistreatment and harassment from their drivers lately. The company had promised to clean up their act, but—

He sensed, rather than saw or heard, movement beyond his desk. When he looked up, Raul occupied his visitor's chair.

"I would like to discuss our lumber supplier," Raul said.

Peter jumped in his seat, knocking his computer mouse to the floor. He retrieved it and wiped his brow with his sleeve. "Where the hell did you come from?" he asked. "And when?"

Raul wiped a burgeoning smile off his face and replaced it with a look of apology and concern. "I am sorry," he said. "You were concentrating so hard. I did not want to disturb you."

"I appreciate the sentiment," Peter said, "but please, next time, knock."

Raul nodded. "Of course. Now, about this lumber supplier. How committed are you to keeping them?"

"I was just working on that, as a matter of fact, and I'm undecided. Why?"

"We have had more complaints about their drivers," Raul

said. "Disparaging, sexist, and even racist remarks. Some rather crude, and…" Raul paused, grimacing. "Now, one directed at me."

"What did he say?"

Raul swallowed hard, his face darkening. "I was helping to guide the driver into the loading dock, signaling while he backed in, and he yelled to me, 'I know what I'm doing. Get out of my way, wetback!' It was very humiliating."

Peter sighed. "Which driver? The regular guy, or a new one?"

Raul shrugged, a prolonged hunch of his shoulders. "I hadn't seen him before, but I am new, so I cannot be sure." He slid a folded sheet of canary-colored paper across Peter's desk. "Here is the delivery slip. It contains all of his information—his name, truck number, time of delivery, bill of lading. I wrote down a description of him on the back, in case you want to follow up."

"Of course. Right away." He opened the page and scanned it. The driver had been the source of several complaints in the past. The company had promised to deal with him, but clearly they had not.

A new shadow darkened his doorway. A sandy-haired man in his late twenties appeared, grinning—another supervisor in Peter's crew.

"Hey, Skip. What's up?"

"Hey, Pete," Skip said. "It's almost five. Join us for Friday happy hour at the pub? You too, Raul. New guy buys, right, Pete?" His grin widened.

"That's the tradition," Peter said, suppressing a smirk. "What did it run you when it was your turn? Couple of hundred?" He stole a quick glance at Raul, expecting a panicked look. Instead, Raul appeared unruffled.

"At least," Skip said. "It took months to pay off my credit card."

Still no reaction from Raul.

"And then," Skip said in mock seriousness, "the strip club crawl nearly killed me. Especially the male vegan strip club."

"We'd better get going, then," Raul said, standing. "Before

the pub gets too crowded."

Standing behind Raul, Skip's jaw nearly hit the floor. "I'll, er, gather up the team," he said. He mouthed to Peter, "Can you believe this guy?"

Peter shrugged and shooed them both out. "I need to deal with these supplier complaints," he said. "I'll catch up."

"What supplier complaints?" Skip asked, re-entering. "What happened now?"

"I will tell him on the way to the pub," Raul said, pulling Skip out by the arm. "We will see you there."

Peter puzzled over this, his hand resting on his desk phone. Skip, the floor manager, should have known about the complaints before Peter. Clearly Raul hadn't followed protocol. He'd have to speak to him about that.

Ten minutes later, his cell phone startled him with a few bars of "Black Magic Woman." "Hi, Christine," he said into the phone. "Miss me?"

"Terribly," she said. "When can I see you?"

"Not tonight," he said. "How's tomorrow?"

"Peter! It's Friday night. Date night. Has it really been that long since you've had a girlfriend?"

"Eight years," he said. "I just got divorced in May, remember?"

"What's so important on your social schedule that you can't see me tonight?" Her voice dripped disappointment.

"Initiating the new guy over drinks," he said. "Or what we call 'informal training.' It's likely to go late."

"Ah, yes. What we called 'hazing' before we knew better. What's on the agenda? Beers, strip clubs, making the new guy pay?"

Peter pulled the phone away and stared at it for a few seconds. "How the hell did you know that?"

"Come now, Peter. You don't think you're the first ones to come up with that plan, do you? People have been foisting vice on the new guy since the first time there was a new guy. Well, have fun. Don't let those lap dancers get too friendly with you. I want you to save it up for tomorrow night, with me."

"Don't worry," he said. "I'll be lucky if I make it in time for the last round. I have to deal with more harassment complaints before I go."

"Not those lumber suppliers again, is it? You really should fire them. That's unacceptable."

"Easier said than done. It's midsummer, our busiest season. I can't afford to have empty shelves while I search for a new firm. Anyone I bring on now would charge twice what I currently pay. And—" Just in time, he stopped himself from blurting out his vacation plans he'd promised Frankie to keep secret from her. "It's just not a good time," he said instead.

"So, Cal-Tex gets away with harassing and abusing your employees with impunity? Peter, I expect greater courage from you."

Silence hung on the line for several seconds. Finally, Peter exhaled a long, slow breath. "Not with impunity. When you and I hang up, I'm calling their office. Which I'd better do soon, in fact, if I'm going to catch them before they close up for the weekend."

"Okay," she said, annoyed. "I know when I'm getting dismissed. Well, don't let me get in the way of business as usual. Have a good weekend."

"Christine! Don't hang up."

"Why not? You're not listening to me anyway."

"I am. It's just…more complicated than it seems."

"No, it's simpler than it seems. Just more difficult. It always is, when you're acting on principle." Another pause. "You are a man of principle, aren't you, Peter?"

He gritted his teeth. "You know the answer to that."

"Do I? Maybe you can show me tomorrow."

"What do you mean?" Alarms rang in the back of Peter's mind.

"I have it on good information that Kyle will be back in Portland this weekend. It's a perfect opportunity."

Peter's blood ran cold. He'd hoped to put off any confrontation with Kyle until he could figure out another plan, if not indefinitely. He hadn't counted on Kyle coming back to town so soon. "This weekend?"

"Wouldn't it be wonderful to put an end to all of this right now? Oh, Peter. You don't know what this could mean to me. To be free of his threats, his stalking. To be able to focus on life again, and give myself fully to the man I love. Don't you want that for me, Peter? For us?"

"Yes, of course. But—"

"Oh, you're so lovely! Listen, why don't you come by in the morning. I'll make you breakfast, we can take a late morning nap…"

Peter's face warmed. He knew what she meant by "nap," and he had to admit, it sounded better than hanging out with the folks from work all night.

"Then," she said, "we can make our plans."

The warm feelings disappeared, and the ice returned. His throat tightened. "I may have to come in to work in the morning."

"To fire Cal-Tex?"

"Perhaps."

"Okay. Well, you call me in the morning and let me know when you're free. Have fun tonight." She cut the connection.

And only then did Peter realize that he'd never told Christine about his problems with Cal-Tex.

Yet somehow, she knew all about it.

Chapter Eighteen

Peter arrived at the pub seething. The phone conversation he'd just had with Cal-Tex lumber had made him look and feel like a fool, and he knew exactly whom to blame.

He spotted Raul in the middle of a long picnic-style table in the back corner of the pub, surrounded by loud, laughing co-workers, mostly from the loading crew. They quieted as Peter strode toward them with his brow furrowed and mouth set in an angry line. Raul, sitting with his back to Peter, turned and stood when Peter reached the table.

"Is something wrong?" Raul asked, his voice calm.

Peter thrust a folded sheet of canary-hued paper into Raul's face, the one containing the report of the Cal-Tex driver's harassment. "Explain this."

Eyes widened around the table. Raul glanced at the page and refolded it. "I've never seen this before. What is it?"

"What is it? It's your first official firing offense, that's what it is. Lying about our supply partners, accusing their employee of—"

"I didn't write this," Raul said. "As I said, I've never seen it before."

"Bullshit!" Peter said.

Gregg, seated at the far end of the table next to Jessica, stood and ambled around behind Raul. "Peter, take a chill pill," he said. "Grab yourself a beer, relax."

"Gregg, you dodo," Jessica said, snapping her gum. How she could do that while drinking beer, Peter could never fathom. "When has telling someone to 'take a chill pill' ever actually calmed him down?"

"Especially Peter," Skip said with a nervous smile. "It takes a lot for him to get mad, but when he does—hoo boy."

"All right, all right," Gregg said. "So, what's the problem, Pete? And whatever it is, why couldn't it wait until Monday morning? It's Friday night, for God's sake."

"Show him the paper," Peter said to Raul.

"Is that one of our forms?" Jessica said, reaching to grab it from Raul. He snatched it away, just in time.

"Guys," Gregg said, "this isn't the place for company business. Nor the time. Come on, Pete. Have a beer."

"Don't you even want to know what your all-star new employee is saying about one of our oldest and most trusted partner?" Peter said.

"Is this about the CalTex thing?" Gregg asked Raul. He turned to Peter. "Raul told me we've gotten more complaints."

"And I followed up on them while you were all here drinking and having a good time," Peter said. "And guess what? It's all bullshit!"

Raul stood, his face turning beet red. He tore the page in half and crumpled the pieces into his fists. "It is bullshit, all right," he said, shaking the pages at Peter. "Invented by you!"

Peter's mouth dropped open. "You are making a huge mistake here, buddy," he said. "Don't make it worse than it already is."

"Give me the papers," Gregg said, placing a hand on Raul's shoulder.

Raul shook the hand off. "This is a frame job. Another frame job—by him!" Again he waved the pages at Peter.

"What the hell are you talking about?" Greg spun Raul around to face him. "What frame job? And what do you mean, 'again'?"

Raul stepped away from the table and turned sideways, as if seeking an escape, but Gregg and Peter blocked his path on either side. "Peter has been against me from the start," Raul said. "He made this up so he could fire me and hire his friend. I have been set up, I tell you! Framed, just like at my trial!" He lunged into a tiny gap between Peter and the neighboring table, whose occupants—four young guys sharing a second pitcher of pale lager—scrambled out of the way. Peter grabbed Raul by the belt as he passed and pushed him, hard. Raul sprawled face-first onto the floor, dropping the torn shreds of paper. He scrambled to his feet and backed away, hands up, then dashed out of the bar.

"What the hell?" Gregg said.

Peter picked up the scraps of paper and waved Gregg outside. "Let's talk."

Outside the pub, Peter stood close to Gregg and spoke in a low voice. "I don't know what's up with this guy, but we made a mistake in hiring him."

"What did he do, exactly?" Gregg's voice echoed off the brick and glass walls. Stark Lumber employees stared out the pub's plate-glass window at them, and passersby turned their heads in the direction of the two men. "He told me on the way over that a driver called him a name, a slur. He didn't want to repeat it to me. Pretty offensive, he said."

"He lied," Peter said

"How do you know?" Gregg asked. "You got proof?"

"I called Cal-Tex," Peter said, his voice dry. "I read them the riot act for ten minutes—then they asked me the driver's name. It turns out they fired the guy Raul named on the report two days ago. I felt like an idiot."

"Why the hell would he do this?" Gregg asked. "It doesn't make any sense."

"The guy's got some weird agenda. I don't know what it is, and I don't care," Peter said. Which was mostly true. Christine had known about the complaint before he told her. It seemed connected to her somehow. But he had no idea of how to explain all of that to Gregg. "Whatever Raul's reason, it doesn't matter. He's made a mess of this situation, and I just want him gone."

"You haven't exactly made a secret of that." Gregg smirked at him. "And I think you're overreacting. But even if you're right, aren't you curious to know what he's up to?"

Peter wiped sweat off his brow, flowing like a faucet had opened up. None of Raul's possible motives appealed to him.

But perhaps it was better to know than to fly blind. He took a deep breath, calming himself a little. "All right, Gregg. What do you suggest?"

"Let's bring him in and talk to him first thing Monday morning. Maybe it was just a mistake—wrong name, or something. Wait—let me finish. If his story doesn't line up with what we know, I'll back you up in firing him on the spot."

"I don't get why it's not automatic," Peter said, his hands spread wide. "You've fired people for a lot less."

Gregg frowned and sighed. "The people upstairs really want him to work out. Pete, look at it from their perspective. He's new, he's eager…maybe overeager. Maybe he overheard some old complaints, mistakenly thought they were fresh, and jumped on the chance to stick up for his staff. We don't know."

"He falsified a legal document! How is that a mistake?" Peter threw his hands up in the air, still clutching the torn-up report. "Why am I the only one that can see this?"

"Great question," Gregg said. "Why are you the only one that has a bug up your butt for this guy? Anyone else, you'd be making excuse after excuse for them. Need I remind you of how you reacted to Frankie's situation? And he was caught red-handed!"

"That's not fair, Gregg."

"You're not being fair. To Raul."

Peter sighed. When Gregg got like this, there was no arguing with him. "Okay. Fine. We talk to him Monday. But if he doesn't have a good explanation—"

"I'll kick his butt to the curb myself." Gregg put a hand on his arm. "Now, come inside, have a beer, and calm down. Okay?"

Peter nodded. A beer did sound good. Especially with Raul gone.

***

Noises in the kitchen startled Peter awake. At first he suspected that someone had broken in, and he reached for his phone to call 9-1-1. Instead of a phone on his bedside stand, however, his hand discovered a white silk blouse. On the floor he found a black skirt and nylons. Near the door, a pair of black pumps with two-inch spike heels.

He was fairly certain they weren't his.

He guessed they belonged to whoever was making a mess of his kitchen at the moment. He fought to remember the evening before, but a pounding headache got in the way. He remembered drinking at the pub with the folks from work. Breaking in the new guy, Raul. But Raul had left in a huff...why? Something about a complaint about a supplier. Something connected to Raul...damn this headache. He closed his eyes.

A moment later the door burst open and Christine entered, carrying a TV tray loaded with eggs, bacon, buttered toast, and, most important, coffee.

"Good morning, Sleepyhead!" She flashed her most charming grin and set the tray on the dresser. Bending over to pour coffee into the mugs revealed that she wore only Peter's loose-fitting Trail Blazers jersey with nothing underneath. He doubted that the exposure was anything but intentional, but his body reacted in predictable fashion. He covered his own naked body to the waist with a sheet.

"What a fabulous surprise," he said, still trying, without success, to piece together the events of the night before. He had no memory of how and when she'd gotten there, but he had a pretty good idea of how little sleep he'd gotten.

"Making you breakfast is the least I could do for my white knight who rescued me on a busy highway at night." She handed him a cup of coffee and brought another one with her to the foot of the bed. "Although with the way you were driving, I had my doubts about our survival at first. How many beers did you have at the pub, anyway?"

"I...I don't know." He sipped the coffee. Perfect. "You say I drove you here?"

"From the side of the road on I-5," she said, "even called Triple-A for me and drove me to the repair shop. I owe you big time." She leaned in for a soft, lingering kiss. Hot coffee splashed onto Peter's bare chest. The kiss continued. Her hand fumbled beneath the sheet, and a low groan emerged from inside him.

Abruptly, the kiss ended. She reached across to the dresser, stretching her fingers to a plate loaded with bacon, again showing off her naked body below the waist, this time from the front. She straightened and pushed a long crispy strip of warm maple bacon into his open mouth. "Stop drooling," she said. "It's only breakfast."

"No, it's not," he said around a mouthful of salty deliciousness. He washed the bacon down with coffee, draining the mug. The caffeine helped. His headache subsided a little, and he remembered what he'd wanted to ask her. "Christine," he said, "do you remember when we talked around five o'clock yesterday, about the Cal-Tex thing?"

"Yes. Open wide," she said, feeding him a forkful of eggs. She took a bite herself. "Mmm. For a change, I didn't burn everything I touched in the kitchen."

"How did you know—" He paused to accept another delicious piece of bacon. "Wow, that's so good."

She giggled. "I haven't cooked breakfast in three years. This is fun." She held a piece of bacon between her teeth and straddled him. He leaned forward and nibbled on the end closest to him. She nibbled on the other end, her eyes boring into his.

"How did you know about all that?" he asked, or tried to. His mouth worked a lot harder on chewing the meat and edging closer to her bright red lips.

"I know everything," she said. A well-manicured fingernail traced the muscles in his chest, and slid downward across his stomach, dancing, pausing, tickling.

He wanted to ask more, but his mind would no longer focus. Besides, she'd answered, kind of, and it all made sense, in its own weird way. And her fingers felt so good, her lips edged ever closer—

He pulled her on top of him. Coffee spilled everywhere, but he no longer cared. His desire took over, overwhelming his hunger for food, for knowledge, for anything except what she was willing to offer, right then, in such abundance.

***

"I think Tuesday would be a good day," Christine said, feeding Peter another cold piece of bacon. They sat up in his bed, propped up by pillows and blankets, their naked bodies touching and sweating in the early morning heat.

"A good day for what?" Peter chewed the salty meat, savoring its sweet maple flavoring and supple greasiness.

"Taking care of the Kyle problem." She offered up another piece of bacon.

"Christine, you can't be—"

She smothered his mouth with her lips and tongue, and somehow managed to climb on top of him again. She broke off the kiss, straddled him, and ground her groin into his, eliciting a very predictable response.

"Think about it," she said. "After Tuesday, you'll have me all to yourself. No more unwelcome distractions." She ground harder into him, kissed him again. "Isn't that what you want? Me, all to yourself, all the time?"

He nodded. Pushed his own body against her. Damn, she felt good. Something nagged at him, in the back of his mind. Something he meant to ask her—

She leaned closer. "Tuesday," she said in a whisper. "On Tuesday, we take care of everything."

His body went cold and sagged backwards onto the bed. She sat up straight and gazed down at him. Her eyes narrowed to slits. She slid to the side of the bed and sat with her legs hanging off the side, looking away from him. "I sense some reluctance on your part, all of a sudden."

He closed his eyes and inched his head from side to side. "Not sudden. Always. I've never liked this idea."

She sighed. "I don't like it, either. But I don't like being scared all of the time, knowing he could be nearby, watching me, waiting for his chance. Would you like that, Peter? Would you like him to get to me first?"

He opened his eyes, saw the fear on her face, the hurt, the impatience. The growing anger. "Of course not. I just—I think you've misjudged me. I don't think I'm your man."

Her eyes widened, her lips drawing into a snarl. She leapt off the bed and pulled on clothes in angry jerks. "I see. Well. Thanks for letting me know." Her blouse covered her back. On came the skirt. She snatched her underwear and shoes off the floor and took a step toward the bedroom door.

"Christine, I didn't mean it like that. Of course I'm your man. I mean I'm just not—"

"Sure. You're my man when it comes to getting your rocks off. Just not when it comes to meeting my needs—at least not the ones that come up outside of the bedroom." She zipped up the back of her skirt and slipped on her shoes.

He rolled off the bed and met her at the door as her hand hit the knob. He pressed one hand against the door, holding it shut. "What I mean is, I want to be with you. And I want to help you. I just—I don't know if I'm the guy who can do this for you. Do the actual deed. You know what I mean?"

She met his pleading gaze with a cool stare, then glanced at the bed. "I guess it all depends on which deed, huh?"

His eyes fell to the floor. "What I mean is, it's not all about sex. I care about you, and I want Kyle gone from your life as much as you do."

"Do you?" She crossed her arms. "Show me. How will you help me get him out of my life—permanently? What other solution do you have up your sleeve?" She tapped her toes on the rug, waiting.

"I don't have a Plan B. Hell, for that matter, we don't really even have a Plan A. No real plan, I mean." He reached out to her, took her hands in his.

Her gaze softened. "That's a fair point. We do need to plan." She thought a moment and smiled. "Why don't we use Tuesday as a planning opportunity, then? We can watch him from a distance, get you familiar with his habits, how he operates. Maybe it'll inspire you with a new idea."

He nodded. "Perfect. Where will he be?"

She drew closer and whispered in his ear. "He'll be wherever I am, darling. You just need to be there first."

Chapter Nineteen

"She's planning something." The shaggy-haired man checked his surroundings again for eavesdroppers. The park bench on which he sat backed up to a paved walkway that sliced through one side of Laurelhurst Park, a well-manicured, tree-lined greenspace occupying a fifteen-square-block strip amidst some of the most expensive housing in Portland. Nearby, a few twenty-somethings wearing T-shirts bearing logos of various local colleges chased Frisbees within an area marked off by orange cones. An elderly couple strolled around the edge of a duck pond clotted with algae and lily pads. Other than that, the park appeared empty.

"What, exactly, is she planning?" asked the man on the phone.

The voice belonged to the shaggy-haired man's client, who for whatever reason preferred to think of himself as his Boss, with a capital B. Some sort of status thing. Whatever. Kyle Campbell paid his bills right now. He could have whatever title he wanted.

"I'm not sure. It involves what she calls a 'permanent solution.' I can't imagine that's good news for you."

Kyle laughed. "I can handle her."

The shaggy-haired, heavy-set man wiped sweat from his neck. Not even ten o'clock and the temperature had already climbed into the 80s. He wished he'd picked a spot in the shade. "She's getting help from Lumpy."

"What kind of help?"

"I think he's the trigger man."

A pause, marked only by some grunts and heavy breathing.

The shaggy-haired man cursed to himself. Here they were, discussing threats to the guy's life, and the damned fool wouldn't even take a break from his precious morning workout.

"Is he a credible threat?" Kyle asked.

The shaggy-haired man shook his head before remembering that Kyle couldn't see him. "I doubt he would be much trouble for you in a fair fight. But she keeps referring to something he did in the past—something bad. He doesn't seem to want to talk about it."

"So what you're saying is, he's a wimp unless he has a gun in his hands." More heavy breathing and grunting.

"I guess so."

"You guess so? I don't pay you to guess. I pay you to know."

Damn him. He took a long, deep breath before responding. "When you pay me, you mean. I haven't seen a deposit into my account this week."

A loud grunt this time, almost a roar, followed by a louder clank in the background, like barbells hitting a gym mat. "I haven't gotten results this week!" More heavy breathing, steady, the sound of anger rather than exertion.

The heavy-set man kept his voice calm, despite the pounding in his chest. "I'm giving you results right now. You always get them as soon as I know something." Sweat poured anew from his body.

"And you get paid when I know something!"

Another deep breath. "And now you do."

This time it was Kyle's turn to pause, accompanied by a clackety-clacking sound of keys on a keyboard. "Okay. Now you've been paid. Happy?"

"Ecstatic." The shaggy-haired man stood and walked toward the shade. "Now, what is my next move, Boss?"

***

After a long, busy Saturday at Stark's, Peter treated himself to a leisurely dinner at a local brewpub, known for its slow service, comfort food, creative beer selections, and wait staff who didn't mind if patrons camped out for long stretches in corner booths, even on weekends. He finished a Michael

Connelly thriller over a burger, Cajun tots and two pints of stout, and looked forward to falling asleep in front of the TV with a full belly. Such a fun Saturday night.

He had almost reached his turnoff into his Ladd's Addition neighborhood in inner southeast Portland when his cell phone chimed the chorus of "Taking Care of Business." He considered sending it straight to voice-mail, but relented. Gregg never called on weekends, and never this late, except in an emergency. He answered and put the phone on speaker.

"Pete! I need you at the store, stat. We've got a problem." Gregg's voice sounded strained, a rarity for him.

"What kind of problem?"

"We had another break-in," Gregg said. "Lots of damage this time, and lots of stuff is missing. Expensive stuff. God, what a mess!"

"I'll be there in ten minutes." Peter swerved out of the turn lane and gunned the engine to zip through the intersection before the signal turned red. His stomach growled, complaining about his greasy dinner. He needed to eat better, get some sleep, and get back to the gym—none of which would happen this night.

He made it to Stark's with time to spare on his estimate and parked in the street, since the police had roped off the parking lot with crime scene tape. Gregg waved to him and said something to a uniformed cop guarding the only opening in the tape. The cop nodded and waved Peter through.

Approaching Gregg, Peter glanced at the front of the store and surveyed the damage. The eight-foot-high windows lining the front wall had become a sea of glass shards in the parking lot and inside the store, reflecting the red and blue flashing lights from police car roofs in kaleidoscopic fashion. Where rows of rider mowers, small tractors, and power tools once filled the store, now only empty shelves, cut security cables and crooked "On Sale" signs advertising early autumn season discounts greeted would-be customers. A few shelves leaned at awkward angles against each other, empty of contents once worth thousands of dollars.

Peter had expected to tease Gregg for hyperbole, but if anything he had understated the situation. A total mess would have been an improvement.

"Whoever it was, they knew what they were doing," Gregg said, handing Peter a paper cup full of black coffee. "They didn't even touch the cash registers, so they knew they'd be empty, or figured it out real quick. But all the expensive stuff is gone. And I mean all of it."

Peter tasted the coffee and winced. Gregg should never be allowed near the coffee pot, or even a drive-through espresso stand. "Looks like they didn't bother with locks, either. Do you have any idea who?"

Gregg shook his head and pointed to an empty brace dangling from the corner of the building near the eaves. "They took out our cameras first and even disabled the alarms. Like I said, these guys are experts."

"Or they knew us really well. Could it be one of our suppliers? I noticed a new guy for Cal-Tex today." Peter grimaced. "Thanks to Raul's bogus complaint yesterday, they assigned us a new driver already."

Gregg shook his head. "Doesn't make sense. They'd have to have known the ins and outs of our security setup. That eliminates a supplier, at least one working alone. Especially a new guy."

Peter hesitated, took a deep breath, expressed thoughts he'd have rather kept to himself. "An employee, perhaps?"

Gregg glared at him. "You can't wait to pin this on Raul, can you?"

Peter held up his hands, as if fending off a blow. "I didn't say that! But after yesterday—"

"It's moot," Gregg said. "He called this morning from a motel in Bend. Visiting some family or something. I already called back to verify—he's still there. He's not our guy. And he apologized for the Cal-Tex thing. Says he was sticking up for one of his crew, didn't realize it was an old complaint." He took a sip from his cup and winced. Even he hated his coffee.

"Okay," Peter said, still unconvinced. Something about that

didn't add up. "But maybe a different employee—or former employee."

"Only supervisors knew our security setup well enough to do this. And I can only think of two of those." He looked squarely at Peter. "Both of them worked for you."

"José, and…"

Gregg's eyes narrowed. "Who else has been hanging around here when he's not supposed to?"

"Frankie? No way. Neither of them—"

"I agree with you about José—he has too much to lose with his new job and all. But Frankie left under a cloud and was just turned away when he tried to apply for José's job. He's also broke, giving him a financial motive."

"He's also crippled, honest as the day is long, and—"

"Crippled I'll give you. But honest? He didn't show it during the harassment investigation." Gregg took a long hit on his coffee.

"I disagree. But regardless, he has an alibi. He was with me all evening."

Gregg gave Peter a long look and shrugged. He finished his coffee, crumpled the cup, and tossed it into the pile of rubble at their feet.

"Hey, this is a crime scene!" yelled a man in a suit. Peter guessed him to be a detective. He finished his own coffee, picked up Gregg's trash, and stuffed it inside his cup.

"Besides," Peter continued, "Frankie wouldn't do anything against Stark's—at least, not as long as I work here."

"Yeah, we'll see. In the meantime, we're going to have to close for a few weeks to rebuild. And when we do, we'll be upgrading our security system. You can bet on that."

"How can I help?"

Gregg pointed to the suits. "The cops still want to interview you. They'll want Frankie's contact information."

"I'm sure he has nothing to hide."

"Good. Then I'll need you here to help me rebuild and restock. We'll have to lay some sales staff off for a bit."

"Yuck. And during our busiest time of year."

The detective waved to Gregg, who turned to Peter. "That's our cue. Let's go tell them everything we know."

Peter shuddered. Telling cops what he knew about crimes remained among his least favorite pastimes.

But at least this time, nobody had died.

Chapter Twenty

Kyle shaded his eyes against the bright sun, hanging in the cloudless sky just above the trees on the western horizon. Even his Ray-Bans couldn't protect his eyes against the intense glare, and he needed to be able to detect the couple the moment they arrived—without, of course, being spotted himself.

Or at least, not identified. The shades could only hide so much. The dark dye in his hair, the idiotic seventies mustache, the dangly clip-on nose ring, and the fake paunch would hide him to a much greater extent. Especially, he hoped, the paunch around the gut.

But the true disguise lay not in his physical appearance, but in his behavior. Like, for example, holding these stupid rent-a-dogs on retractable leashes. Two disgustingly cute, puffy little mutts, designer dogs of some sort. Dee-John Freezays, or some such nonsense. He'd forgotten their names, too, but they responded to treats, which he dispensed with near reckless abandon any time he spoke or they came near. Whatever. Disgusting creatures. They could eat until they puked and then some, for all he cared. They weren't his dogs. God forbid.

He shuddered at the thought of having dogs around on a permanent basis. Smelly, hairy creatures, and so damned needy. Worse, they reminded him of his equally needy, idiotic brother, who cried for days when their foster parents put down their stinky old mutt after she'd attacked the postal worker. Kyle neither understood, nor much cared for, his brother Earl. He had no doubt that his brother felt the same way. How two people could share so many common experiences, and so much DNA, and look so much alike, yet turn out so different—

His phone vibrated in his pocket. He clicked on his wireless ear bud to answer.

"They're here," the voice said. His man. "They're parking."

"Good. Get ready."

"I was born ready."

Kyle clicked on the ear bud again to hang up, gritting his teeth. God, how he hated clichés.

He scanned the parking lot. The small loop of pavement held less than a dozen cars, despite the popularity of the trail head, one of the many feeding the beautiful expanse of the 5,000-acre Forest Park in northwest Portland. The lot was full, but a slow parade of hikers approached in clumps of twos and threes from Northwest Upshur Street, many carrying backpacks, water bottles, and walking sticks. He chuckled at the sight. The gentle slopes of the park's trails wouldn't challenge even the most casual gym rat, but these Portland wimps dressed and equipped themselves like they were about to climb Mount Fuji.

The woman he sought, of course, would do no such thing. Fit as a drum from her daily five-mile runs and obsessed with appearances, she would never burden herself with such crap. Not when she could show off her amazing body with tight shorts, a tank top, and a stylish set of tennis shoes.

As if summoned, she appeared, dressed exactly as predicted, with her nerdy-looking boyfriend in tow. He, of course, dressed like the other idiots all around them, and already huffed and puffed like he'd just run five miles instead of walking a block or two from his car. He looked ordinary, a slice of white bread compared to the croissants and panini that typified Christine's finer tastes. He reminded Kyle of the goofy kid on that old black-and-white TV series he used to watch as a kid. Lumpy. Perfect named for this oaf.

They walked a foot or two apart, her maybe a half-stride ahead, chatting about something—probably the weather or something equally mundane. Whatever drones like him found interesting.

He called the dogs and tugged on the leash, rewarding them with yet another crappy little treat when they bounded near. He rubbed their backs like the cute gal at the pet shop had showed him, and the dogs responded with their stupid, excited yips, so he stuffed their mouths with treats again. To the casual observer, he appeared to love his adorable little pups.

Yuck.

He tugged the leashes again, leading the dogs toward the sidewalk at an angle that he hoped would give the impression of heading to the parking lot. From the corner of his eye he tracked their progress into the forested section of the trail. They did not look toward him, nor, even, seem to look around the park. No awareness at all of their surroundings, potential threats, escape routes. Oblivious.

That didn't square with Kyle's knowledge of Christine. If nothing else, she was a hyper-alert person. Which meant one of two things: either she really loved this Lumpy guy—the odds of which he put at roughly zero—or she was up to something.

He unlocked the black rental SUV, put the dogs inside, sat on the open tailgate, and made a phone call. "Get into position."

"I already am."

He hung up.

Show time.

***

"You really think he'll follow us here?" Peter huffed and quickened his pace on the narrow path to keep up with Christine, who always seemed a step ahead of him. In so many ways.

"I'm certain of it." She slowed her pace a bit, allowing Peter to close the gap behind her.

"Have you spotted him yet? I don't see anyone matching—"

"Did you see the big guy with the two little dogs?"

Peter nodded, then remembered she couldn't see him. "Yeah. That's him? I thought he had blond hair."

"You've heard of hair dye? The ugly mustache was a dead giveaway." She chuckled and shook her head.

"I didn't take him to be a dog person."

"He's not. They're not his. Did you see how awkward he was with them?"

"I confess, no, I didn't pay much attention to him." The path widened and he caught up to walk next to her. "What's his next move?"

"Typical bully, he won't want to confront me if you're with me. He'll look for a chance to find me alone." She stopped at an overlook with a view of the stream below and the path behind them.

"So, we stay together, right?" He checked their surroundings again. A young couple with toddlers ambled up the hill at a two-year-old's walking pace. A shaggy-haired, heavy-set guy with a walking stick passed them, smiling at the toddler, and strode past Peter and Christine without a glance. No sign of a tall dark-haired guy with a moustache or dogs.

She glanced sideways at him. "You're forgetting our objective. How would you observe him in action if we stay together? No, we need to separate before he separates us."

His head jerked back involuntarily, and he blinked, twice. "Doesn't that leave you exposed? What if he tries something?"

She turned toward the stream again, her eyes focused on something far in the distance. "He won't. Even though this place seems isolated, there are too many people around for him to take any chances." As she spoke, the young family passed behind them on the path. "And I don't want you to go far. Stay within sight of me, and keep your smart phone ready. Be sure to get a picture of his face."

He searched the forest in front of them. This plan of hers seemed too risky, but he had no better ideas. "Are you sure about this?"

She shook her head. "I'm not sure of anything. But he's not going to show his face unless I leave myself vulnerable—in appearance if not in fact." She touched his arm and faced him again. "Stay close, okay?"

He nodded. "I will."

"And, Peter?" She held his arm in a tight grip. "Watch him carefully. Study him. How he approaches me, his body language, the distance he keeps, the sudden moves. He tries hard to be unpredictable, but he's not, really. Just…different."

Peter studied her dark eyes for a moment, then nodded. "Okay. Be careful." He kissed her forehead, stepped back, and watched for a few seconds more before heading up the trail without her.

***

The shaggy-haired, heavy-set man lowered his binoculars and speed-dialed his phone. "She's alone."

"Good. Where's Lumpy?"

"Who?" Frigging Kyle, always coming up with derogatory nicknames for people. He wondered what Kyle called him behind his back.

Laughter. "The guy. The meathead boyfriend."

"He went on ahead without her. She's overlooking the stream, about a hundred yards past the bridge." He peered through his binoculars again until he spotted Peter walking on the trail. "He's probably fifty yards from her and still walking."

Rustling noises came over the line. Probably Kyle fussing with his stupid earbud again. "Okay. Find a way to lure him further away. I'm coming in."

"Got it." The shaggy-haired man hung up and put away his phone. He had an idea.

Chapter Twenty-One

Peter rounded the corner of the trail's gentle switchback and snuck a peek toward Christine. Tree branches thick with leaves temporarily blocked his view of where he'd left her, but he assumed she'd remained there. At least, that's how he understood the plan. He'd have to continue to climb another forty or fifty yards to regain a clear view of her. He reached into his pocket, pulled out his phone, and opened the camera app. He wanted to be ready, just in case.

"Help!" A man's voice yelled out from the wooded slope above him. "Someone help me! I'm stuck!"

He searched the woods uphill of the trail. Thirty or so yards uphill and fifty feet to his left, someone—a man, by the sound of his voice—thrashed in the thicket of trees, ferns, and shrubs crowding the landscape.

"Where are you?" Peter shouted. "Are you hurt?"

"My ankle's twisted. I–I can't walk. I'm stuck. Help!"

Peter glanced around, saw no one else around. Even the young family had disappeared from view ahead. More than likely, no one else could hear the man. "I'll come up," Peter said. "Try not to move." He stepped off the trail into a narrow gap in the underbrush and poked his way in the direction of the man's voice. He should call Christine. He paused and opened his Contact list on his phone.

"Hurry!" the man shouted. "This hurts like hell. I think I might have broken it. I might...pass...out..." His breathing grew loud and ragged.

"Hold on!" Peter put the phone away and hastened his pace, no longer bothering to try to protect the fragile, native plants that filled the forest floor. If caught off trail, he could be penalized with steep fines, but an injured man in distress, he reasoned, ought to exempt him. "I'm coming!" Peter yelled again. "I'm getting clo—"

Pain seared the back of his skull. His knees buckled, and he sank to the spongy forest floor. Tall, thick ferns filled his view. The green fronds swayed, going in and out of focus.

Then, everything went black.

***

Christine perked up when shouts echoed through the trees uphill to her right. Two men shouted, their voices muffled by the soft, irregular shapes and background noise of the wooded trail. One of the voices sounded familiar. She listened a bit more.

It sounded like Peter. Dammit!

She had no choice but to surrender her strategic vantage point overlooking the stream and head up the trail toward the shouting men. No sense shouting back, with the terrible outdoor acoustics deadening all sound. She hustled to the sharp turn of the switchback and stopped, facing up the trail.

Empty. And the shouting had stopped. When?

She took careful steps forward, listening, making as little noise as possible, assessing, observing. Peter shouldn't have gone any further ahead than this. Just far enough to give the appearance that they'd gone their own separate ways, but close enough to observe, and to race down to rejoin her in case of emergency. She looked for broken branches, gaps in the underbrush, trampled ground cover, any sign that he'd left the trail. She peered closer at what appeared to be a footprint in the moss to her right.

A strong hand clamped onto her shoulder from behind. "Peter?" She said before turning. "I was just—"

"Oh, so that's his name? I was just getting used to calling him Lumpy."

She completed her turn, and nearly fainted. Blocking her view stood the smirking, unwelcome sight of the man she most feared and reviled in the world.

"Kyle?" Even though she'd spotted him earlier, seeing him

up close, she almost couldn't believe it. He'd chopped off the long blond locks that once flowed to his shoulders, and now sported a short, military-style haircut, with stiff brown hair clipped close to his scalp. The ridiculous moustache, a dark caterpillar, covered his upper lip. His nose appeared twice the size of normal. His eyebrows, usually invisible, now nearly connected over his nose, darkened by mascara or dye.

But the sardonic, lazy, smart-ass grin remained, exposing two gold caps glistening in the sunlight. His trademark Ray-Bans hid his eyes, and his musky scent filled the air. He grinned at her and held her left forearm in his muscular grip. "Long time no see, beautiful," he said. "Aren't you going to kiss me hello?"

"What have you done with Peter?" She wiggled to free her arm, but he redoubled his grip. She winced in pain.

"I haven't done anything to your lumpy little lover boy." Kyle tossed his head in the downhill direction. "Come, let's stroll while we catch up on old times, and perhaps we'll spot him. I bet he just took a little nature break." He tugged her down the trail. Resisting, she stumbled into him, and he caught her full in his arms. He squeezed hard, knocking the wind out of her. "A hug? Now, that's more like it. I missed you, too."

"Let—me—go!" Christine managed to push free of his grip, gasping for air, bent at the waist. She took a few steps away from him, but he caught her, wrapping an arm around her waist. He pressed his body against hers and dry-humped her from behind.

"Nice of you to offer such a tempting target, but is this really the time and place?" He laughed. "You always did like it outdoors."

"Get away from me!" She slapped at him, kicked his shins, and pried his fingers off of her. He released his hold and pushed her down into the weeds along the side of the trail. She scrambled to her feet, then realized she was heading downhill, just as Kyle had suggested.

He stepped toward her, still blocking the trail. "Keep going. We have a good half-mile walk to my car."

"I'm not going anywhere with you!"

He stepped closer and pushed her again. She fell, landing

hard on her butt and elbows. He grabbed her shorts by the waist and lifted her to her feet one-handed, spun her around so she faced downhill, and pushed her again. "Come on, get going, I'm tired of screwing around with you."

She took a long, awkward step down the trail, keeping an eye on him. He followed, his eyes fixed on her. She took another step, then noticed movement behind him: the image of a thick, leafless tree branch, swaying in the wind.

Except that it swayed downward.

Fast.

And there was no wind.

Crack! The branch landed square on the top of Kyle's head, snapping in two. The end of the branch skittered into the brush. Kyle collapsed in a heap on the trail. Behind him stood a husky, sandy-haired man, breathing heavily, the balance of the branch gripped in his large hands like a baseball bat.

Christine stared at him, then at the fallen body at her feet. Still breathing, but out cold. "Who the hell are you?" she asked the man holding the tree branch.

"Most people might start with 'Thank you'," the man said. "But since you asked, my name's Frankie. I'm a friend of Peter's."

"I've heard of you," Christine said. "You used to work for Peter, right?"

"I've known Peter since we were twelve. Yes, I used to work at Stark's...Christine."

She held out her hand. He shook it. She held on a moment. "Thank you. Where's Peter?"

"Up the trail a bit, recovering from a conk on the head. Now, as for this guy..." He threw the stick to the ground and checked Kyle's pulse. "He'll be all right."

"Pity."

Frankie grinned. "Only if he doesn't get up. This must be Kyle."

"You know a lot."

"Like I said. Friend of Peter's. Come on." He walked up the hillside without checking to see if she followed. She did, losing sight of him momentarily around the sharp turn in the underbrush.

"Hey, you're not supposed to go off the trail," she said, her voice faltering under Frankie's withering glare.

"You want to help me here, or what?" Frankie approached a thick clump of ferns and hoisted Peter to his feet. Peter stumbled and rubbed the back of his head. "You all right?" Frankie said, still holding Peter up. Christine waited on the trail below where Frankie had left her.

"Other than a massive headache. What happened?" Peter stumbled down the hillside toward Christine with Frankie's assistance. When they reached the trail, Christine allowed Peter to lay one arm across her shoulders, with Frankie supporting him on the other side.

"Some dude hit you and ran," Frankie said. "I was too far away to do anything. I thought about going after him, but I thought I should check on you first. Then Kyle caught up with Christine, and—"

"Kyle found you?" Peter leaned harder on Christine. Damn, he was heavy.

"Yes, briefly. Frankie knocked him out. He should be right—"

They turned the corner to where Kyle's body had been moments before. But the trail was empty.

Christine halted in her tracks, forcing the others to stop as well. "What the hell?"

"Told you he was all right," Frankie said.

"Someone please explain what the hell is going on," Peter said.

"Hear, hear," Christine said. "Let's rest a minute and talk, shall we?"

They sat Peter on the ground along the side of the trail. Frankie squatted next to him, an arm resting on his friend's shoulder. Christine stood on the trail, arms crossed.

Frankie checked Peter's eyes. "You gonna be okay? Maybe we should get you checked for a concussion."

"I'll be fine."

"Frankie's right," Christine said. "Good Sam is close by. You should go to the E.R."

"I'll be fine!"

"Peter." Frankie shook him by the shoulders. "You either go to the E.R., or I knock you out again and take you there unconscious." Christine smirked.

"You would, too." Peter shook his head, an embarrassed grin easing onto his face. "Okay. But where's Kyle?"

"That coward?" Christine shook her head. "The moment he knew he'd be fighting someone his own size, he ran. But he'll be back."

"We'll be ready for him," Frankie said. "But for now, let's take care of Peter. Get up, man. We're taking you to the hospital."

Chapter Twenty-Two

"Dammit, Shaggy, I told you to take care of him!" Kyle peeled the fake mustache off of his lip, wincing as the spirit gum tore at his skin. Glancing into the mirror, he winced again at the dark hair covering his scalp. That ugly brown had to go, pronto. He yanked off the prosthetic that had enlarged his nose, resulting in more spirit gum-induced pain and redness. None of it, however, could match the pounding that split his skull where Christine's bodyguard had slugged him. His own fault, that: he should have known she wouldn't leave herself that vulnerable.

"I did. I knocked him out cold." The shaggy-haired, heavy-set man sat on the bed, his fretting image taking up a corner of the bathroom mirror serving Kyle's de-costuming purposes. An open sliding door separated the two rooms. Kyle peered at Shaggy in disgust. His ripped, shirtless body put Shaggy's shapeless form to shame. That, more than the man's formless hairdo, prompted the nickname, recalled from the character on that silly Saturday morning TV cartoon. That and the fact that the doofus better fit the role of the slightly stupid sidekick, rather than a thinker or doer in any group situation. Even a group of two, like now.

"Apparently he didn't stay knocked out for long." Kyle scrubbed the sticky glue off of his nose and lip with a wash cloth loaded with cheap hotel soap. Not good for his skin, but effective, and skin lotion would take care of the damaged pores later.

"I tell you, there's no way he got up on his own power and hit you. Not that fast." Shaggy picked up the TV remote and pointed it at the TV. Blaring voices filled the cramped space.

"Turn that stupid thing off. I need you to focus. Now!"

Shaggy cowered and, after a moment's hesitation, clicked off the set. "Okay. I'm focusing." He tossed the remote onto the bed.

"Obviously, then, she's got more help. We need to neutralize them, however many there are." Kyle splashed water on his face and rubbed lotion onto his sore skin. "We need to know how many and who they are."

"I'm betting it's the big Polish guy. Lumpy's friend."

"The cripple?"

"He doesn't seem crippled to me. He only uses the cane when he's asking for something. To gain sympathy, if you ask me."

Kyle paused over the sink. Clever. He admitted, to himself only, that he'd been fooled by the act. "Okay. So, we need to take him out. Both of them."

"They're going on a road trip next week. We could do it then."

Kyle, patting his face with a towel, exited the bathroom. "How do you know that?"

A shrug. "Surveillance. That's what you pay me for."

"Does she know?"

"Doesn't appear to."

"Perfect." Kyle smiled, and remembered the lesson from his online Leadership for Dummies class: compliment the crew. "Good work, Shag. And good idea. Can you take care of it?"

Shaggy frowned. "Not alone. I'll need help. And money."

Kyle waved a hand at him. "Do it. Use the expense account I set up for you. I don't want either of them coming back here, at least until I'm done with her."

Shaggy smiled, displaying uneven, brown teeth. "They won't come back at all."

***

"How the hell did Frankie know where we were?" Christine asked Peter once he'd checked in at the emergency room admissions desk. They sat side by side in the crowded waiting room amidst various injured softball players, industrial workers and do-it-yourself gardeners while Frankie parked Peter's pickup in the garage.

"I thought we might need backup. And as it turns out, I was right." Peter held an ice pack rolled into a towel against the back of his head, which felt like someone had drilled into it with a dull masonry bit for an hour.

"You didn't feel that was important enough to tell me first? Do you realize how dangerous a move that was?" She spoke in a low voice, too soft for anyone but Peter to hear, in a tone— just in case—that sounded reassuring and caring rather than angry. "If Kyle had spotted him first, he could be lying in a ditch right now. And so could we."

"But he didn't."

"That's not the point!" Her voice rose to a squeaky pitch and near-conversational volume. She calmed herself and leaned closer. "We need to work together on this. Full disclosure, always. Okay?"

His head pounded. He really didn't want to argue, but dammit, something wasn't right here. "That goes both ways. You haven't told me everything, either."

"That's ridiculous. Of course I have."

Frankie appeared in the doorway and made his way over to them. He squatted in front of Peter and placed a giant paw on his shoulder. "How are you holding up?"

"He's in pain," Christine said before Peter could answer. "Don't make him talk—it only makes it worse."

Peter glared at her, which only made his head ache more. Suddenly she cared about how talking pained him? "I'm fine," he said. "This is a waste of time." The invisible low-speed drill pushed the mortar bit deeper into his skull. He lowered his head to take the pressure off, stared at the floor.

"You're probably right," Frankie said. "Once they look at your noggin and discover you don't even have a brain to concuss, you'll be back on the street in no time."

Peter grinned in spite of the pain. "Thanks, pal."

"Anytime."

"Here comes the nurse," Christine said.

"Hot damn," Frankie said. "She's a looker."

A short, buxom, brown-haired woman in a white lab coat approached. She glanced at a clipboard in her hands, then screwed her face into a puzzled frown. "Peter Robertson?"

Peter raised his hand, recognition dawning on his face. "Angela?"

"Peter, what the heck happened to you?" Nurse Angela Wegman sat next to Peter on the side opposite Christine and examined the bump on his head. "Tsk, tsk. We're going to need to scan this and run a few tests. Who did this to you?"

"Wait, you two know each other?" Frankie spread his hands and exchanged a surprised glance with Christine.

"Peter and I go way back." Angela tapped Peter by the elbow. "Come on, let's get you taken care of. Your friends can come back with you, if you like." She indicated Christine, then Frankie, with an uncertain nod.

Peter stopped her with a hand on her shoulder. "That's okay. I'd rather go by myself. These two would have me on life support for a hangnail." He allowed Angela to help him up. Nausea swam in his stomach, and he swooned a bit. Angela steadied him with a hand on his back.

Christine's face darkened, glaring at Peter. "Fine. I'll get to know Frankie a little better." She turned to Angela. "Take good care of him."

"I will." Angela guided Peter toward a set of swinging double doors.

Christine patted Peter's now-vacant seat and raised her voice to be heard across the room. "Come, Frankie. Tell me all about your lifelong best friend."

***

Nurse Wegman guided Peter to a small examination room and set him on the hospital bed. "We're going to need you to get out of those clothes and into a gown," she said, popping a thermometer into his mouth. "Will you need assistance? I can send in a male nurse."

"No, I'll be fine," he said around the thermometer. "Are you moonlighting here, too? Seems like I run into you everywhere."

She laughed. "Yes, I'm still trying to save money for that trip to Europe. Normally they wouldn't allow it, but there's a serious nursing shortage, and I've been able to bring a few OHSU nursing students over for training shifts, too." The thermometer beeped, and she checked it. "Normal. Let's take your pulse." She pressed her finger onto the inside of his wrist for fifteen seconds, timing it with her watch. "Seventy-six. A little fast."

"I've been under some stress lately."

"Yes, but your body could also be reacting to a concussion. Let's get your blood pressure." She wrapped the wide black strap around his arm, pumped air, and listened to his arteries with a stethoscope, frowning. "One forty over one hundred. Elevated. Another bad sign."

"I'm okay, really."

"I'm sure you are." She smiled and laid a hand on his shoulder. When she smiled, Peter realized, she could be quite pretty. "Go ahead and get into the gown. The doctor will be here shortly." She headed to the door.

Peter nodded. "Thanks. And, Angela?"

She turned. "Yes, Peter?"

"I'm sorry I haven't called."

Her smile turned bittersweet. "It's okay. You've obviously met someone. I understand." She exited, closing the door behind her.

Peter sat still on the bed for several seconds, his mind a blur. Yes, he'd met someone. But was it the right someone?

Chapter Twenty-Three

After a series of tests and interviews, the hospital released Peter into his friends' care with the diagnosis of a mild concussion and a prescription for painkillers aimed at helping him sleep. "If you experience continued pain, any dizziness, memory loss, or balance issues, or find that you can't focus, come right back in here for further analysis," Angela advised him in the examination room. "And, Peter." She locked eyes with him and squeezed his hand. "Call me—as a friend. Tell me what's up with your mom once in a while. Okay?"

He nodded. "I will."

With the painkillers starting to kick in, Peter dozed as Christine drove him home in his truck. She helped him upstairs, tucked him in, and sat on the bed next to him. "How do you feel?"

He groaned. "Like I've been hit by a train."

"I'm sorry. I should have realized that Kyle wouldn't come alone." She rested her hand on Peter's chest, caressing him. It felt…nice.

"Well, we achieved one goal: we learned more about his tactics." Peter covered her hand in his, eyes closed. Unbidden images of Angela Wegman filled his imagination. He blinked his eyes open and focused on Christine.

"We may need more help, too," she said.

"We have Frankie."

"I mean professionals."

He propped himself up on one elbow, nearly fell over,

steadied himself. "You mean, hit men?"

"I mean, security professionals. People trained in surveillance and personal protection."

"Isn't that kind of risky, given what you want to, er, accomplish?"

She shrugged. "I need witnesses who will confirm what I've been saying. That he's stalking and threatening me—and now, physically attacking me, and those I love." She planted a dry kiss on his forehead. "I don't want anything more to happen to you. And Frankie—I can't protect him, Peter."

"Frankie can take care of himself." His voice slurred. He licked his dry lips. Angela Wegman had said something about water. Drink more. Or less. He couldn't remember.

"Really?" Christine patted his knee. "You're okay with risking Frankie's life over this, too?"

He sank back into the pillows and closed his eyes. "I probably couldn't stop him if I tried."

"He's a loose cannon. He makes me nervous."

Peter chuckled. "You think he's bad now? Watch him drive sometime." His mind drifted off, the effects of the painkillers really taking hold. Her fingernails drew small circles on his chest, a wonderful, tickly feeling. He owed her, big time. She'd probably saved his life out there. Then she'd treated him so well at the hospital. So caring. So professional. And all of her help when Mom got sick months ago, and—

Wait. That was Angela. This, here, now, was...that other brunette. The pretty one on the jury. Smart, too. With the red lipstick and the delicate perfume. And the freckles. That she'd worn since they met at college...no, wait. That was Marcia, his ex-wife. Who was this, then? He fought to remember her name. Nellie...no. Nielsen. Mrs. Nielsen, his favorite teacher. No. No. What was her name?

"Goodnight, Peter," a familiar female voice whispered. And then, all the world disappeared into darkness.

***

The doctor confirmed the diagnosis of concussion the next day, and Peter, much to Gregg's chagrin, followed their orders to take some time off of work. Frankie, however, couldn't conceal his excitement.

"Rooooad trip!" He loaded two coolers filled with ice, food, and beer into the bed of Peter's pickup, then stowed sleeping bags, fishing gear and two small suitcases around them. He tied them all down with bungee cords and slammed the tailgate shut with relish. "This works out perfect. Three extra days!"

Peter held his head in his hands. Frankie's shouts reverberated inside of his skull, still sore from getting clocked by Kyle's muscle in the woods. "Not so loud, okay? And there are no extra days—just different days. I need to be back by next Wednesday."

"Come on. A few extra days won't kill you."

"No, but Gregg would, and my mom would kill you if I missed a visit. Speaking of which, I need to stop by Sunset on our way out."

"It's completely in the opposite direction!" Frankie, who had started to climb in the passenger side, jumped back out and slammed the door shut with extra energy.

Peter winced. "Easy," he said. The sharp slamming pierced his brain, and he wished he could take more painkillers, but he needed to be alert for his visit with Thelma.

"Sorry, I forgot. Give me the keys and get in. I'll drive."

"It's my truck," Peter said in protest, but Frankie climbed in on the driver's side before Peter could stop him. Ah, well. Driving would only made his headache worse anyway. He handed over the keys and climbed in the passenger's side.

With Frankie's NASCAR-style driving, they made it to Sunset in time to have lunch with Thelma, who babbled on about her upcoming doctor's appointments and about how Ruby Tuttle had cheated to win at Bingo the night before. She seemed not to notice Peter's grogginess and barely acknowledged Frankie's presence. Frankie, for the most part, kept quiet and ate his grilled cheese sandwich on white bread with a great show of fake enthusiasm.

Once back on the freeway, Frankie's good mood no longer had to be faked. "On to Coeur D'Alene!" he shouted out the window and hooted like a cowboy.

"What is there to do in Idaho, anyway?" Peter asked. He swallowed two of the pills and washed it down with a sip of Frankie's Coke. It smelled, and tasted, of bourbon.

"Nothing," Frankie said. "That's the point. We'll be drunk by nightfall and fishing by morning."

"I hate fishing."

"That's because you do it wrong." Frankie zoomed around a driver stupid enough to drive only five miles per hour over the speed limit.

"You're crazy. The few times we've gone, I've always caught more fish than you. How could I be fishing wrong?"

"Not enough beer and women!" Frankie laughed and hooted again.

Peter shook his head, leaned back, and closed his eyes. Some things, and some people, never changed.

***

"Where is he?"

"On his way to Idaho. Should I follow?"

Kyle smiled into his phone. "For a bit. Let them get a few hours out of town. Then…I have an idea."

***

Peter's cell phone chimed the chorus to "Black Magic Woman," waking him from a comfortable slumber in the passenger's seat. He reached for it in his pocket, but Frankie slapped his hand away.

"Don't answer it."

"She'll just keep calling back."

"Turn it off, then." He cranked up the volume on the stereo and started singing off-key to an old Van Halen tune. He shoved cheese puffs from a half-empty bag into his mouth, then drained the rest of a Coke and tossed the can onto the floor of the truck, already littered with empty snack bags.

"You know I can't do that," Peter shouted above the noise, then turned the volume down halfway to normal. "I'm my mom's emergency contact."

The song played again. Frankie grimaced. "Send it to voice
mail, then. If it's anyone but your mom. And I know whose ring
that is, so don't go answering it."

Peter pulled the phone out and tapped the "Ignore" button.
The tinny chiming ceased, and he had to admit, he felt better
immediately. "Where are we?"

Frankie yawned. "We're almost to the Tri-Cities. We can
stop for dinner in Spokane in about two, maybe three hours, if
that works for you."

Peter picked up a few empty cellophane bags that once held
barbecue-flavored potato chips, pretzels, and other fried junk.
"I can't believe you can even think about dinner after all this,"
he said. He pulled a plastic trash bag from the glove box and
cleaned up the cab as best he could.

The phone chimed again, this time playing an excerpt from
"Mr. Postman," an old 1960s tune. He hunched his shoulders, a
question for the driver. Frankie frowned, then shrugged. "At
least it ain't her."

Peter smiled and tapped the "Voicemail" button, then
"Speaker."

"Darling?" Christine's voice whined between them. Frankie
cursed and pounded the wheel. Peter batted his hand away from
the radio's volume control. "Can we do dinner tonight? My treat.
Call and let me know how you're doing. I'm worried about you."

Frankie cheered. "You really didn't tell her we were leaving,
then?"

Peter shook his head, stopped after two wags. His head still
hurt like hell. "As we agreed. But I'm beginning to think it was
a mistake."

"No, it wasn't. It's for the best. You need a few days away
from her to get your head on straight."

"But Kyle's in town. He could be stalking her right now."

"And I'm telling you that's not your—"

The Santana tune played again. After a moment's hesitation,
and amidst much cursing from the driver's seat, he clicked it
through to voicemail.

Frankie grinned in surprise. "Good boy!"

"I'm not so sure. But one thing I am sure of—I need a rest stop. Take the next exit. We can get gas, too."

"I will if you promise to leave the phone in the car."

Peter sighed. "Fine." But when Frankie looked away, he slipped it back into his pocket.

***

Christine hung up without leaving a second message. His not answering struck her as worrisome, particularly since she knew he'd stayed home from work. He could be unconscious, or awake but out of it—the side effects of concussions were scary and unpredictable. Frankie had promised to stay with him, but she didn't quite trust him.

She checked the time: five o'clock. She'd done all the advertising and PR work she could for the day. She grabbed her purse, left her office, and dashed to the parking lot. She reached her Miata and beeped it open—

But it was already open. With the top down, in fact. In the driver's seat sat an athletic, blond-haired man with a laconic grin.

"Baby," Kyle said. "I wondered if you'd ever leave work today."

"What are you doing here? Get out of my car. I'm calling the police!"

"Oh, I don't think so," Kyle said.

He tapped his cell phone, and her own voice played from its speaker. "Darling? Can we do dinner tonight? My treat. Call and let me know how you're doing. I'm worried about you."

Kyle sneered. "Even the police would have to agree, that sounds an awful lot like an invitation."

"How did you—"

"It was so sweet of you to call. Now, how about you get in and we can catch up a bit before dinner? We have so much to talk about."

"I have nothing to say to you."

"Oh, but you do. There's so much new going on in your life. New boyfriend, for example."

"That's right, I do have a new boyfriend. He's not going to be happy knowing you're here. And he has a nasty temper. All I have to do is call him and—"

"And what? He turns his car around and drives three hours back to rescue you from—what? Dinner with an old friend?"

"You are not my friend!"

He tapped his phone again. "Darling? Can we do dinner tonight? My treat." He cocked his head. "Sounds like we're really good friends…darling."

She backed away from the car. "Get away from me!"

He narrowed his eyes and got out of the car. She took another step back. He followed her. She turned and broke into a run. His footsteps pounded the pavement, got closer. A hand grabbed her shoulder. She twisted away from his grasp, scanned the area while she ran. How could the lot be so empty at this hour? Her colleagues all remained inside their air-conditioned offices, working far too late as usual. She headed to the front door of the building, readying her electronic ID that would open the door. She reached the doorway and pushed the ID close to the small rectangular scanner on the wall, but a hand grabbed her again, this time by the arm holding the ID, and she couldn't reach it. He spun her around, pushing her against the wall, and pointed the silver barrel of a 9mm Beretta between her eyes.

"Let's try this again, shall we?" He lowered the pistol to her abdomen and pressed it into her, hard. With his other hand, he held his phone in the air. Once again she heard her own voice: "Darling? Can we do dinner tonight? My treat."

"How about it, then?" He smiled, an expression of utter cruelty. He leaned close. "Or do I have to use my little persuader here, darling?"

Trembling, she slid down to the ground, her back to the wall, tears pouring down her face.

Where the hell was Peter?

Chapter Twenty-Four

Parking the truck alongside the gas pumps, Frankie grimaced at the garbage bag full of fast-food wrappers at Peter's feet and patted his belly. "You fill the tank. I gotta take a serious dump," he said. "Find a place to get comfortable. This could take a while, and it's gonna get ugly." He limped off to the men's room.

Peter shook his head in amazement. He disposed of the garbage, filled the tank, and whisked in and out of the men's room while Frankie squirmed, still waiting for a stall. Poor bastard. He left Frankie there, found a booth in a coffee shop, and listened to Christine's voice-mail message. Feeling guilty, he took advantage of Frankie's absence and called back.

The ringing stopped after a few seconds, replaced by scratchy scuffling noises and muffled voices. A male voice for sure in the mix. Maybe only the one male voice. His blood pressure rose. He hadn't been gone more than three hours, and already she'd found someone else?

"Hello? Christine?" He listened a few moments longer to the muffled noise. Then the connection dropped. He called back, and his call went straight to voice mail. "Hey, it's Peter. Sorry I haven't called you sooner—"

A sequence of chimes interrupted, indicating receipt of a text message. He read the text on the screen: "SOS." Then, moments later, "911."

Both from Christine.

His heart racing, he redialed, and again the call went straight to voice-mail. He texted, fumbling with the tiny keypad on the screen: "Where R U?" Sixty seconds went by. Ninety. More. No reply.

"What's wrong?" he texted. Heart beating faster. Harder. Again, no reply.

He left his untouched coffee on the table and ran to the men's room. A short line of men of various ages, sizes and dress stood waiting for an open toilet, but no tall, sandy-haired men with canes. "Frankie?"

"Sorry, dude." Frankie's voice echoed off the tile walls. "I'm kinda having some issues here."

"We have to go back to Portland," Peter said. "Christine's in trouble." The men in line studied him in curious silence.

"What? No, man. Come on. Don't to this to me." A toilet flushed, and a man emerged from one of the stalls. Not Frankie.

"She just texted me an SOS. And a 911. I've got to go help her!"

"Dude, she's manipulating you again. Ahhh." Something splashed. Peter tried not to think about it. Frankie groaned. "Finally. Look, man. Just call her, okay? And leave me alone. I need a few more minutes of peace here." He grunted again.

"I'm telling you, she's in trouble. We have to go, now. Or as soon as you're done." He cringed and forced a sheepish smile at the men listening in on their conversation. One, a short African-American man sporting a crown of short gray curls, made eye contact and smiled as if he sympathized.

"Dude, it's a three hour drive from here. Even if we left right now, whatever trouble she's in—if any—will be over before we can get there."

"We've got to try!"

Frankie groaned and sighed in response to another splash. "Dude, you're not thinking clearly. We can't help her. Call the cops if you're so worried. And leave me the hell alone!"

"Give me the keys, then."

"No freaking way."

"It's my truck!"

"Tough shit." He laughed. "Literally."

The men ahead of Peter in line shuffled forward, filling in empty stalls as other men finished their business. Peter fretted and fumed but remained in line, realizing that he needed to empty his bladder again. In a few minutes he'd relieved himself and washed his hands, and considered one last appeal to Frankie, still ensconced in a closed-door stall somewhere, but decided not to risk angering him any further. He returned to the coffee shop and checked his phone. Another cryptic text from Christine: "Pls. Qkly."

"Where exactly do you need to go?"

Peter turned to find the source of the voice. The gray-haired African-American man from the restroom stood beside his table.

"Portland," Peter said. "And fast. But I probably can't get there fast enough."

"Not by car," the man said. "But there are other options." He handed Peter a business card. "Cleo T. Randolph, Private Pilot."

"How long—"

"A little over an hour in the air. Not to PDX, but there are plenty of private airfields. How soon would you want to go?"

Peter hesitated. Frankie would kill him, and even an hour-long flight might get him there too late. But he had to try.

"What will it cost me?"

Cleo smiled. "Your friend is in danger?"

Peter nodded.

"True, physical, fear-for-her-life danger?"

Peter showed him the text messages. Cleo nodded, a grave expression on his face. "To be honest, I was headed there myself today with an empty cabin, so...just the cost of my fuel, then."

Peter extended his hand for a shake. "Cleo, you've got yourself a passenger."

***

Frankie emerged from the men's room about fifteen minutes later and scanned the lobby for his friend. He checked the lines at the coffee shop and fast-food joints. Stepped outside, into the heat. Ambled over to Peter's truck. Scanned the lot.

No sign of him.

He checked his cell phone. One text message waited, unread. He tapped the icon, saw that Peter had left a terse note. "Sorry.

Gotta go back. Have fun fishing. See you next week."

Frankie closed the app, clenched the phone in his fist, and shouted at the sky. "You son of a bitch!" He kicked the side of Peter's pickup with all the force he could muster. Pain shot up his leg from his foot, and flared with intensity where the fractures had only recently healed from his crippling car accident two months before. He cried out in pain and fell against the truck, unable to stand under his own power.

"Stupid, stupid, stupid!" He banged on the truck with his fists, then pivoted away and kicked the truck again. Agony engulfed his entire leg, and, gasping, he collapsed to the scorching hot pavement.

Chapter Twenty-Five

Cleo had Peter in the air less than thirty minutes after leaving the rest area. "Lucky for you," he shouted over the roar of the Cessna's twin engines, "I had already confirmed my flight plan. I'm picking up a client in Clackamas for a flight to the coast."

"That explains the big discount," Peter said with a wry smile. He waited for Cleo's thumbs-up, then gazed out over the parched brown flatlands of eastern Washington, a stark contrast to the lush green hills and valleys of the western part of the state. Like Oregon, Washington's eastern half consisted mostly of high desert dotted by small towns and cities, oases amidst the harsh brown landscape.

"I hope we make it in time to help your friend," Cleo said. "Sounds like her ex is a real piece of work."

"Let's put it this way." Peter turned back so that he could see Cleo's face and raised his voice to shout over the churn of the engines. "If this were a military plane, I'd want to go in with guns firing."

"I've got a chute," Cleo said, grinning, "in case you want to save a few minutes by jumping."

"Out of a perfectly good airplane? No, thanks!"

Cleo snorted. "Who says it's a perfectly good plane? This is a rental, man!"

That shut down Peter's short-lived light mood, and he rode in nervous silence until they reached the steep, green cliffs of the Oregon Cascades, towering over the broad blue waters of the Columbia River. "I've never seen the gorge from above," he said. "It's even more beautiful from up here."

"You should see it in winter, when those hills are

snowcapped." Cleo pointed west, toward a cone-shaped white peak rising above the forested hills. "They all look like miniature versions of Mount Adams there."

Peter shielded his eyes from the harsh glare of the sun, sinking low over the horizon. "Will we make it by sunset?"

Cleo nodded. "Easy. And I arranged a cab to bring you wherever you need to go, so—assuming you know where to find her—you'll be right on your way."

"Thanks. You're amazing."

"Not at all. You find that creep, and hit him once for me, too. And once for my little girl."

Peter snapped to attention. "Why's that?"

Cleo's lips curled into an angry sneer. "My daughter lived for four years with a prick who thought hitting women made him a big man." He shook his head, and a tear slid down from behind his sunglasses. "One day I found her in a pool of blood, bones broken, barely breathing. He'd hit her with an axe handle because she bought the wrong brand of milk. If I ever get my hands on that son of a bitch, I will arm this plane. With machine guns, so I don't miss."

***

Christine shivered in the brisk air blowing onto her from the window AC unit perched in the old house's wooden double-hung window a few feet to her right. Kyle sat across the kitchen table from her, pointing a Beretta at her torso. The house sat on a large untamed lot outside of Oregon City, some fifteen miles south of Portland, on a gravel road just wide enough for two cars to squeeze past. Or one tractor, the more likely vehicle to traverse the pothole-flecked surface. The nearest neighbor sat across an empty lot behind her, over a hundred feet away.

"Are you cold?" Kyle asked.

"A little." She rubbed her bare arms. "Could you turn down the air a bit?"

Kyle pondered her request. "Afraid I can't. I'm not used to the heat here. Weird, isn't it, that Portland would be hotter than northern California?" She didn't answer. An evil smile curled onto his lips. "But if you want me to warm you up a little…"

She made a face, wishing she could spit out the vile taste in her mouth. "I'd rather freeze to death."

His smile faded. "That can be arranged."

She shivered again. "What do you want from me?"

Kyle slammed the handle of the gun onto the table. The loud thud echoed off the kitchen's bare walls, and a white divot appeared where the metal struck the dark wood of the table top. "I want my life back!"

She edged her chair away from the table. She bit her lip to keep it from quivering. "You have your life. It just doesn't include me anymore."

"You call what I have a life?" He stood and leaned over her, glaring. "I have people following me and tracking my every move. I have to report in any time I want to leave the crappy little town I live in. I have to document my every waking moment to some control freak magistrate once a month. No woman will come near me once they discover the bullshit charges you've leveled against me—which takes about five seconds on Google. I lose business left and right to people who can't see past the legal restrictions I live under. I'm under constant surveillance. I have no privacy, no freedom of movement. You call that a life?" He slammed the table again, the loud crack even more painful to her ears than before.

"Your argument is with the court, not with me."

"The court did what you told them!" He towered over her, his face inches from hers. Spittle dotted her face when he spoke. "You created this problem for me. You ruined my life. You! You! YOU!" He pushed her by the shoulders. Her chair tipped backwards onto the floor. Her head landed on the stone tile, hard. Pain shot through her skull. The kitchen, Kyle, and the table all blurred together, spun around her, and faded into blackness.

***

Kyle's phone buzzed. His man in the field, according to caller ID. He glanced at the bitch in the chair, who pretended to sleep. He strolled into the living room, reclined in an easy chair, then answered. Wind whipped in the background on the caller's side.

"What's up?" he asked. "You sound like you're standing in a wind tunnel."

"I'm at the airport outside the Tri-Cities area. Our boy's in the air, headed your way."

Kyle bolted upright in the chair. "What? How? Are you sure?"

"Three hundred bucks cash to the flight controller on his smoke break, it better be good information. By the way, I'll be expensing that."

Kyle cursed, in reaction to both the information and the expense. "Where's he headed, exactly? Which airport?"

More wind, then: "A private airstrip in Clackamas County. He should be touching down in about a half hour."

"Crap. Of all the geeks she could have hooked up with, she had to find Clark Kent. Well, we need to get rid of him."

"Already taken care of. I used that credit card you gave me and sent an Uber driver over to wait for him and take him to the House." Shaggy chuckled. Proud bastard.

And an idiot.

"You moron. I'm at the House."

"What? You said—"

"Never mind what I said! Change the destination. Tell the driver to take him home, or to Timbuktu, for all I care. Just not here."

"But I thought—"

"Do I pay you to think? Huh?" Kyle gritted his teeth and squeezed the phone with crushing force. "Get. Rid. Of. Him. Now!"

The whipping wind noise disappeared, and the line went dead.

***

"Screw you, Kyle!" Shaggy jammed his phone into his pocket and stormed over to his vehicle. He'd had enough of Kyle's abusive crap. Job or no job, he didn't have to take that from anyone.

And he wouldn't. Not anymore.

Kyle owed him money—plenty of money—for the past few

weeks' work, but more important, he owed him respect. He'd worked hard. Done everything asked of him, and then some. Gone above and beyond. Took initiative. Made good things happen.

But money be damned. Kyle had to learn to treat people better. And that treating people like dirt had consequences. And those consequences needed to be felt.

In the present situation, that meant that he wouldn't be calling the stupid Uber driver back to change their destination. No, sir. He'd keep everything as is. Lumpy would go on over to the House. Maybe confront him. Maybe even kick the crap out of him.

Whatever. Let the chips fall where they may. He was done with Kyle and his abuse.

And he'd find a way to get paid. He knew of a few people with money who might even enjoy seeing Kyle suffer a little bit, too. One person in particular.

And as luck would have it, he knew right where Kyle was keeping her.

Chapter Twenty-Six

Cleo set the Cessna on the ground at the North Clackamas air strip with the sun still hanging well above the western horizon—and blazing right in their faces. "How can you even see well enough to land this thing?" Peter shouted above the engine noise.

Cleo grinned and tapped the dark sunglasses that hid much of his face. "There's a reason they call these aviators, my friend." He taxied to a stop as close to the terminal building as he could get and shooed Peter out of the plane. "You've got bad guys to catch," he said. "Don't waste time here on formalities."

Peter didn't wait to be told twice. He raced through the gate into the parking lot out front and scanned the taxis idling in the waiting area. Sure enough, as Cleo had promised, a driver held up a sign with his name on it. He raced over and jumped into the back seat.

"No luggage?" asked the driver, a short, fleshy man with stringy, shoulder-length brown hair and matching facial hair. He wore a jeans jacket over a flannel shirt that hung over beige khakis.

Peter shook his head. "Say, is this really a taxi? There are no markings anywhere."

The driver laughed and buckled up. "I get that a lot. I'm with Uber. See the sticker on the back window?"

Peter glanced around, spotted the sticker. "I've never used you guys before. How does this work?"

"The drivers are all contractors, and we use our own cars," the driver said, combing the fingers of one hand through his beard. "I guess your friend who arranged this ride for you didn't mention that?"

Peter shook his head. "I guess I get to pay extra for this privilege."

The driver started the car and gave him a puzzled glance in the rearview mirror. "You really don't know how this works, do you? It's prepaid, by your buddy who arranged the ride."

"How does that work if you don't even know where I'm going?"

Another puzzled look. The driver pulled the vehicle into the airport exit lane. His GPS speaker intoned in an Australian accent, "Turn right in three hundred feet, then continue four point seven miles."

"Of course I know where you're going," the driver said. "He told me that, too."

Peter leaned forward, his forearm on the top of the seat in front of him. "Then why don't I know where I'm going?"

The driver stopped at the exit and gave him a long over-the-shoulder stare. "Seriously?"

"Seriously. This is freaking weird. Where did Cleo tell you to go?"

"He said—wait. Did you say 'Cleo'?"

"Yes. My pilot. He arranged the ride for me."

The driver shook his head and eased into traffic. "Some taxi driver's gonna be hating on Cleo tonight, because his fare's not going to show. My friend, the name of the person paying for this ride isn't Cleo."

"Then what is it?"

"Close to Cleo, I guess. The name on the credit card is Kyle."

***

The driver let Peter out at the corner of a two-lane collector street and a narrow cul-de-sac in a quiet suburban neighborhood with quarter- to half-acre lots, only about half of which sported houses. The modest, ranch-style homes all dated from the 1960s and 1970s, and all of them needed work. The address Peter sought sat a long block down the eastern side of the street. He had no plan, no strategy, not even an idea of what he intended to do. But he knew he needed to go there.

After asking the driver to wait on the corner, he made his approach with as much stealth as he could, crouching close to the homes and scampering between them after brief pauses to make sure he hadn't raised any suspicions. The house in question sat on an extra-large lot, devoid of trees, with a weedy, unkempt yard, packed with white-topped dandelions and tall brown grass. Wood shake siding long ago needed a fresh coat of white paint, and moss-caked roof shingles peeled up from the roof. A panoramic set of double-hung windows wrapped around the back corner of the house, opening to a small wooden porch rimmed by a waist-high plank rail. That, he decided, would be his way in.

He crept around the side of the neighbor's house, which appeared vacant, judging by the bright green notice tacked to the front door. The entire place smelled of urine. He slid along the side toward the back yard and peered across to the house where Kyle had sent him. An athletic, blond-haired man at least six feet tall stood in what appeared to be the kitchen, his back to the window, holding a cell phone to his ear with one hand, gesturing now and then with the other. He wore a tight-fitting tank top and workout pants that showed off his impressive physique.

If he turned around, he'd see Peter, without a doubt. Which meant Peter had to move, sooner rather than later.

Peter remained crouched but took long, quick strides on a diagonal trajectory toward the front edge of the kitchen's wraparound windows, hoping the tall weeds would camouflage his approach. He kept one eye on the man, whom he guessed to be Kyle, and one on his path forward. He still had no plan, except to improvise. One step at a time.

He'd gotten about halfway across the lot when the blond man turned to his left. Peter dropped into the grass, watching. The man gestured again, turning further to his left, his face now visible through the glass. The sun setting behind Peter would create a glare in the man's eyes if he looked in his direction.

Sure enough, the man shaded his brow and turned away again. Peter stayed low in the grass, sucking in deep, steadying breaths. The blond man stepped deeper into the kitchen, his back still turned. Peter rose to his hands and knees, then crab-walked to the side of the house, his eye on the kitchen window the entire time. The man did not turn before Peter reached the spot below the windows. Peter flattened himself against the siding, catching his breath.

The man's voice became audible—through an open window, Peter guessed. "Well, where the hell is he, then?...Don't give me that 'how should I know' crap. You should know because it's your damned job to know!...I'll pay you at the end of the month, like we agreed...I know you have expenses. So do I. A deal's a deal...Don't you hang up on me again! Damn you!"

A door slammed. Footsteps pounded on the tiny back porch. Kyle must have stepped outside. Peter rose up from his crouch so he could peek inside the kitchen. No sign of Kyle there, but a dark-haired woman sat with her back to him in a ladderback chair in the middle of the room, several feet away from the kitchen table, her hands tied behind her back.

Christine.

She turned, as if looking out the window, right above Peter's head. He rose up a few inches more to make his entire face visible to her. Her mouth gaped open, her eyes wide. "How did you find me?" she mouthed. Peter shook his head. Not a good time to chat, Christine. She nodded and glanced out back. "Kyle," she mouthed.

"I know," he mouthed back. He pointed to the back: "Is he still out there?"

She nodded. "Help me."

He gave her a thumbs-up and started to mouth out a new question, but something moved at the back of the house. Footsteps! He plunged flat to the ground. Moments later, Kyle leaned on the rail of the porch, staring into his cell phone, punching in numbers, or perhaps a text message. He finished, looked away from the phone to his right, away from Peter.

Then, left. Right at Peter.

Confusion, surprise, then recognition washed over Kyle's face. "What the hell?" he said.

Peter didn't wait. Didn't think. He stood, ran, and reached

the back porch in three long strides. Kyle leaned further over the rail, shouting. Peter raised his right fist and swung in stride, connecting a vicious roundhouse blow to the blond man's temple. A cry of pain, and Kyle went down in a heap.

Peter climbed over the rail, landing with both feet on Kyle's back. Something cracked—he guessed one of Kyle's ribs—and air gushed out of the man's mouth. But he didn't move.

Peter opened the kitchen door and rushed to Christine. "Let's get out of here, before he wakes up," he said, tugging at the rope tied around her hands.

"How did you—where's—I don't—"

"Shh." He kissed her, a quick peck on the lips, the kiss of a man in a hurry. He fussed with the rope, but couldn't budge the knot. He opened a drawer, found a sharp knife, and moments later she was free.

She wrapped him in a tight embrace, crushing his own ribs. He patted her back, then pushed her back a step. "We've got to go."

"Where?"

"To the corner. I have a car waiting." Out on the back porch, Kyle stirred, raising himself up onto his hands, wincing in obvious pain.

"I don't have shoes. He took them from me."

"Then I guess you're going barefoot." He grabbed her hand and pulled her through the house. She grabbed her purse off the floor in the living room and followed him out the front door. Still no shoes. He took her hand, tugged her toward the sidewalk.

Footsteps thudded around the outside of the house. Peter pulled her back to the front of the house, up against the wall, and signaled Christine with a silent finger. Wait. He edged to the corner of the house and crouched into a three-point stance like a defensive lineman. He listened, waited…then pounced.

His timing was perfect. His arcing fist collided full force with Kyle's nose. Kyle spun and tumbled onto his back, legs splayed wide. Peter stepped forward and kicked him in the crotch, hard. Kyle screamed and curled into a fetal position. Peter lifted his heel and crushed it into Kyle's skull.

Peter waited. Kyle didn't move.

"Is…is he dead?" Christine crept up behind Peter and rested a hand on the small of his back.

Peter watched Kyle for a moment. "No. He's still breathing. Let's go." Pain leaked up from his hand. His knuckles bled and felt like he'd hit them with a hammer.

"Go?" Christine grabbed Peter's arm and spun him around. "What do you mean, go? Aren't you going to finish him off?"

Peter shook her off his arm. "What are you talking about? I didn't come here to kill him. I came to rescue you."

"But if we let him live, you'll be rescuing me every week for as long as we live. Come on, Peter. Now's our chance!"

Peter stared at her in disbelief. "I won't kill a man in cold blood!"

She wrapped her arms around him, held tight, drew her lips close to his. An embrace of control, not one of romance. "Of course you will. Wasn't that the plan?"

Peter shook his head, pushed her away. "It's your plan. It was never mine."

"But you said—"

"Forget what I said!" He pointed to the end of the sparse cul-de-sac. "A car is waiting. If you want to get out of Kyle's clutches, come with me."

"What about Kyle? Are you just going to leave him here?" Her voice softened, disbelieving.

"I'll call 9-1-1 if you want. But my work here is done." He turned and walked toward the car.

Moments later, footsteps padded up behind him. She caught up to him and hooked his arm with her own, limping in silence next to him toward the Uber vehicle. "I can't believe this. Our perfect opportunity, and you're walking away."

"That's right. Do you understand now? I'm not your hit man." He quickened his pace, dragging her along the sidewalk.

She hopped along barefoot for several more steps, but about fifty feet from the end of the street, she stopped. Tugged at him, making his stop. "I have to go back."

"To the house? Are you crazy?"

"I can't leave my shoes here. What if he dies? The police will find them and accuse me of killing him!" She limped back down the street toward the house.

"We'll call the cops and tell them what happened," he said. "Come on. We need to get out of here."

"I want to call them now. I want him arrested, at the very least. He kidnapped me, for God's sake!" She kept walking.

"Fine, call the cops. But not here. In the car."

"I want to stay close by, so when the cops come—"

"What is wrong with you?" Peter shouted. He strode toward her, closing the distance between them. "He could come to at any moment, and things might not go my way in a fight next time. Let's go!"

She looked over her shoulder at him, held up one hand. "Just wait here. Okay?" Kept walking. He stopped, stared after her. She made it back to the house, keeping a wide berth around Kyle's fallen body, still unmoving on the grass. She bounded into the house, then out again moments later, shoes on her feet. Sensible flats, for a change. She skipped past Kyle and ran toward Peter, surprisingly fast.

"You're crazy, you know that?" he said as she approached. "What if he had come to?"

She stopped about six feet away and stared at the ground for a long time. "I'm s-sorry, Peter," she said. "With everything that's happened, I'm not thinking clearly." She held her arms out toward him, tears streaming down her face. "Hold me, Peter? Please?"

He drew in a deep breath, let it out in a slow, controlled sigh. She stepped closer, and he opened his own arms wide, inviting her to collapse into him.

Instead, she reached into her blouse and pulled out a dark object. Moments later, he was staring into the barrel of a cannon.

"We're not leaving until we finish this," she said.

He kept his arms wide. "Where the hell did you get that?"

She gripped the gun with trembling hands but kept it pointed at his head. "Kyle dropped it when you knocked him out on the back porch. Now we can use it on him, and be done with him forever."

"This is ridiculous." He licked his lips, heart beating double-time. He looked for the safety, but with his limited knowledge of guns, couldn't make it out. Keep calm, boy. Think. "For one thing, you're not going to shoot me. At least not with all of the neighbors looking on." He gestured to his right, toward the houses on the west side of the street.

Her eyes flickered to the side for the briefest moment, then returned to focus on him. "You're bluffing. Nobody's looking, because nobody cares."

"You say so." He lowered his hands, not quite to his sides. His pulse slowed a little. Keep her talking. "But you're also not going to shoot him in the middle of the street. And even if you did, what makes you think you'd ever get away with it? If nothing else, the Uber driver is a witness, and he knows my damned name. And yours."

She squinted at him, as if concentrating—or, knowing her, calculating something. Some odds, some angle. "You amaze me," she said. "Kyle meant to use this gun on you. Oh, yes. You didn't really think he would fight you armed only with his fists? No, my friend. He wanted to kill you."

Peter swallowed. He hadn't considered that possibility. The pain in his hand doubled and shot up his arm.

"But," she said. "You're right. I'm not going to shoot you." She lowered the gun.

"In that case," Peter said, his heart rate slowing, "we should get out of here. You can call the cops from the car." With his good arm, he gestured toward the Uber car. They walked together in silence for a few seconds.

She put her arm around his waist, pulled him close, smiled at him. Smiled, of all things! "I have to give you credit," she said. "You didn't even flinch when I pointed the gun at you."

Finally Peter's steady demeanor had paid off with her in some way. Still, he played it cool. "Remember what you told me on the night Kyle broke into your house?"

She pondered a moment. "I said a lot of things. What in

particular helped you tonight?"

He shrugged. "You've never shot at a person, and even at paper targets, you're a terrible shot."

She grinned. "Me and my big mouth. Well, I had to try. Now, how about we head back to your place? I owe you big time, and I think I know just what to do." Her smile turned mischievous. Her hand rested on the curve of his back, then slid inside the waistline of his jeans, giving him a pretty good idea of what kind of thanks she had in mind.

Unbelievable.

"Of course, I might not be able to focus on that," she said, "if I was constantly thinking Kyle might be on his way over."

"Oh, for God's sake." He pushed away from her, saw the gun still in her hand. Christ, she'd had the gun in his pants. He grabbed it from her. She let him, a slow smile creasing her face. "What are you doing?" she said in a sly voice.

He walked back down the street toward the house, gun in hand.

"Peter," she said. "Are you doing what I think you're doing? I love it! You naughty, naughty man!" She laughed. A jittery, uncertain laugh, despite her brave words.

He kept walking. When he reached the house next to Kyle's, he stopped. Stared at Kyle, lying on the ground. Stared at the Beretta for a moment. Found a latch, released the magazine from the handle. Turned it upside down. Emptied the bullets into the tall grass of the neighbor's yard. Tossed the magazine into the bushes.

"What are you doing?" she called out to him, her voice shrill now, angry. Footsteps pounded on the pavement.

He reared back, gun in his right hand, and tossed it onto the roof of the neighbor's house.

Chapter Twenty-Seven

After a long night of tossing and turning in bed next to a silent, angry Christine, the next day went by in a sleep-deprived blur. He left her sleeping in her bed and took another Uber to work, arriving an hour later than his usual 7 a.m. start time. Gregg, busy with managing the remodel of the store, hardly noticed, and greeted him without commenting on his early return from vacation. To make matters worse, his cell phone had gone missing.

Crews with tool belts appeared at every turn, and everyone worked at top speed. Power saws whined, compressors chugged, and nail guns blasted fasteners into fresh shelves, counters and half-walls dividing the redesigned showroom into small sections. The pounding of hammers and crowbars echoed inside Peter's aching head, doubling the intensity of his sleep-deprivation headache. Coffee, even Gregg's industrial strength mud, offered little relief.

"What's the big hurry?" he asked Gregg around mid-morning when they crossed paths between meetings with separate groups of contractors. "Did the insurance company give you a deadline or something?"

"One of the great advantages of being a lumber supplier," Gregg said with a grin, "is that we know all of the best contractors in town, particularly the ones who owed us favors. I just reminded them of the many times we rushed their orders, alerted them to upcoming shortages, and extended discounts during lean times. So, let's just say, they're motivated."

"But why the frenzied pace?" Peter said, pressing thumbs into his temples. "It's like a war zone in here. The pace they're working, they put the Army Corps of Engineers to shame."

"We want you back in business ASAP," said one of the contractors who'd ambled close and overheard their conversation. "I'd just as soon never step foot in Lumber City ever again. No offense, Raul."

"None taken," Raul said, appearing out of nowhere. He shot Peter a dirty look, then plastered a fake grin on his face. "I am a Stark's man now." He trudged off, carrying a half-dozen two-by-fours over his shoulder and barking orders in Spanish to one of the crews.

Peter's main responsibilities—rearranging stock to temporary locations to enable construction, and furnishing and tracking supplies to the contractors—didn't tax his time the way his regular job did, and as the day wore on, Gregg often snagged him to help supervise other odd tasks. "So glad you changed your vacation plans," Gregg finally said late in the afternoon. "I'd never keep up with this project without you."

One new task Peter wished he could have avoided was overseeing the security system upgrade. He hated the idea of having cameras recording every corner of the store every second of the day, and he tried to convince Gregg to cut back. But his pleas fell on deaf ears.

"We've been robbed and vandalized a dozen times in the last two years—four times in the last two months," Gregg said after Peter pitched a reduction in alarm sensors for cost-cutting reasons. "I consider every penny of this system money well spent." Ditto for the contract with the new security agency, which would provide undercover "secret shoppers," as well as 24/7 monitoring and backups of the sound- and motion-activated cameras and microphones mounted all over the building. Gregg approved installing devices not only in the retail section, but in the offices as well—even his own. "They've been inside jobs," Gregg said. "I want to catch the son of a bitch responsible and pin his or her ass to the wall with the evidence. No more of this crap on my watch!"

"It just feels like overkill," Peter said. "I mean, I'm bummed about the break-ins too, but is any of this even legal?"

"According to the legal-beagles, yes," Gregg said. "Oregon's a one-party-consent state, so the lawyers are drafting agreements that all employees will need to sign—or they can drag their asses out the door and find jobs somewhere else. I'm out of patience!"

Peter sighed. Gregg never had any patience to begin with.

Worst of all, the security crew worked late. Peter kicked them out at 6:30 over their protests, but too bad. He needed food and sleep—alone. And soon.

He exited the side door of the building—and spotted his truck, parked in the back of the employee lot. He stumbled toward it. An angry, familiar voice stopped him.

"Aren't you the least bit surprised to find your truck here, waiting for you? Or do your vehicles always magically transport themselves two hundred miles overnight?"

Peter froze. Frankie stepped around him from behind and blocked Peter's path to his truck. Keys dangled from Frankie's hand, but nothing else about him appeared casual. Dread and shame flooded through Peter's body.

"I'm so sorry," Peter said. "I can explain." Which was a stretch, at best. In his exhaustion, he'd clean forgotten about leaving his truck and his best friend in eastern Washington, a three-hour drive from Portland.

"Let me guess," Frankie said, sarcasm dripping from his voice. "Your manipulative little brunette gave you a booty call, and suddenly the planned vacation getaway with your lifelong pal is long forgotten. Well, was it worth it? Did you get any?"

"It's not like that. She was in trouble, Frankie. Serious—"

"She wasn't in trouble. She is trouble. For you. Don't you see that?" Frankie stepped closer, pointing a finger into Peter's chest. "She's making a total mess of you, and ruining your life. Hell, she's ruining you. What's happening to you, man? A month ago, you'd never have pulled something like this." Frankie rolled the key ring around one finger, the keys jangling. Peter grabbed for them, but Frankie yanked them away. "Oh, no. You want these, you gotta earn them."

"Frankie, listen to me. Kyle kidnapped her. He had her locked up in a house—"

"Oh, really?" Frankie spread his feet wide, hands on hips. "Funny thing. I didn't see a story on the news about any kidnapping. Wasn't on the radio or in the papers, either. Curious, such a major crime being kept so quiet, isn't it?"

Peter's shoulders sagged. "He didn't hold her long. I got her out of there, but—"

"What? You? How?"

Peter smiled and leaned sideways against the truck door. "Believe it or not, I slugged him. Twice. Knocked him out cold." He held up his knuckles. No visible cuts or bruises, although they still felt plenty sore.

But Frankie would have none of it. He doubled over with loud, sarcastic laughter. "You? Hit a guy? With what, your tire iron again?"

"Shush!" Peter reached for Frankie's mouth, but Frankie squirmed free. Peter grabbed for the keys again, missed. "Dammit, Frankie. What the hell are you doing?"

"I'll tell you what I'm doing!" Frankie's voice thundered over the parking lot, echoing off the nearby buildings. He stepped toward Peter and leaned into his face. "I'm stopping this lunacy, right now. My next call is to your brother, and the one after that is to the cops. I'm ratting you out for what you did last November. It's the only way I know to get you away from this bitch and her crazy schemes!" He held his cell phone up over his head with his free hand, breathing heavily and glaring at Peter.

"There's no need, Frankie. It's over. The whole thing is over and done with."

Frankie froze, staring open-mouthed at his friend. "What are you saying? Wait, did you—? I thought you said you just popped him in the kisser once or twice. You didn't—"

"No, I didn't...do what you're thinking. I knocked him out, yes. But I left him there alive. And I told Christine that I wasn't going to go after him anymore. I left him unconscious, on the ground, but breathing, and very much alive."

"Jeez." He rubbed his chin, keeping his eyes on Peter. "What did she do?"

Peter shrugged. "Freaked out, for a minute. Even pulled a gun on me."

Frankie stared for several seconds. "No shit?"

Peter smiled. "No shit."

Frankie looked him over. "She must not be a very good shot."

Peter laughed. "I didn't say she pulled the trigger. But no, apparently she's not. Anyway, I got the gun away from her and we got the hell out of there. She even came on to me a little bit. That gal, man—the weirdest things make her horny."

Frankie's face brightened, and his mouth split wide with a toothy grin. "You dog, you! How in the hell—? That's amazing!" He clapped Peter on the back, then bear-hugged him. "That's so awesome!"

"I know, right? I wish I'd just done that to begin with." Her horniness hadn't lasted long, unfortunately. But no sense correcting Frankie's false impression and spoiling his fun. He held out his hands. "Now, may I have my keys back, sir?"

Frankie sighed and handed them over. "I'll need a ride home, if you don't mind."

Peter clicked open the truck and climbed in. He waited for Frankie to limp around to the passenger's side and haul his large frame up into the seat. When he started the truck, a soft "ping" sounded from the console between the seats. He glanced down. The end of a white charging cord lay buried beneath a half-empty bag of cheese puffs. He moved the bag and saw the object being charged.

His phone!

"So that's where it is!" He checked the charging icon: 45%. He'd missed several calls and text messages since the previous evening.

"Yup. And yet again, you owe me big time." Frankie grinned. "You're lucky I found it. If I hadn't tried to call you last night, it'd still be in the weeds in the middle of nowhere."

Peter gave him a quizzical look. "What do you mean, in the weeds? Didn't I leave it here, in the truck?" He backed out of the space and headed for the exit.

"Nope. Found it on the ground."

"On the ground where? Eastern Washington, at the truck stop?" He signaled a right turn and pulled into traffic.

"Hell no. I'd have never found it there."

"My house?"

"Uh-uh." Frankie took far too much delight in this game.

Peter didn't. "For God's sake, Frankie. Are you going to tell me where, or make me guess all night?"

Frankie laughed. "I think it'd be fun to make you guess."

Peter glared at him. "You have a bizarre idea of what 'fun' is."

"Come on. Guess."

Silence. Peter drove, stopped at a red light, continued through on the green.

"I'll give you a hint. It was on a cul-de-sac."

"Thanks. That narrows it down to almost every suburban neighborhood on the planet."

"Really? How many cul-de-sacs have you been on in the last twenty-four hours?"

Peter shrugged. "Technically, one. But I can't imagine you went to North Clackamas any time recently."

"Then you'd imagine wrong!" Frankie laughed and pounded on the dashboard. "See? Wasn't that fun?"

Peter froze and nearly forgot to brake in time to avoid colliding with the car in front of him. "You went to Kyle's hideout? Why?"

"Looking for you."

"How?"

"Long story. Can we change the subject? Let's put on some tunes." Before Peter could protest, Frankie clicked on the radio. A female singer belted out a song of freedom and empowerment. Frankie swore and punched another preset.

A male reporter's somber voice intoned over the speakers. "...On site here in east Portland. Police found the body of a California man in this Mount Tabor neighborhood—"

"Forget that crap," Frankie said, reaching for the presets.

Peter batted his hand away. "Wait! I want to hear this."

"—identified the man as thirty-five year old Kyle Campbell," the reporter said.

"What?" Peter shrieked.

"You know him?" Frankie asked. Peter shushed him.

"The man's body was badly beaten," the reporter said, "and police say he may have been left there for as long as twelve to twenty-four hours."

"Holy shit!" Peter slowed the truck and pulled over to the side of the road.

"Dude. This Kyle Campbell—is that 'your' Kyle?"

"Sh!" Peter leaned in to listen. Peter recognized the next voice as belonging to Officer Tennyson Howard, the same cop who had responded to the break-in at Christine's. "It appears that the victim was beaten to death by a blunt object, possibly after a roadside scuffle," Howard said. "We see evidence of a possible collision, or of a vehicle swerving off the road adjacent to the victim's car, which we found abandoned nearby."

"Anyone with information," the newsman said, "is asked to call the Portland Police. In other news…"

"Wow." Peter clicked off the radio and sat in stunned silence. Frankie stayed quiet also, even seemed a little tense. Peter cleared his throat. "If you're wondering whether I had anything to do with this—"

"I'm not," Frankie said in a quiet voice. A puzzled expression occupied his face. "I know you. You wouldn't."

Peter met his gaze, lips pressed together, and nodded. He extended his hand. "Thanks. That means a lot."

Frankie accepted the handshake, held his hand in a firm grip. Started to say something, stopped. Then smiled. "How about you get me home? Maybe you want some alone time. Get your story straight before the cops call."

"I don't need a story. I didn't kill him!"

"I know, I know. I mean…well. They're going to call. You know that."

"Yeah."

"So. Home, then? I can imagine you've got a lot to think about."

Peter nodded. "My friend," he said, "that may be the understatement of the year."

They drove the rest of the way in silence.

Part Three

Framed

Chapter Twenty-Eight

After letting Frankie out at home, Peter drove aimlessly around Portland. Too restless to go home, too upset to even think about eating dinner. Kyle, dead. He suspected Christine, of course, but for some reason he couldn't shake the idea that Frankie had somehow been involved, or at least knew something. He'd gone to Kyle's house, for God's sake. But the body had been found in Portland, a good twenty miles away. Beaten with a blunt object, after a roadside scuffle.

Sounded all too familiar. And very few people knew how a story that familiar might affect him.

His phone sang the familiar, scratchy refrain to "Black Magic Woman." He let it ring. Play. Whatever. He should change the ringtone. Hell, block the damned number. Delete it even.

It chimed again. He picked up the phone, pressed the button to send it to voice mail. The ringing stopped. He sighed, paused at a four-way stop. Waited for the beep that indicated a waiting message.

Waited.

"Black Magic Woman" played for the third time.

"Crap!" He grabbed the phone again. No sense putting this off—she'd just keep calling. He answered. "Yeah."

"Darling!" Christine sounded so chipper, he wanted to puke. "I can't thank you enough!"

"Thank me?"

"For Kyle. You lovely man. To think I'd almost given up hope."

"You have nothing to thank me for," Peter said. "I had nothing to do with Kyle's death." Even though his windows were shut, he checked the area to make sure no one could overhear him.

Christine laughed like he had told her a hilarious joke. "Peter, my dear. It's me you're talking to. You don't have to deny anything. Take credit for it! Remember, silly man, I'm the one who asked you to do it. And after what you did yesterday, I thought—"

"Christine." Peter lowered his voice and held the phone closer to his mouth. "I know how this must appear to you. But I swear to God, I have been nowhere near Kyle since we left him unconscious on the ground in North Clackamas. I've been with you, then at work. Lots of people can verify that, if that's what it comes down to."

"Perfect." She cooed rather than spoke the word. "You are so good at this!"

"What are you talking about?" Peter gripped the phone—no, crushed it. His voice went tight, tension stretching it like the skin of a drum. "Good at what?"

She laughed again, almost a giggle. "Setting up alibis, of course. You've covered your tracks perfectly."

"I'm telling you—!" Peter calmed himself. Shouting hurt his throat. A passerby gave him a curious look, then signaled that he wanted to cross in front. Peter flipped his hand in an angry wave: go. Go!

He took a breath to calm himself. "Listen to me, Christine. I. Did. Not. Kill. Kyle. All right?"

She sighed. "If you say so." She didn't sound convinced. "I must say, I'm disappointed in you, Peter. I thought you'd be proud."

"Proud?" Shouting again.

"And a little more forthright with me. After all, we are partners."

"I am being forthright!" He took another deep breath. Easy, boy. Easy. "I am telling you. I had nothing to do with it."

"Then who did?" She sounded curious now, a bit surprised, like maybe she even believed him a little bit.

"I don't know. I thought you might."

"Peter. Don't be silly. Just like you, I've been nowhere near him. With you, then in meetings at work." Her voice turned light again. "Oh, I know. You hired someone, didn't you?"

"Of course not!"

"Peter! It's brilliant. Making sure you had an airtight alibi, then—"

"Christine. This conversation is over. And you know what else is over? Us. You and me. I'm done with you. Don't call me. Ever." He hung up, expecting the phone to ring again immediately.

But it remained silent.

***

Shaggy limped along on the sidewalk lining the modest, well-kept homes of Ladd's Addition, a neighborhood that had once been a gold mine of affordable three-bedroom homes for Portland's middle class. In recent years, however, a housing shortage had led to skyrocketing prices that left thousands of newcomers scrambling to buy or rent dilapidated shacks in outlying suburbs for amounts that made realtors and bankers drool. Himself one of those newcomers two years before, Shaggy found rents and mortgages in the city well beyond his reach, even at the exorbitant rates he charged clients like the late Kyle Campbell.

But those skyrocketing prices meant windfalls for many Portland homeowners, who could refinance almost at will, pocketing wads of cash that bought consumer goods like TVs, game consoles, jewelry, and other easily-fenced goods. And easily-fenced goods often made up for hard times, like the ones he faced now.

Lumpy had plenty of easily-fenced goods. And exorbitant rates, he'd learned, only mattered if one actually received payment. Which tends not to happen when a client suddenly dies.

As he neared the bungalow, he slowed his pace. He peered out from under the broad brim of his baseball cap, giving his eyes a chance to focus in the sharp shadows of the early summer evening. The bungalow sported a shallow front porch behind a white wooden railing, with wide steps leading up to a heavy wooden door, secured by a deadbolt lock and metal plate guarding the antique brass handle. Front door entry was not an option at this hour. Nor the big picture windows, as tempting as they were. Too visible. The tiny fifty-by-hundred-foot lots put curious neighbors within easy sight and earshot of everything that happened on every front porch on the street. No, he'd need to use the back entry, as before.

Even so, nosy neighbors might look askance at a stranger wandering around Lumpy's yard. He glanced up and down the street. A few kids played some sort of bouncy-ball game in the street a few houses further down, but if they saw him, they ignored him. No adults seemed available to supervise them. He shook his head in mock disgust. Parents should be much more careful. One never knew what kind of people might come around.

He chuckled to himself, pleased with his private little joke, and glanced toward the detached garage at the rear of the house. He'd cased the property a few weeks before and knew that the owner always parked his truck inside. He glanced through the street-facing window on the side of the garage. Empty. Good. Lumpy wasn't home. He turned to walk up the alley separating Lumpy's house from his neighbor's, and nearly jumped out of his shoes when a burst of canine noise exploded from behind the twisted-wire fence that ran along the alley. A ball of black and white fur pranced along the fence, barking with a furious vengeance, now and then slamming its front paws on the pole rail running horizontal to the ground about four and a half feet high.

"Shut up, Gypsy!" A man's voice shouted from inside the neighbor's house. "Settle down!"

The shaggy-haired man sidled up close to the bungalow, trying to blend in among shrubs in dire need of a late-summer trim. The idiot dog barked louder, jumping side to side, apoplectic. Stupid thing risked giving itself a heart attack, smashing into the fence with its claws, its body, even its teeth a few times.

"Gypsy!" The man's voice got louder. A storm door squeaked open, and a balding, apple-shaped man in a white ribbed wife-beater and plaid cargo shorts appeared on the back stoop. A cigarette dangled from one side of his mouth, his puffy face red with rage or exertion. He yelled at the dog again, something unintelligible.

Shaggy dove for the dirt, scrambled behind the bushes, and pressed himself against the house. The man squinted away from the dog, shading his eyes from the sun. He scanned the bushes, inhaled on the cigarette, and frowned. "It's just a damned squirrel, Gypsy," he said. "Come on inside, girl."

The dog glowered at its owner. She took a step or two sideways, and emitted a long, low growl, and burst into her crazed barking again. The man threw his hands up, cursed, and stomped down the steps. He waddled over to the dog, who slowed her barking and cowered low to the ground. Apple-belly raised a hand in the air, as if to strike the dog. Shaggy gritted his teeth and made a mental note: if Lumpy's place didn't pan out, Apple-belly's would be next. Anyone who mistreated a poor, dumb animal deserved it, and worse.

The dog whimpered and flattened herself to the ground. Apple-belly grabbed her by the collar and dragged her toward his house. Shaggy breathed easier. In a moment, this distraction, this threat, would be gone.

The low hum of a combustion engine, paired with tires rolling on asphalt, emerged from Shaggy's right, toward the front of the house. The apple-shaped man stopped and waved in that direction. The sound grew louder, partially masked by the dog's renewed devotion to shrill barking. Through the branches rolling wheels appeared, attached to a silver truck body. They rolled past, then stopped. The rattling whir of the garage-door opener joined the medley of sound.

Lumpy was home.

Shaggy flattened himself against the house. Clearly his mission was over. So he had two choices: wait until Lumpy and Apple went back inside, or make a dash for it now, hoping their current distractions would provide enough cover for a getaway.

Waiting seemed prudent on its face, but what if the two men got to talking about sports, or barbecue grills, or the weather, or God knows what? He could end up stuck there for hours. Then the damned dog would bark again, and sooner or later they'd think to look in the bushes, and he'd be done for.

He could easily outrun Apple-belly. And Lumpy was still parking his truck.

The garage door rattled again. Closing, then, hopefully with Lumpy still inside. His window of opportunity.

He crawled behind the bushes to the front corner of the house. The dog's barking reached a fever pitch. He sprang to his feet and ran.

"Hey, you there!" the fat man called after him. "Stop!"

Shaggy almost laughed. Sure, man. I'll stop. Because you asked so nicely.

He stumbled and landed hard on the sidewalk. Rolled to his feet, looked back. The fat man, the dog, and even Lumpy stared at him. He ran, expecting to hear footsteps behind him, but none came. Just the sound of that nasty, yippy little dog.

He turned the corner, slowing a bit to take one last look behind him. No one followed him. Good. He ran down to the end of the block, gasping for breath, turned toward his vehicle, parked a few hundred feet away. He reached into his pocket, fumbling for his keys.

Not there.

He slowed his pace, checked the other pocket.

Nope.

Oh, for the love of all things chocolate, as his mother used to say. Where the hell were those keys?

***

Peter watched the man go, too startled to move. He turned toward his neighbor. "George, did you see—"

"I sure did," George said, stomping out the cigarette on his porch. "Should we call the cops?"

Peter shrugged. "For all we know, he was a cop."

George cupped his hand over Gypsy's mouth to stop her from barking. "Naw, I don't think so. Portland don't let cops grow their hair like that."

Peter left his doubts unspoken. "Could you ID him? Did you see his face?"

George shook his head. "Just got a glimpse. Still. He might come back."

Peter nodded and looked in the direction the man had run. Something glistened in the sunlight on the sidewalk. He strode over and picked it up.

"Oh, he'll be back," Peter said with a grin. "If he wants his keys."

Chapter Twenty-Nine

Peter popped the cap off of an India Pale Ale and returned to his front porch, sitting on an Adirondack chair to wait for the return of the man who'd fled his property earlier that evening. He took small, slow sips, savoring the balance of sweet malt flavor and the hop bitterness. The sun had sunk low over his neighbor's roof by the time he finished the beer, and it made him hungry. Time to fix some dinner. The shaggy-haired man, perhaps, would not be returning after all.

He stood to toss the empty into the nearby recycling bin when a Portland police cruiser slowed to a stop in front of his house. He dropped his empty bottle into the bin and took slow steps toward the vehicle. Neighbors tending their flower gardens pretended not to watch the potential drama unfolding in this otherwise quiet neighborhood, but their kids playing in the street gawked without shame. Peter, in turn, ignored them all.

The cruiser's driver-side door opened, and a uniformed officer Peter recognized as Patrolman Tennyson Howard climbed out. Moments later his young partner exited the passenger side. Tens tipped his cap and circled around the car to the curb. "Evening, Mr. Robertson."

"Officers. Did you come back for these?" He held up the keychain, out of the officers' reach.

The two cops exchanged puzzled glances. "No," Tens said. "I keep my keys on my person at all times. Why?"

Peter chuckled. "I know they're not your personal property. But perhaps the man you had staking out my house will want these back. Assuming he wants to drive anywhere soon."

Tens shook his head. "I don't know what you're talking

about. We aren't staking you out. At least not to my knowledge. And trust me, I'd know."

Peter tucked the keys into his pocket. "I see. I'm supposed to believe that you showing up here twenty minutes after we flush a man out of hiding in my bushes is a coincidence?"

Tens glanced at his partner, then back to Peter. "Do you want to file a report?"

Peter laughed. "You're sticking with your story, then? That wasn't you guys?"

Tens smirked and leaned against his car. "Sorry. That's not our M.O. But you raise an interesting point. Should we be watching you?"

Peter's pulse quickened. "No, no," he said. "But now I'm curious. Why are you here?"

Tens smiled—an unfriendly, if not downright hostile smile. "Mr. Robertson," he said, shifting his weight away from the car, "we need you to come downtown."

Alarm bells rang in Peter's head. Had Christine turned him in for Alvin Dark's murder after all? He glanced from Tens to his young partner and back again. "You mean to the Justice Center? Why?" Their expressions told him nothing.

"We've just arrested a friend of yours for murder," Tens said. "We think you may be able to clarify a few points for us."

"Which friend?" Sweat trickled down his sides and back. He guessed Christine, and she wouldn't wait ten seconds before spilling what she knew—or whatever fit her needs, whether she believed it or not—to save her own skin. He tensed, ready for flight. But to where? How? Either or both of these cops could outrun him, and they carried sidearms. He'd get nowhere, except maybe to jail, or the morgue.

Tens narrowed his eyes and cocked his head. "I find it interesting that you ask which friend, but not who the victim was."

"Maybe because he already knows who the victim was," his partner said, menace dripping from his voice.

"I sure as hell hope there's only one recent murder victim in my world," Peter said, irritation rising. "Or have you guys let crime get so out of control here in Portland that I need to check in on my friends' vital signs every few hours?"

Tens smirked. "Touché. The victim is Kyle Campbell." He paused, as if expecting a response. "You don't look very surprised."

"I heard you on the radio a short while ago. I guess the shock is wearing off. So, who's your suspect?" His voice rose again, despite his best efforts to stay at even keel. He reminded himself that they didn't suspect him. This was about Kyle, not Alvin.

Still. His heart beat double-time, and if his sweat glands didn't slow down, he'd dehydrate in the next five minutes.

"You really don't know?" Tens asked. "Seriously?"

"How should I know? Hell, I'm surprised you even have a suspect this fast."

Tens checked his watch. "Yeah, we're moving right along on this case. Of course, it helps that we have a witness."

"A witness? Someone saw it?" Peter could not keep the excitement out of his voice. If someone actually saw Christine do it, his troubles might be over.

Tens held up his hands in self-defense. "I didn't say eye-witness. But the tip we got put the suspect at the scene. Really, it would be better if we could talk downtown." He gestured toward his cruiser.

"I'll drive myself, if I go," Peter said. "But I'm not yet convinced I should. I mean, you think you already know who did it, anyway." He hoped he appeared calm, despite the tangle of nerves closing in around his throat.

Tens thought a moment, nodded. "We know who killed Kyle Campbell," he said.

Peter waited, his heart pounding so loud he could barely hear the man speak. "And?"

"And you know the suspect pretty well too, so I hear." Tens smiled, an expression of steely grit.

Peter's pulse somehow quickened even further. He imagined Christine behind bars, dressed in prison garb. With some shame, he pictured her in tight-fitting overalls, smiling through her trademark red lipstick, looking as pretty as ever. A ridiculous image. He really needed to stop watching late-night crime dramas.

But if she'd been arrested, his own drama might be over. His mood lifted…just in time to crash around his heels.

"The suspect," Tens said, "is Frankie Kowalczyk."

***

"This is crazy!" Peter pounded the table in the police interrogation room with his bare fists. "Frankie was nowhere near Portland last night. I should know. I left him in eastern Washington myself!"

Tens leaned against the pale green cement block wall several feet away, shook his head, and smirked at the police detective seated across from Peter at the table. Detective Davont'a Collins, a graying beach ball of a man with chocolate-hued skin and deep-set black eyes, leaned back in his chair, arms folded. "You managed to get back here before sunset, by your own admission," Collins said. "Why couldn't he?"

"Because he was driving my truck, and I flew back," Peter said for the sixtieth time. "I've given you the pilot's name. Why don't you call him?"

The detective shrugged. "I will. Right now I'm talking to you. Now, here's the thing, Mr. Robertson. We know your friend drove the truck back. We also know he possessed it until at least late this afternoon."

"Yeah, about six o'clock. He brought it to my work place. I told you that, too."

Collins leaned forward. "We also know that he drove said vehicle to the scene of the murder. Which is why we're sweeping your truck for evidence as we speak."

"Pure coincidence. Frankie didn't even know the victim. Why would he go anywhere near him, much less kill him?"

"That's what we're trying to find out from you," Tens said, his first spoken words in over an hour. Collins hushed him with a wave of his hand.

"What's becoming clear to me, Mr. Robertson," Collins said, "is that while Frankie may not have known Mr. Campbell, he did know that you and the victim had quarreled—apparently over a Ms. Christine Nielsen."

"We did no such thing."

"Witnesses say you two had a fistfight in the front yard of a house he rents in Clackamas."

"He kidnapped Christine! I was there to rescue her."

Collins shook his head, amused. "No one reported any kidnapping to us." Collins tapped a pen on the table, a paragon of patience and calm.

"That's ridiculous. Christine called 911 in the cab going home."

Collins checked a printout in a manila folder on the table, then closed it again. "No, sir. We've checked every transcript from the 911 center from yesterday evening. No such call was ever received."

Peter leaned in, his voice rising. "I was sitting right next to her when she called!"

Tens pushed away from the wall, arms still folded. "But who was she talking to? Did you watch her dial the numbers?"

"Well, no." The policeman's words sank in, and Peter's stomach collapsed into his feet. Of course they were right. She'd never had any intention of calling it in—and she hadn't done so. She'd decoyed him. He collapsed back into his chair and rubbed his temples, hard. "Dammit. I can't believe it."

"So, shall we start over?" Collins rested his elbows on the table, his hands folded. "Did you or did you not have a fist fight with Kyle Campbell in the front yard of his rental house in Clackamas yesterday evening?"

Peter expelled air through his lips and propped his chin up with an open palm. "There wasn't much of a fight. He ran at us. I punched him, knocked him out. Then we left."

"You hit him once? That's it?"

Peter shrugged. "Maybe a couple of times. Like I said, it was quick."

Collins wagged his head, as if impressed. "Are you a boxer, Mr. Robertson?"

Peter glared at him, gave him his best withering look. "Of course not."

"Do you usually go around knocking guys out with one punch?"

Peter waved him off. "I got lucky. Hit him blind-side in the temple. And I guess I was pretty amped up."

"Bare fist?"

Peter lifted a shoulder, let it fall. "Yeah. Why?"

The two cops exchanged glances. Collins stood up and paced away from the table. "I don't see any scrapes or bruises on your knuckles. Seems like a punch to the temple might hurt a little."

Peter wagged his hand, fingers dangling. "They sting a little yet."

Collins turned back to him. "Are you sure you didn't use a bar, or club, or something of that sort to knock him out?"

Peter nodded. "I'm sure."

Collins strode back to the table, leaned over him. "You didn't use a tire iron, for example?"

Tire iron! Peter's head swam. Not that again! He shook his head. "No. Nothing. I punched him, with my fist. Once—no, wait, it was twice. Once when I was trying to get into the house, he jumped me—"

"Seems to me, if you were breaking into his house, wouldn't he be a little bit justified in defending himself?"

Peter stood, stared eye-to-eye at Collins. "He had Christine! She was his captive! How many times—"

"All right, all right, calm down," Collins said, waving off Tens, who had pushed away from the wall again with a menacing stare. "We'll see what your girlfriend's story is, see if yours checks out with hers." He fixed Peter with a level stare. "But maybe, just maybe, if you'd have stayed clear of Mr. Campbell's house, he'd be alive to tell his own side of the story."

Peter started to object, but decided against it. He'd probably already said too much. Maybe he should get a lawyer.

Collins, meanwhile, returned to his seat. "So, you've got an alibi for the time of death, and a witness to corroborate it. If it checks out, and let's assume for the moment that it will, then you've got a different problem. Namely, why your friend, who you say was in eastern Washington and didn't know the victim, was seen at the same house, driving your truck, less than an hour before the body was found. And he left prints and other physical evidence at the crime scene. Got any answers for that?"

Peter shook his head, confused. "There has to be some kind of mistake."

"Oh, there were lots of mistakes made," Tens said, earning another sharp look from Collins. He continued anyway. "Most of them by you and your buddy."

"I just can't think of a reason why he'd even go there," Peter said. "I'd have never found it myself if Kyle hadn't sent an Uber driver to the airport for me."

"See, that doesn't add up for me," Collins said. "If he kidnapped your girlfriend, as you say, why would he send a cab to bring you there? It doesn't make sense."

"It doesn't make any sense," Peter said, "but it's true."

The two cops exchanged a long look. Finally, Collins rose to his feet. "Sit tight a few minutes," he said. "I need some coffee."

Peter could have used some too, and some dinner for that matter, but he knew that wasn't in the cards. The two cops headed to the door, but Tens waited there after Collins left. "Here's something else I don't get, just between us girls," he said, facing Peter. "That night I came to your girlfriend's house a week or two ago. You said that was the same guy as the victim. Right?"

Peter nodded. "Yes. Kyle broke in, and—"

Tens interrupted him with a slow wag of his head. "No, sir."

Peter frowned. "What do you mean?"

"I mean," Tens said, a smirk rising on his lips, "the man who broke into Ms. Nielsen's house that night—if 'breaking in' is the term to describe it—was not Kyle Campbell. The prints, the DNA—none of it matches."

"That's not possible."

Tens chuckled. "My friend, it's more than possible. It's the God's-honest-truth. And something tells me that your girlfriend may already know this." He paused, holding the door open. "That's something that you might want to find out." He nodded once and left the room, closing and locking the door behind him.

The click of the lock echoed in Peter's ears—the sound of freedom slipping slowly away. Meanwhile Christine, with her double-crosses and twisted schemes, remained free, somewhere outside of those thick, concrete walls.

Suddenly the room felt smaller, stuffier and a whole lot warmer.

Chapter Thirty

Christine hummed to herself as she walked toward the setting sun in Portland's bustling and hip Pearl District. Shoppers ducked in and out of the chic shops selling upscale clothing, artisanal chocolates and locally-produced pinot noirs. Pub-goers stumbled across the narrow, busy cross streets into high-end restaurants. Money flowed like the abundant streams pushing summer rains down West Hill slopes toward the Willamette and the once-mighty Columbia River. Christine drank it all in—the urban excitement, surrounded by natural beauty and the odd, almost beatnik optimism of the locals. She breathed a satisfied sigh. The move to Portland four years before had worked out well for her. And now, with Kyle gone, she no longer would have to live in the constant fear under which she'd labored for the better part of a decade. Finally, amidst all the beauty and abundance, she would enjoy her freedom—if only briefly. It would be a shame to leave it all behind.

First, she needed to change her pattern of bad luck with men. Peter hadn't worked out quite the way she'd hoped, but she could live with the way that had turned out. Kyle was gone. Not by Peter's hand, as she'd hoped, but he'd serve as a perfect scapegoat, if she needed one. For now, his idiotic friend Frankie filled that role, and that, too, worked well for her. Frankie had escaped justice for sexual harassment a few months before. If he took the fall for Kyle's murder, well, call it karma.

She reached her destination, an ATM outside a local bank branch that held her reserve funds under an assumed identity, untraceable back to her. She checked the balance, made a note to engineer the complex series of transactions that would, over the next several days, boost the balance to its targeted level. No rush. She couldn't go anywhere just yet, anyway. Running too soon would only make the wrong people suspicious.

She turned the corner to navigate the entrance to one of her favorite wine bars, but stopped when a faint ring tone leaked out of her purse. She retrieved it, read the caller ID, cursed, and answered. "This call," she said, "is a very bad idea."

"So is making me wait for my money," the man said.

"Nonsense," she said. "You'll be paid exactly when, and in the manner and amount, in which we agreed."

"I need it now! And I need more. I've had expenses."

"*When-and-in-the-amount-agreed!*" She spit the words into the phone, tucked low into her shoulder to prevent her voice from projecting into the crowds around her.

"Are you sure this is wise?" he said, his voice tinged with sarcasm. "I know things…you don't want to keep that knowledge hungry. A man could get desperate."

"That cuts both ways," she said, slowing her walking pace. She hadn't paid much attention to her surroundings. Not good. "You know, most people don't even know you exist. Which is how you like it. What a shame it would be if all that were to suddenly change."

"After what I've done for you—"

"You—!" She caught herself and lowered her voice from the loud, high pitch it had quickly reached. "Look. You did well. You'll be paid well. But the timing is important. If we rush, it will only raise suspicions. This whole thing could unravel. Is that what you want?" She looked around and realized she'd taken a detour down a dark, unfamiliar street, with few people around. More private, but not safe for a woman on her own. She reversed direction back toward the busy, well-lit shopping district—

And nearly crashed head-first into Raul Vasquez.

"I gotta go," she said into the phone.

"But—"

She hung up. Raul, hands in his back pockets, grinned. "Did I surprise you?"

"What is this, stupid night?" She tossed her phone into her purse. "What the hell do you think you're doing? Following me?"

Raul shrugged. "Following? No, no. By pure coincidence, I saw you at the bank machine, and I thought you must be getting my money. So, for your convenience, I thought I would say hello and maybe save you a trip."

"Your money?"

Raul spread his hands wide. "Two weeks I have been working for you, but I have not been paid."

"We agreed on a monthly stipend. That assumes a month's work. We also agreed not to meet in person—ever. Yet here you are. What were you thinking?"

Raul sighed, dropped his hands to his sides. "I see. So it is to be like this. Well, so be it."

She started to push past him, then stopped. "What do you mean, 'So be it'?"

He stepped aside for her. "I guess it means, I must continue to wait. And you, also, must accept the consequences."

She turned to face him, forced a smile onto her face. "Consequences, Raul? A man with your history has the nerve to talk to me about consequences?"

Raul's expression darkened. "I must warn you, I do not respond well to threats."

She laughed and reached for his button-down shirt, holding the seam between loose fingers, tugging him toward her. "Threats? Oh, my. Now why ever would you assume I would threaten you? What information could I possibly have that might put you in jeopardy?"

He batted away her hand. "I was acquitted by a jury of my peers. A jury that included you, I might add!"

She widened her smile and winked at him. "So it did, Raul. So it did. So. Where does that leave us? Right where we started, I think, before you made the unwise choice of following me." She leaned in close, pressed her hand on his sturdy chest. "If you want things to go well between us, you won't make that mistake again. Will you, Raul?"

He glared at her, but said nothing.

She smiled sweetly at him, pure saccharine. "Be careful, Raul. Be very careful."

She stepped around him and resumed walking toward Glisan Street. After taking several steps, she stole a glance behind her. Raul had disappeared.

She sighed in relief and walked toward the bright, busy street.

***

The police released Peter after another agonizing and repetitious hour of questioning, apparently satisfied enough with his alibi to conclude that he couldn't have done the deed or even witnessed it. "But don't stray too far," Tens said when he let him go. "Check in with us before heading out of the area."

"Am I still under suspicion, after all that?" Peter asked, an edge in his voice.

"Just don't go buying any airplane tickets in the coming few weeks, okay?"

Peter stomped out of the Justice Center and up three flights of stairs in the nearby parking garage, then slammed his truck door shut behind him. He hadn't eaten dinner, and it was past nine o'clock. He put the truck in gear and suppressed every urge to burn rubber down the garage's spiraling exit ramp. He behaved himself in traffic, wary of giving Tennyson Howard any more reason to harass him, and pulled into a short line at a Burgerville drive-up window on the Eastside just as Carlos Santana began playing on his cell phone. He put the call on speaker. "Yeah, what's up?"

"What's up? Geez. I'm happy to hear your voice, too, darling."

"Don't 'darling' me. I told you not to call me."

"Of course you weren't serious," she said in a mocking tone. "A lonely man like you?"

"Damn right I was serious. And I'm in no mood for any more of your crap. I just spent three hours getting grilled by police about Kyle's death thanks to an 'anonymous tip.' Gee, I wonder where that came from?"

"Welcome to the club. I was at the police station all day,

starting at ten a.m. I somehow earned the privilege of identifying the body. So much fun for me, huh?"

The line of cars in front of him dwindled to one. He pulled up behind it, contemplating his order. "Well, get this. They're blaming, not you, but my best friend for this murder. How do you think they got that idea?"

"Peter!" she said, mock aghast. "You didn't slough the dirty work off to your best friend, now, did you?"

"Of course not! Wait—that's not—"

"I can't tell you how happy I am that you did this for me," she said. "Especially after you left him lying there—"

"I did not do this for you! For God's sake!" He drove forward, following the car ahead of him, and stopped next to the ordering kiosk.

"Peter," she said in a soothing voice, "if not for me, then for whom?"

"For nobody! I didn't do it for anybody. I didn't do it, period! Jesus!"

"I can take your order anytime you're ready," a teenage boy's high-pitched voice said amid a cacophony of static.

"I see you're taking yourself out to dinner to celebrate," she said. "So fancy."

"I am not celebrating anything!" Peter shook the steering wheel. He would have torn it off if he could.

"Sir?" the teenager said. "I didn't quite get that."

"I'm shocked," Christine said. "I expected to find you someplace fancy. Pazzo's, maybe, to commemorate our first date. Or, maybe, Florentino's?" She laughed as if she hadn't a care in the world.

"There is nothing to celebrate," he said through gritted teeth. "A man is dead, my best friend is accused of killing him, and why I didn't just turn you in for it, I still don't know."

"S-sir?" the disembodied static said.

"We both know why you didn't do that," Christine said. "Unless you really do want to talk to the police about Alvin Dark."

He took a deep breath and tried to focus on the LED lights

that, in some universe, formed words on a menu. No luck. "Maybe I should."

"Peter, you're being a petulant brat."

"Yeah, well. Love you too, Killer Queen."

A sharp intake of breath, followed by several seconds of dead air, let him know that his comment had left its mark. He smiled. If she ever heard her ring tone, she'd have a heart attack.

"Well," she said after a long pause, "I can see that I've misjudged you. I thought you were a man I could count on through the rough patches. A team player. But apparently—"

"We are not a team!" He caught himself yelling again. Static coughed out of the drive-up kiosk's speaker.

"Sir? Could you repeat your order, please?"

"You're right, Peter." All lightness of tone left Christine's voice. "We're not a team. We never really were. I thought you might have helped me out with Kyle, but I can see you never really cared about my problem."

"Of course I cared," Peter said. "I just didn't agree with your solution."

"You lied to me, then."

He gritted his teeth, exhaled noisily. "You gave me no choice."

"Well, then. I'm glad I had other options. More reliable men. More…loyal."

"More lethal, you mean."

"Apparently, yes. But at least they told me the truth."

"You're no one to talk about lying." His voice grew hoarse with anger. "About being deceitful. How about that night you said Kyle broke into your house, eh? Utter bullshit."

"You were there. You saw—"

"I saw a man, yes, but it wasn't Kyle. The police proved it. So, who was it, Christine? One of your 'other options,' I take it?"

She made a noise like she'd sucked air in between her teeth. Her voice came back, sharp, accusatory. "So, what are you saying? I staged a break-in at my own house, using a Kyle look-alike?"

"Something like that." Hearing her say it actually calmed him for some odd reason. "Actually, now that you've laid it out so clearly, yes. Exactly like that."

"Ridiculous."

The speaker coughed again with growing impatience. "Sir?"

"Give me a minute," Peter said out the window.

"I've given you too many minutes," Christine said, venom in her voice. "Too many hours, and too many days, and too many fucks. And you know what, Peter? I no longer give a fuck about you or anything that happens to you."

Silence hung in the air for several seconds, broken up only by the static in the speaker outside his car window. "Sir? Would you like to—"

"Forget it!" Peter put his truck in gear and drove forward, too fast. He jammed on the brake, stopping just in time, inches from the bumper of a car collecting their order from the service window.

"Forgetting it is great advice for you to take," Christine said. "Forget everything you know about me, and us. Forget it all. Do not let a single word about me pass your lips to anyone—most of all, the police. Do not even think about creating problems for me. Because if you do, Peter, I'll know. And as you're now quite well aware, I take care of my problems. And when I do, my solutions are quite final."

The line went silent, then dead.

***

Christine downed the rest of her drink, vodka with too much fruit juice, in one swallow. The drink boiled in her otherwise empty stomach, much like the blood racing through her veins. Damn that man! How could she have chosen such a useless jerk for this critical mission?

Lesson learned. Leverage, even deadly leverage, was not enough.

Kyle was gone. No thanks to Peter, as it turned out, and in the end, she'd simply replaced one enemy with another. A much less dangerous enemy, to be sure, but even so, a problem.

Still, she knew how to deal with problems. Sometimes

dealing with problems like these involved a little bit of pain, and too often, that pain was self-inflicted.

But the pain, too, would pass. And soon, freedom would return.

***

Peter inspected the repairs to the front windows and doors at Stark's and gave an approving nod to the contractor standing next to him. "Great work," he said. "I couldn't even see the alarm sensors at first."

"That's the goal," said the graying, short-haired man. His nametag read "Shawn Dekum—Safe Buildings, Inc." He noted something on his clipboard as he spoke. "If you can't see them, neither can intruders."

"I'm confused," Peter said. "I thought the idea was deterrence. For that, don't the security measures need to be visible, front and center?"

"We've got those," the security man said, pointing to video cameras mounted on the soffits twenty feet above. "Plus we'll add lots of signage, additional lighting, and alarms. There'll be plenty of deterrence."

Peter nodded. If anything, the system was overkill. "What about the insider aspect? Gregg's convinced one of our employees had a hand in this."

"More cameras, plus voice-activated audio recorders, both in every office, hallway, and retail zone," Dekum said. "Phones are monitored and all calls centrally recorded. Access to the building will require sign-in codes and IDs unique to each employee. If someone on the inside is involved, we'll know."

"You're taping our phone calls? Where do all these recordings go, anyway?"

Dekum smiled, revealing chipped, yellowing teeth. "A secure, offsite data center, connected by a dedicated gigabit data line. We store it all digitally for fast, secure retrieval at our facility. You want to see who said what and when, we'll have it on demand. We'll train you on the retrieval software."

Peter shuddered. "We all love Big Brother, right?"

Dekum gave him a puzzled look. Peter waved him off.

Education in the classics, his father had always railed, had gone all to hell.

A dark green Impala with government plates pulled into the parking lot. Peter made eye contact with the driver, a uniformed African-American woman whose head barely cleared the top of the steering wheel. She said something to her passenger, a tall, husky Caucasian with close-cropped gray hair and black horn-rimmed glasses wearing a similar uniform. The driver parked and the two got out, staring straight at him. The man in uniform carried a large, closed, yellow envelope.

"Looks like someone's about to get served," Dekum said.

"Are you Peter Robertson?" the man called out to him.

"I am." Peter excused himself and approached the pair. "Who wants to know?"

"I'm Richard Gray, Deputy Marshall of Multnomah County Court. This is my partner, Alyssa Jaycock. Could you verify your address for me, please?"

Peter rattled off his address, then asked, "What's this all about?"

Gray removed papers from the envelope and scanned them, then handed Peter the documents. "You are hereby served notice by Multnomah County, on behalf of the State of Oregon."

"Notice of what?" Peter glared at Gray, who merely pointed to the pages in Peter's hand.

Peter read the opening paragraph of the court order. His jaw dropped.

Christine had taken out a restraining order on him.

***

Back in his office, he slammed the door shut and paced the cramped room.

His mind reeled. He couldn't believe his eyes. It wasn't enough that she'd blackmailed him for weeks, then somehow managed to get his best friend locked up in jail, accused of her own crime. Now she'd filed a civil complaint against him to the court, alleging that he'd been stalking, harassing, and threatening physical harm against her. The complaint alleged that he presented a clear and present danger to her person, and demanded that he cease and desist from attempting any contact with her or from going within two miles of her house or office. The order compelled him to appear in court on a Monday some two weeks out to answer charges, or stipulate to the charges and pay a huge fine. Penalties for violating the order were severe and included additional fines, possibly jail.

The order included specific complaints against him: that he'd not only threatened violence, but had actually assaulted her on multiple occasions. It referenced medical reports that documented bruises, scrapes, her hair being pulled out by the roots. It alleged he'd forced himself upon her sexually, that he'd committed "unnatural acts," and threatened further violence if she ever told anyone. She alleged that he'd called her dozens of times, day and night, harassing her, stalking her, interrupting her sleep and invading her privacy.

All the things that she had done to him.

The woman was crazy. And paranoid.

He sat at his desk, calmed himself with some deep breathing. On the one hand, the order wouldn't have much impact. He had no intention of contacting her, or of being anywhere near her. She'd asked the court, in effect, to enforce his own self-imposed ban.

He could almost hear Frankie cheering his good luck. If they allowed cheering in jail.

On the other hand, it angered him. She'd taken a pre-emptive strike in her own defense, effectively getting the courts to label him a violent man. A threat.

Just like she'd done to Kyle!

He stopped pacing, letting that realization sink in.

Was he next on her hit list?

Chapter Thirty-One

"Dude, thank you so much for coming to visit me. I can't tell you how much it means to me." Frankie sat opposite Peter, each man cradling the beige phone handsets close to his face. A thick wall separated them, and gray Formica-topped counters gave them a place to rest their elbows. Short extensions divided the space along the counters into separate carrels, most of them empty, except for the ones at each end, occupied on the visitors' side by an elderly African-American woman at one end and a white man in a blue suit on the other, both speaking in hushed tones.

"I'll be here every day," Peter said. "Until they let you out, I mean." Technically he'd missed a day already, but only due to visiting hour restrictions.

"They ain't letting me out," Frankie said. "Not until my arraignment, anyway. Sam said that'd be sometime next week." Frankie wore a pale orange jumpsuit with black digits printed across a white rectangle sewn or pressed across his chest. A light stubble dotted his cheeks and chin, and his blond hair looked like the county had mopped the floor with it, then put him in a wind tunnel to dry.

"Sam?" Peter said. "Who's he?"

Frankie grinned, the first positive expression he'd shown since Peter arrived. "Not he. She. Samantha Pullen. My lawyer. She's a real hotshot. Just won a big case way out in central Oregon. Man, did I ever luck out in getting her."

"Oh, right. I've heard of her. So she's that good, huh? Better than all the under-employed lawyers in Portland?"

Frankie shrugged. "Donna at Stark's recommended her. I guess they went to high school together. She says Sam has never lost a felony case. But man, that ain't even the best part." He leaned closer to the glass, as though to confide a secret, even though their voices traveled only through the phone. "When I say hotshot? I mean, she's hot."

Peter shook his head, but smiled anyway. "Frankie, if there was ever an irrelevant fact about a lawyer—"

"It ain't irrelevant when I get to meet with her, and all I get to look at in here are stinky men's butts," Frankie said. "I tell you what, man. Whatever she says, I lap it up like a dog in heat. Because at that moment, I am."

Peter sighed, not bothering to correct him about which gender of dog goes into heat. "Well, if she's as smart as you say, that's good—you should do whatever she tells you. It'd be a nice change of pace for you."

"Shut the hell up. You're one to talk, never listening to me about hanging out with Christine."

"I'm listening now. I should have listened sooner."

"Finally! Then ditching me in eastern Washington like that. If you'd have stayed with me—"

"I said I was sorry."

"We're gonna need a lot more than sorry to get us back to even. Hell, it's because of that I'm in here now in the first place." Frankie's voice broke and he put the phone down on the shallow counter.

Peter waited for him to collect himself. "I wanted to ask you about that. How did they come to charge you with this, anyway? I mean, you didn't do it, did you?"

Frankie jumped up on his feet, stretching the phone cord taut. "Hell no! Of course not! What the hell kind of question is that?" Frankie's shouts attracted the attention of the uniformed policemen guarding the corners on either side of the plexiglass wall dividing the long, narrow room. Frankie held up his hands, as if to signal that all was okay, then sat back in the chair. The guards relaxed again, but the one on the inside kept his eye on

Frankie.

"So how did they decide to charge you?" Peter asked. "They told me they had an anonymous tip. Someone saw you at the house in Clackamas."

"Dude. My lawyer told me I can't talk to anyone about this stuff. Even you." Frankie slumped in his seat, eyes toward the floor.

"That's ridiculous," Peter said. "I'm never going to rat you out, no matter what you tell me."

"All I can tell you is that it's a total frame job," Frankie said. "I didn't kill nobody."

Peter sighed. He wanted to believe Frankie, but he had a track record of denying the obvious—most recently when Stark's managers caught him having sex with his own employee on the job. Still, just because he broke employee conduct rules didn't mean he'd kill someone. He tried a different approach. "How'd you even think to go there? Hell, I'd never have known how to find it if Kyle hadn't sent a damn car to pick me up at the airport."

Frankie sat up in his seat. "What? Seriously?"

"Yeah, it was freaky. I still don't get why, unless he was trying to lure me into some sort of trap."

Frankie laughed. "Probably was. I'm surprised you went."

Peter waved him off. "I had to. Or so I thought. They had Chr—uh, anyway," he said, his face warming with embarrassment, "why did you go there? And how in the hell did you find it?"

Frankie took a deep breath and leaned back in his chair, rubbing the bridge of his nose, eyes closed. "Dude, I can't talk to you about it."

Alarm bells rang in Peter's head. Frankie didn't often lie outright, but he often got evasive when the facts looked bad for him. But he knew how to tease information out of his friend. "I know you can't talk about the case and all," he said, "but the murder didn't even happen there. The cops said it was somewhere in Portland, near Mt. Tabor."

"Yeah, so?"

Peter eyed the security guards. At the moment they seemed more interested in the African-American woman, who had hung up and headed toward the exit. He lowered his voice. "So, Clackamas is a long way from Mt. Tabor. How'd you know to go there? I mean, jeez, last I saw you, you were a three hour drive away."

Frankie grimaced at Peter, shaking his head. "After you ditched me in that truck stop, I drove your truck right back to Portland, with every intention of forcibly dragging your sorry ass back to Idaho like we'd planned. On the way, I noticed a black Ford following me. Nice car, too—a black GT500 coupe. Hard not to spot it, you know? I got a bad feeling about it, even moreso when he just happened to take the same exit when I stopped for a bite to eat, and left right after me, too."

"I don't see how that gets you to Kyle's house in North Clackamas."

Frankie held up his free hand, palm out. "I'm getting to that. When I got off the highway in Portland, I'd had enough of his crap. I ducked into the Lloyd Center parking garage and stopped, blocking the entrance. He was stuck in the traffic lane a couple of cars behind me, and I wouldn't move until he left— and he had to. Everybody's honking at him and stuff. He had to blow. I figured he'd circle around, so I hid the truck real quick in the lot across the street. Sure enough, he comes back, but can't find me. When he gave up looking, I followed him."

"The pursuer becomes the pursued."

"Exactly. He clearly didn't expect it, because he drove straight to the house where Kyle was." Frankie grinned, pride all over his face, sitting straight up in his chair.

Peter shook his head. "Or, he did expect it, and led you right to him on purpose."

"Why the hell—"

"Kyle wanted leverage over Christine. Me, you, anything to keep her close."

Frankie's grin faded, and he slouched back into his chair. "I hadn't thought of that."

Peter's heart sank along with his friend's posture. He didn't need to make things worse by pointing out the flaws in Frankie's tactics. He noticed that the man in the suit had stood up, and he waited for the man to leave so he and Frankie could have the room to themselves. "It's okay, man. I'm probably over-thinking this. What happened at the house?"

"Well, as I said, Sam told me not to talk about this, but...hell. I have to talk to someone. And I trust you more than my own mother." He leaned in again and lowered his voice. "I parked up the street, ready to take off at a moment's notice, but I can see everything, you know? So the dude I'm following finds Kyle laying in the yard, half-dazed. He rouses him up, they go inside, and only Kyle comes back out. Kyle drives off in the GT, but just as he does, he sees me, and recognizes me. I think, oh, shit. I gun it, but now he follows me."

"Into Portland?" Peter kept his voice light. Conversational. Keep Frankie talking.

"Yeah. I thought I could lose him, but he's a crazy son of a bitch. He ran me off the road on Mt. Tabor, then he gets out, all pissed off. And he's got a freaking gun."

"Holy crap! Have you told the cops this?"

"Of course. They were all, like, 'So, you're going with a plea of self-defense?' I could have punched them!" Frankie punched the air instead.

"Why not? It seems—"

"Because I didn't kill him, that's why!" Frankie's shouts echoed off the dim concrete-block walls, drawing stares from the guards. One of them pointed at Frankie, shook his head. A warning.

"So what did happen? How'd you get out of there?" Peter kept his voice low, hoping it would calm Frankie.

It worked. Frankie slumped back into his seat. "He got a little too close. I guess he didn't recognize me from that day in Forest Park."

"Yeah, he never really saw you there, from what Christine told me. You conked him from behind."

"Right. So he's all aggressive, trying to push me around, and I'm all like, Dude, just chill, okay? So he left me an open shot, and I took it. One punch and old Mr. Glass Jaw is on the ground, out cold. Just like you!" He grinned and glanced at his knuckles, a few of which sported light scabs, still healing. "I even scraped my hand."

"What happened to the gun?"

"I tossed it into the bushes."

"You touched it?"

Frankie sighed. "Yup. Stupid, I know. Here's the worst thing." He hung his head, took a deep breath. "I had to get your truck out of there, so I moved his GT first, 'cause it was blocking me in."

"So your prints are everywhere."

"Literally. And I guess even my DNA. My hand bled all over his car. Fibers from my clothes came off onto him, and onto the seats. I–I screwed up, Peter. Bad."

Peter cringed and pressed his palm up to the glass. Frankie, after a moment, pressed his own to the glass opposite Peter's. They locked eyes for several seconds.

"I'm so sorry, Frankie."

"I know, man."

"I'll get you out. I'll do whatever it takes."

"Don't worry, man. My lawyer's taking care of it."

Peter shook his head. "I want to help. I got you into this. I need to get you out."

Frankie started to object, stopped. "It's all right, man. It's my own fault."

"Way more mine than yours." Peter's voice cracked. "You were helping me out. Now it's my turn to help you."

The guard on Peter's side of the room approached. "Time's up, Mr. Robertson."

Peter held up an "OK" sign to the guard and turned back to Frankie. "I gotta go. I'll come back tomorrow if I can."

Frankie nodded. "Yeah. My lawyer's supposed to be here any minute anyway." He paused, fighting for words. After a long silence, he offered a sad smile. "Be good, man."

"You, too." They sat in silence, phones to their ears, for several more seconds. Finally, Frankie's sad smile crumpled. He slammed the phone into its cradle, then buried his face in his hands. Peter stood, pretending not to notice, and trudged to the door. The guard escorted him into the waiting area, a small rectangular room with chairs aligned along a pale green concrete block wall.

A blonde woman in a skirt suit folded her laptop into a briefcase and stood when Peter entered. About thirty-five, she looked movie-star pretty, with bright blue eyes, a slender nose, and a trim, proportional fix-foot five-inch frame. With her friendly smile, she reminded Peter of the actress Elisha Cuthbert.

"Mr. Robertson?" She extended her right hand, and he shook it. She held on an extra second with a firm grip and smothered his hand in both of hers. "Thank you for coming to see Frankie today. He's told me a lot about you."

"And likewise," Peter said. He couldn't take his eyes off of hers—so bright, so blue, so intelligent. So…intense. "Frankie's my best friend. I feel responsible for him being there."

Her eyes darkened a bit. "Sorry to say, I agree with you on that." She released her grip on his hand and gathered up her purse and briefcase.

A lump rose in Peter's throat. "I'm going to do everything I can to help fix this. I know he didn't do it."

"You know it? With certainty?" She cocked her head. "How so?"

"Ahh, well…I just know Frankie, that's all. He'd never—"

"Of course." She smiled. "Mr. Robertson, you're a key pl—ah, witness in all of this," she said. "You wouldn't happen to be able to provide Mr. Kowalczyk with an alibi for that night?"

"Unfortunately, no."

The attorney pursed her lips and nodded. "I see. Where were you that night, if I may be so bold? Weren't the two of you supposed to be off camping in Idaho together?"

"Ah…well, I had to come back to Portland. There was, an, um, emergency."

"Emergency. I see." She looked him over, as if assessing him. "Mr. Robertson, I'll be blunt. I understand this is not the first time you and Frankie have been on opposite sides of a legal dispute."

"We're not on opposite sides! I want to help him!" Peter's voice echoed off the walls of the tiny room. His hands shook. It occurred to him that she might try to blame him for Kyle's murder. "I have some information that could help clear all this up, I think. I just need to make sure of a few details—"

Pullen held up a delicate hand, perfectly manicured. "Yes. Well. On that front, I think it'd be best if you left his defense to the professionals."

"I didn't mean I wanted to be his lawyer," Peter said with an uneasy chuckle. "I just meant that I want to help clear his name. I know some of the people involved, and I have some ideas regarding the real killer."

"I have a few thoughts on that myself," she said, fixing Peter with an intense stare. Her eyes pierced his like lasers, and he took a step back from her. She softened her gaze. "We'll want to depose you, and those other people," she said. She put her hand on his back and walked him toward the exit door. "Would you be able to supply me with contact information for them?"

"Sure!" Peter said. His spirits lifted at the thought of working with her to help Frankie. "In fact, I could talk to them—"

"That'd be a big help. Their contact information, I mean." She handed him a business card. "And while I do appreciate your offer to help, I'd prefer you leave the investigation to me."

"I'll email you," Peter said. "But I think I can help in other ways, too. For instance—"

"Mr. Robertson, please. I was trying to say this nicely, but perhaps I need to be a bit more direct." She lowered her voice and placed a gentle hand on his arm. "Please, do not interfere with the investigation. That means not talking to potential witnesses or tampering with evidence, or anything. In fact…" She fixed him with a plaintive gaze. "It would be best if you could avoid all further contact with Frankie until after the trial. I hate to ask this, knowing how close you two are and how much your support means to him, but the potential for contaminating your testimonies, for coordinating your stories, is too great."

Her voice took on a steely edge. "That would hurt, not help, Frankie's cause. Do I make myself clear?"

Peter, taken aback by her words and forceful tone, nodded. She smiled, and in an instant her pleasant charm returned. "Thanks, Peter. I look forward to seeing you again soon." She disappeared through the door to the visitors' area.

Peter stared after her, dumbstruck. He saw why Frankie admired her. She was smart, tough, and charming. In front of a jury, she'd likely be unbeatable.

But as for her request to stay away, he knew he would not comply.

Chapter Thirty-Two

Peter navigated from the waiting area to the Justice Center elevators in a numb haze. Sam Pullen's directive to cut ties with Frankie complicated matters. For one thing, he had information relevant to the case. But he could not share with her, except as a last resort. Not unless he wanted to risk rotting in the cell right next to him. She'd be watching. He'd have to be careful.

But if he could use the information himself, maybe cause Christine to make a mistake, he could help Frankie. So long as he wasn't in jail himself, that is.

The elevator door opened. A uniformed cop and a shorter African-American man in a rumpled suit stepped out. Peter stepped aside to let them pass, but they remained in front of the open doors, blocking access. Only as the doors closed behind them did Peter recognize their faces and realize why they blocked his path.

"Good evening, Mr. Robertson," Detective Collins said. "You remember Tens—er, Officer Howard?" He gestured with his elbow toward the taller man. Tens stood to one side of Collins, arms folded across his chest, his feet shoulder-width apart. Even in his uniform, his tapered physique created an intimidating presence. Unlike Collins, however, he did not even try to fake a smile.

"Detective. Officer." Peter gave each a curt nod. "Can I do something for you tonight, or—"

"Do you have a minute to chat, Mr. Robertson?" Collins asked. "We have a few questions for you."

Peter sighed and reached between them to push the elevator call button. "I've told you everything I know about Kyle Campbell's death, Detective. And when I learn something new, I'll—"

"It's not about Kyle Campbell," Tens said.

Collins glared at him a moment. "Officer Howard is correct. There's another case we'd like to revisit with you. A cold case that we've been led to believe you might know something about."

"Cold case?" The term matched the temperature of Peter's blood at that moment.

"That's right," Collins said. "I believe you were a juror in the case. The murder of Alvin Dark."

***

The interview room was no better lit, no more comfortable, and no better heat controlled the second time around, Peter discovered several minutes later. He sat on the hard wooden chair facing a rickety table across from Collins, with Tens again guarding the door, mute. The mirrored wall opposite Peter reflected his sweaty, tired face and the thin layer of dark hair matted to his skull. He wondered how many more detectives sat behind the one-way glass, observing and recording his every word.

"Interesting that you drive a silver pickup truck," Collins said. "Just like the defendant in the Alvin Dark case."

"It's not an unusual combination."

"But it's quite the coincidence, particularly since your ex-wife was also in the restaurant where the victim and the defendant quarreled that night." Collins slouched in his chair, awaiting a response.

Peter took a controlled, deep breath. "Was she?"

"Don't play games, Mr. Robertson. You know she was. And so do we."

Sweat coated Peter's scalp and ran down the taut muscles in his neck. "H-how would I know this?"

"Because you were there. Weren't you, Peter?" Collins fixed him with a level stare. Tens seemed to grow a foot and hover

over him, despite not moving a single one of his well-conditioned, ample muscles.

Peter shrank in his chair. The room seemed to close in on him. The air grew thick and hard to breathe. He forced his lungs to work anyway, inhaling, exhaling, then inhaling the same hot, stale breath again. He wiped a layer of sweat from his brow, only to be replaced by another layer a moment later.

He steeled himself for the pressure, strategized. Give nothing. Find out what they know. He tried an easy grin, probably failed. "I suppose you have some sort of evidence to support such a claim?"

"We do." Collins waited.

Peter took his turn at the level stare, directed it to Collins. "Anyone I know?"

Collins leaned his head back. "Let's call it, for now, an anonymous tip."

Anonymous—what crap. This sounded like a Christine move. Peter frowned in mock concern. "Anonymous tips make poor witnesses."

Collins scowled, stood, stretched. "You're making me wonder, with your evasive answers, whether my anonymous tipster isn't right on the money. Why don't you want to tell us what you know?" He pressed his hands flat on the table, his face level with Peter's. "What are you hiding from us?"

Peter's heart pounded. A drop of sweat curled inside his earlobe, creating an uncomfortable itch. He looked away from Collins to Tens, who stared back, an intense once-over that went on forever. Peter folded his hands, considered his situation. Decided.

"I'm not hiding anything from you," he said after an eternity. He leaned forward until their noses nearly touched. Collins backed off and straightened. A win.

Peter smiled again, this time with confidence. "Detective, you are probably aware that I served on the jury for the trial of the man accused of killing Alvin Dark."

"Yes." Collins drew out the word in a condescending tone. "And we're aware that you later hired Mr. Vasquez at Stark

Lumber. We find that very unusual, to say the least. A little too coincidental, perhaps?"

"Believe me," Peter said with conviction, "he wasn't my first choice."

"Did he get to you?" Collins asked. "While you were on the jury, I mean."

"No," Peter said. "I'd never actually met or spoken to the man before he interviewed for a job with us."

"Are you sure?" Collins said. "Because if he tampered with the jury, his acquittal could be tossed."

"I'm sure." No hesitation. Only after he spoke did it occur to him that Raul could have tampered with other jurors—such as Christine. But he had no evidence.

Collins stared at him for a long time. He paced the room, arms folded, fingers tapping on his forearms. He paused, thinking. "So. Straight up. Were you there, at Florentino's? Or anywhere near that murder scene? Come on, man. Help us out. If you know something, you need to tell us."

"And if you don't," Tens said, "you're obstructing justice. Withholding evidence. That's a crime, you know."

"Which we'll nail you on in a heartbeat," Collins said. "Come on. Spill."

Peter just stared at him, not knowing where to begin, or how.

"For God's sake, man! Who are you protecting?" Collins threw his arms up in the air, as if following the rising volume of his voice.

"Nobody." Except himself. And his mother, from his brother's neglect and anti-science paranoia. He drew a breath. "Okay. I went to Florentino's. I never went in—I sat in my truck and spied on my cheating wife, Marcia. Through binoculars. When she left, I followed her and her lover. Or tried to, anyway. I lost them in traffic. So I went and had beers with my work pals at a darts tourney, which we lost. Then I caught up with my wife at home, just in time for her to dump me. End of night, end of story. Hell. End of my life, really." His expression soured. He wanted to spit.

Collins sat again, jotted some notes on a legal pad. "Did you see Raul Vasquez that night?"

"No."

"Alvin Dark?"

Peter, unable to respond verbally, shook his head.

"Anyone else who might have wanted Mr. Dark killed?"

He cleared his throat. "No. Detective, I knew nothing about Alvin Dark until the trial. And that's the complete, absolute truth." Which it was. Technically.

Collins and Tens exchanged glances. A silent signal passed between them. Collins stood and extended a hand while Tens held open the door. "Mr. Robertson, thank you. I'm sorry to have wasted your time."

Peter stood and accepted the handshake. "Officers, I confess. When you said you wanted to speak to me, I assumed your interest was in Kyle Campbell."

"Why?" Collins held onto Peter's hand in a firm grip. "Do you know something you've, er, forgotten to tell us?"

Peter shrugged and ended the handshake. He glanced at Tens, whose face could not have expressed less interest in anything Peter had to say. "Nothing new, per se. But there is a connection between the two cases."

"Yeah." Tens sneered. "Your best friend killed one, and your employee killed the other. But," he added, his voice dripping with sarcasm, "of course you have nothing to do with either one."

"Well, Raul Vasquez was acquitted, and I think Frankie will be, too," Peter said, trying to keep the heat out of his voice. "But you're missing another obvious link: Christine Nielsen."

Collins froze. Tens laughed. "How interesting."

Peter cocked his head to one side. He'd expected a very different response. "How so?"

Tens shook his head, said nothing. Collins cleared his throat. "Let's just say, we're keeping her in our sights as well."

That confirmed, in Peter's mind, that Christine was their anonymous tipster, trying to save her own skin by deflecting attention onto him. She had nothing to gain by holding back now, after all. Kyle was dead, and she needed a scapegoat.

Tens indicated the open door, which he still held open. Peter moved through it to the hallway, still focused on Christine. She'd obviously not shared everything she knew about Peter's connection to Alvin Dark. Her tip was just her opening salvo—a warning: if Peter moved against her, she'd spill more details, increase the pressure. He needed more information, more concrete proof, about her role in Kyle's death.

"Mr. Robertson," Collins called out behind him. "Remember, don't leave town anytime soon. We…might have more questions."

Peter walked on down the hall without responding. He was in no mood to make any promises to anyone.

Chapter Thirty-Three

Peter exited the parking garage in a numb haze. Entering traffic, he cut off a silent Prius and earned a well-deserved toot of its tiny horn. Then he enraged a couple of Subaru drivers on the next block by straddling the white lane stripes. He came within moments of entering the freeway going the wrong direction with no clue of how he'd even gotten there, much less why. To describe him as rattled by his interview with the police would be the height of understatement.

He needed to settle himself down. He considered stopping somewhere for a beer, but he hated drinking alone. Besides, he needed to talk to someone. Frankie, his only true confidant, was obviously unavailable. His judgmental brother and sister, six hundred miles south, would respond with unwelcome lectures, or worse.

But he had one other person he could turn to. Who never judged him—well, not in recent years, anyway—and who loved him unconditionally. Even in her most senile moments, his mother's presence always brought him some peace. It wasn't his usual night to visit, but she wouldn't mind.

He navigated to US Highway 26, clogged with dinner-hour traffic, but for once he didn't mind. The stop and go pace presented less risk in his current state. Even so, the exit crept up on him sooner than it should have, and he had to beg a Honda Prelude driver to let him over.

He parked on the far end of the lot at Sunset and savored the long walk toward the entrance. The sun sank low in the western sky, accompanied by a welcome breeze. A perfect summer night.

Except for it being absolutely horrible.

He entered the facility and wandered down the drab, familiar hallways, smelling of institutional decay and disinfectant, an aroma unique to terminal care facilities. Many people lived in Sunset, but many simply waited to die. Some had been abandoned by busy families, who shoved aside the onerous responsibility of caring for sick, elderly relatives in exchange for enormous monthly wads of cash. A pang of guilt stabbed at Peter's conscience. His weekly visits seemed paltry all of a sudden. Pathetic. Thelma had given him life, made sacrifices all of her life for him and his siblings. Surely he could spare more than an hour per week to visit her.

Tonight, he would start to correct this. Yes. This visit was a good idea.

"Peter!" Angela Wegman called to him from the far end of a long hallway, one which, he suddenly realized, did not look at all familiar, despite the crushing sameness of every hallway in the building. Only the colors of the walls varied. He'd wandered into the Pink wing. Thelma lived on Blue. How long he'd wandered, he had no idea.

Angela smiled and bounded toward him, her arms outstretched, the universal warning that a huge hug lay in his immediate future. Her brown eyes sparkled, and her face shone with surprise and joy. "What are you doing here? Is Thelma ill? I haven't seen any reports—"

"No, no," he said, returning her warm hug. It felt absolutely amazing. He held on a bit longer. He could get used to this. "I just got lost, that's all."

"Lost? Here?" She glanced around, amusement bubbling up in her dark eyes. He reddened. The building's floor plan, a figure-eight of hallways with resident apartments lining the exterior walls and communal rooms circling a pair of interior courtyards, could not be simpler. "Come on, then. I'll show you to Thelma's room, since you can't seem to find it on your own." She hooked her arm through his and guided him down the hallway in the direction from which he'd just come.

"You're working a lot of shifts here lately," he said to fill an awkward silence. Her arm felt warm on his. Comforting. "You must be building up quite the war chest for your Europe trip."

"Every little bit helps," she said. "It's expensive, traveling alone. But it's getting to be too much. I could use a night off soon." She squeezed his arm and made eye contact. Smiled. "And, you know, my schedule is really flexible. Especially on weekends." Her gaze lingered.

"Well, um, that's…great." He cleared his throat. "Maybe we could have coffee or something next weekend."

"I'd love that!" Her eyes shone like a beacon, her smile radiant. "Saturday?"

"S-sure. Hey, let's make it brunch. Nine?"

"It's a date." She stopped and pointed an open palm at Thelma's closed door. "We have arrived, kind sir."

"Thanks. Um, I'll call you. To get your address."

Her smile turned wistful. "For real this time?"

He reddened. "I'm sorry. I've been busy."

She waited a few moments while he squirmed. She lowered her voice. "So, uh, is that other woman out of the picture, then? The one who brought you to the hospital?"

He could have kicked himself on the spot. He'd forgotten she'd met Christine. Crap. "Um, yes. She is. Totally. We, uh, we're not a good match."

Angela grinned. "I could see that a mile away." Her smile faded. "I'm sorry. That was mean."

"No, no. It's fine. You're not the only one to say so." Of course, the other, Frankie, stewed in jail at that moment because of it. He shuddered.

"Are you okay?" Concern clouded her face. She rested her hand on his arms, which he'd somehow folded across his chest.

"Yes, yes. Just…glad to be moving on." He smiled back at her. She relaxed, then grew serious.

"Peter, can I ask you something?"

"Sure. Anything." He unfolded his arms, tried to figure out what to do with them. In the end, he put one hand in his pocket, the other on his hip.

"I got a call yesterday from the police about my friend who got killed last year. His name was Alvin. Do you remember me mentioning him?"

Peter froze. Numbness washed over him. He leaned against the wall, both to appear casual and to prevent himself from falling over. "Y–yes, sure. So sad, isn't it?"

"Beyond sad," she said, bitterness edging her voice. "Senseless and tragic. Anyway. I guess they're reopening their investigation, and they asked if I knew some of his acquaintances. And—here's what's weird." She stood directly in front of Peter and took his hands in hers. "They asked if you knew him."

Peter's knees wobbled beneath him. "M-me?"

"I told them I didn't think you did. They asked me if I was sure. I didn't know what to tell them." She gazed into his eyes. "Did you know Alvin?"

Peter took a deep breath and bit his lip. What could he tell her? That he'd met him only once, beaten him up by mistake, and left him for dead, never knowing his identity until he helped acquit Raul for the same crime? That Alvin's face had tormented his dreams for the better part of a year? That his murderer— whom she held in her hands that very moment—walked free in the streets?

He could not. For his own sanity, and for hers. But he could share a few things.

"I served on the jury last spring," he said. "For Raul Vasquez."

He eyes widened. Her face went white. Her lips formed a small "O" before she covered them with her hand. Tears welled in her eyes. "Tell me," she said. "Was he really innocent?"

"I believe he was," Peter said after a long pause. "What I can tell you for certain is that the prosecution did not prove him guilty."

The tears fell from her eyes, washed out by a hundred more. She collapsed into his arms, sobs wracking her body. He held her, providing what comfort he could, but he felt like a complete fraud, even as she gripped him tighter, held onto him as if for dear life, crushing the air out of his lungs.

Still he patted her back, rocked her body from side to side until her sobs subsided. She turned away, wiping her eyes. "I'm so sorry," she said. "I just—I was surprised, that's all. I didn't know."

Sadness fell over him. No, not mere sadness—despair. In that moment, witnessing the sadness of this kind, gentle woman, the pain he'd caused the world became too evident. Too much to bear. He had to set it right—even if it meant risking the end of his own comfortable, privileged life.

Which meant, ironically, that he needed her help more than ever. He took her in his arms again and looked into her tearful eyes.

"Angela," he said. "Promise me something."

Confused, she blinked another tear onto her cheek. "What? Peter, you seem so...agitated."

"Promise me," he repeated, "that, whatever happens to me, you'll take good care of Thelma. That no matter what happens, you won't let anyone take her out of Sunset. Not my brother, not the state, no one. Will you promise me?"

Her eyes grew wide, her expression one of fear overtaking sadness. "What do you mean? What's going to happen to you? Peter, are you sick?"

"No, no, I'm fine. Just promise me."

She stared at him, then allowed a slow nod of her head. "Okay. I'll do whatever I can. But Peter, you have to tell me—"

"I can't. Not yet. Maybe someday. But Angela...Angela. Thank you."

He felt like scum, asking her for help after what he'd done, and with the secrets he still kept from her. And he only felt worse when, seconds later, she kissed him, then slowly, silently, disappeared down the hallway.

Chapter Thirty-Four

"Ladies and gentlemen! Stark's Hardware and Lumber Supply is once again open for business!"

With that pronouncement, Gregg cut the ceremonial ribbon stretched across the brand-new hardened glass double doors at the store's customer entrance. The small crowd, comprised mostly of employees, a few local reporters and photographers, and a handful of customers, reacted with polite applause. Gregg and Jessica pulled both doors wide open, swept their arms across their waists, and bowed in mock grandeur. The crowd accepted the invitation by filing two and three across into the gleaming, well-lit store. A completely rearranged showroom welcomed guests with large, colorful signs boasting of deep discounts on practically everything, with free lemonade and coffee rewarding everyone who shopped at the Grand Reopening.

"I was hoping for a bigger crowd," Gregg confided to Peter after the two dozen or so people spread through the store. "Especially after the great press we got."

"It's early," Peter said. Gregg had insisted on conducting the ceremony at the retail store's usual opening time of 7:30 a.m. "Talk to me again at noon."

"You ain't kidding," Jessica said, steadying herself on three-inch spike heels. "Who holds a party at seven in the morning? Half the birds in town haven't even finished their worm omelets."

Gregg protested Jessica's complaint, but Peter tuned out to the argument when he spied Raul wandering the store, hands clasped behind his back. He approached Raul with forced nonchalance and faked a smile. "Not too busy this morning on the loading dock, I take it?"

Raul snapped to attention, then relaxed again. "No," he said. "We got all of our shipments in yesterday so we'd have full shelves for customers this morning. And no trucks to clog up the parking lot."

"In that case, can we talk? Privately, in my office?" Peter gestured toward the 'Employees Only' area. Raul half-bowed, half-nodded, and preceded Peter down the hallway.

Moments later, Peter closed his office door behind them and pointed to his guest chair. Raul sat, hands folded on his knee, and Peter leaned against his desk, hovering over him, arms crossed. For the first thirty seconds or so, they stared at each other, expressionless, while Peter searched for an entrée to the difficult conversation neither wanted to begin.

"You said you wanted to talk?" Raul said at last.

Peter cleared his throat. "I want to ask you something. About your relationship with Christine."

Raul shook his head. "There is not much to tell. I have barely seen her since I started working here."

"But you've talked."

After some hesitation, Raul nodded.

"I chased a man from my house the other day. He was hiding in the bushes."

Raul stared at him, a blank expression on his face. He said nothing.

"Friend of yours? Co-worker, so to speak, in the employ of Christine Nielsen?"

"I'm employed by Stark's now." Raul dropped his hands to his side and gripped the chair for dear life. "Not—"

"How much is she paying you to spy on me?"

Raul blanched, then recovered. "Heh, heh. Spying? I am not a spy. She just helped me—"

"Cut the crap, Raul. Ever since you started working here, she's known my every move. Knows things that happen here, and to me, long before I tell her. You want me to believe that's just coincidence?"

Raul opened his mouth as if to speak, but no words emerged.

"You can either admit it," Peter said, "or I can check the PBX history database. If you've used a company phone, I'll find every call made to her in twenty seconds." A complete bluff. He had no idea of how to do that, if it was even possible. But Raul probably didn't know either. "And under the terms of your probation here, I can get your cell phone records, too. In fact, the police will be requesting those from every employee. I spoke to the detectives yesterday handling the investigation of our break-ins." Another bluff. He had done no such thing, but he made a mental note to do it later. "And if I do find something, your employment experience here will be over faster than you can drop a two-by-four. Am I clear?"

Raul scowled, then emitted a small, bitter laugh. "Okay, señor, I might as well tell you, since it will all be moot soon." He refolded his hands and leaned back in his chair. "I have been observing you, yes. Not spying—just watching. And yes, I've told Ms. Nielsen a few things. She is very interested in knowing things about you."

Vindication! Peter hid his feeling of triumph and maintained a skeptical exterior. "Such as?"

"Where you go, who you see, who you talk to." He smirked and lowered his voice. "She is a very jealous lover for you, is she not?"

Peter barked out a laugh. "Cut the crap, Raul. We both know better than that. She's not worried about my love life." He leaned over Raul, their faces inches apart. "We both know things we're not telling, don't we?"

Once again, his bluff worked. Raul broke into a nervous laugh, and Peter joined him. He circled his desk and sat in his chair, feet propped up. "So," Peter said. "Why don't you just level with me? What does she want?"

Raul stared at a random spot on Peter's desk, eyes glazing over. A long moment passed. Then, Raul met Peter's gaze. "I suppose it no longer matters," he said. "It is all about over anyway."

That caught Peter's attention. "What's over?"

Raul spread his hands wide. "This. All of this. I will be

leaving here soon. My work here is done."

"You're quitting Stark's? Just like that?" He hoped he'd kept the jubilation he felt out of his voice.

"Stark's…Christine…you." His lips curled into a snarling smile. "You are right. Christine hired me to watch you. And when she pays me, I will go away—as far away from you as I can, gringo." He shook his head. "This was a very bad idea."

"On that, we agree."

"You do not know the half of it, hombre." Raul inched forward in his chair. "Every minute I have been here has been a living hell. A reminder of the worst day of my life—and, I am sure, of yours."

Peter's blood iced in his veins. Frozen in his seat, he somehow managed words. "H-how so?"

"Come, gringo. Do not pretend with me. I was there last November, and I saw what you did to Alvin Dark."

Chapter Thirty-Five

Peter's heart raced. Frozen to his chair, unable to speak, scarcely even able to breathe, his hands gripped the arms of his chair, his legs locked into place.

The man who had been falsely accused, tried, and—thankfully—acquitted of Alvin Dark's murder, the man for whom Peter had sat in judgment, who stared into the jury box daily and saw Peter's face—knew that Peter had actually committed the murder. Claimed, even, to have seen him do it.

"I followed you," Raul said. "Alvin took a sudden turn, and you stayed with him, but I missed the turn and had to double back. At first I kept my distance, watching you. You were so intent on your fight with him, you never noticed me. But I saw you."

Finally Peter's vocal chords worked again. "You knew this, all during your trial? Even as I heard evidence against you, and could have sent you to prison forever—maybe to death row—and you said nothing? Why?"

Raul smiled. "Strategy, my friend. Oh, I told the police over and over again that they had the wrong man, but they ignored my pleas. They were convinced of my guilt from the first moment. But once I recognized you on the jury, I knew my freedom was secure. If your conscience bothered you, you would secure my acquittal. If you dared convict me, I had perfect grounds for appeal. Either way, I would go free."

"Your lawyer agreed with this strategy?"

"My lawyer worked for the state. I could not trust her with

this information. No, I pursued this on my own. And it worked perfectly."

"Wow." Peter wiped sweat off his brow. Raul was a much cooler, savvier strategist than he'd ever imagined. "And then, you were still okay—knowing what you know—coming to work here for me? To have a man supervise you, when you knew what I'd done?"

Raul shrugged. "There are other things I know, gringo. Things that change everything."

"Like what?"

Raul considered him for a moment. Made a decision. "Since we're nearly done here…and we are alone…" He glance around, ensuring their privacy, Peter guessed. "Señor, you have suffered a long time. Too long. And in truth, I owe you a great debt of gratitude for what you have done for me."

"You mean, for acquitting you? Or for–for–Alvin?" Peter's throat tightened around the words, as if to choke them out of existence before he could utter them.

"For providing me cover." A grim smile occupied Raul's face. "For creating doubt. Noise. Evidence that pointed, just enough, away from me."

"I don't understand."

"You have lived with the belief that you are guilty of murder—of killing a man you did not know, for reasons I cannot imagine."

Peter started to interrupt, to explain that he'd meant to follow his cheating wife's lover, that he hadn't realized that he'd fought and killed the wrong man. But something stopped him. A realization. What Raul had said.

"Wait." Peter sat up in his chair. "You said I 'believed' in my guilt. Why did you say it that way?"

"Because it is true. You do believe it."

"Shouldn't I?"

Raul emitted a nervous laugh. "No, gringo. Oh, you tried. And you very nearly succeeded. You beat him very badly. Of course, you had every right. He attacked you. I saw him come after you with the iron bar. You acted in self-defense. I knew

Alvin well, and there is no doubt, he would have killed you."

Peter nodded. That proved it: Raul was there. But still, his assertion made no sense. "So, you saw me do it. Why, then, should I not believe that I did it?"

"Oh, you should believe that you tried," Raul said, his voice even and as hard as steel. "But you did not succeed. You left a badly beaten man to die, but he did not die. Not by your hand." He stood and leaned over, his hands resting on Peter's desk, and spoke in a low voice. "You left the job unfinished, you see. And that I could not abide."

"Y-you?"

Raul nodded. "I, señor. I finished what you could not. I made sure that Alvin Dark would breathe his last that night. That he would never steal another man's woman. That he would pay for his crime against me!" Raul pushed himself away from the desk and stood. "So you see, all this time you thought that I had suffered for your crime. But instead, the opposite is true. And, as they say, history has a way of repeating itself, does it not?"

Peter rushed around his desk, his face inches from Raul's. "What's to stop me from going to the police with what you've told me?" he asked.

Raul shrugged. "Go ahead. The rules on this are quite clear. No double jeopardy. Once acquitted of a crime, I cannot be retried for it again. And as for Kyle Campbell—unlike you, my hands on that are quite clean." He gave a curt nod, and pulled open the door. "Have a peaceful life, señor." He disappeared down the hall, leaving Peter to his heavy, conflicted thoughts.

Chapter Thirty-Six

Peter slumped into his chair, speechless, allowing Raul's shocking words to sink in. His heart thumped in his chest. His head felt heavy and numb.

He'd spent the better part of the past year, as Raul had said, convinced of his guilt of a heinous crime. He'd barely slept, couldn't focus, suffered nightmares, and, on nearly a daily basis, considered turning himself in.

But then his rational, responsible side would battle back against his emotions. He'd remind himself of his commitment to his mother's care, to keeping her in a facility like Sunset. He'd shouldered the bulk of the expense to keep her in a familiar, comforting environment, one in which she felt safe and loved. One that also kept her close to the expert, state-of-the-art stroke center at OHSU, who could keep her alive and revive her faculties with cutting-edge rehabilitation unmatched anywhere. One she'd lose in a heartbeat if Peter went to prison and his brother Jimmy took over her care.

For months he'd lain awake at night, weighing one side against the other, torn by guilt no matter which way he turned. When he did manage to sleep, usually out of sheer exhaustion, nightmares filled his sleep with demonic images of his fight with Alvin Dark. Images of an angry man emerging from his wrecked red Camaro, swinging a tire iron, attacking him with rage and determination. How he'd fought back, his own rage taking over, pushing him well past self-preservation to exacting what he'd imagined was his own revenge against the man who he'd thought had stolen his wife. The anger, blood, and violence filled his nightmares until he woke, sometimes only minutes after falling asleep, drenched in sweat, heart racing, his soul begging for relief.

And now he knew it was all a lie.

Well, not all. They had fought, and he had left Alvin bloodied and unconscious on that remote wooded road.

But not dead. Had Raul not intervened, Alvin might have lived.

Peter's hands trembled as the realization settled over him. He was not a murderer. The guilt he'd carried for the past nine months, and in particular since the trial, had all been for naught. He was not a killer.

Which meant Christine no longer had leverage over him.

The trembling extended from his hands, up his arms, to his entire body. To his own amazement, he found himself laughing. Giggling, really. Shaking, from head to toe, as his body released the stress that had bound his nerves for months. The giggles built to out-loud laughter, to side-splitting guffaws. Howls, accompanied by tears of joy splashing down his face.

After several minutes, the laughter subsided, and the shaking stopped, replaced by a cool serenity, a stillness that calmed both his mind and body. It finally sank in, mentally, physically, emotionally.

He was free.

***

Peter found Raul an hour later, alone in the tiny office he shared with Skip, another supervisor who also reported to Peter. Peter entered without knocking, finding Raul alone, and closed the door behind him. Raul paused in the midst of packing personal items into a packing box on his desk.

"Wasting no time, I see," Peter said, pointing at the box.

Raul cast his eyes down and to the side. "As I said before, I am done here. You have never made me feel welcome. And now that you know my secret, how can I ever feel at home here? What opportunity would I have to succeed? None. So. It is time." He picked up a framed photo from his desk of a dark-haired woman and gave it a long, wistful look.

"I see," Peter said. "Well, before you go, I have something

to ask you. About something you said before."

"I said many things. Too much." Raul set the photo in the box and continued clearing his desk.

"But this one thing in particular." Peter paused to recollect the exact words, failed. "Something about how I thought you'd suffered for my crime, but 'history has a way of repeating itself.' What does that mean?"

Raul's face creased into a sly smile. "You thought I was being tried for your murder. Now, you and your friend will be tried and convicted for another's. The murder of Kyle Campbell." He laughed and opened his desk drawer, scooping out its contents and dumping them into the box.

"Wait. You know who killed Kyle?" Peter grabbed Raul's lapels, shaking him.

"Of course I know. As do you. Or at least, we know who is responsible." Raul brushed his hands off of him and pushed him away. "The one who has forced both of us, and so many others, into doing her bidding. She may not have pulled the trigger, but she made sure it would happen."

Peter scoffed. "Pulled the trigger? He wasn't shot. He was beaten. Just like how you—"

"Figure of speech, señor. I know how he died. And I know how you will die. In prison, from a lethal injection. And when that happens, I will stand in the distance and laugh." He picked up his box and pushed his way out the door.

Peter stared after him, then stumbled to Raul's desk and sat on the edge. So, Raul knew that Christine had killed Kyle, just as Peter had suspected. But he'd offered no proof. And Peter, too, had none. So far as he knew, neither did the police.

That would have to change. But how?

Part Four

Revelations

Chapter Thirty-Seven

Christine adjusted the brim of her hat, pulling it down to shade her eyes and cover more of her face. She'd left her sunglasses behind somewhere—her office, probably, or at the bank. She'd drained her "operations" account and needed to get the cash to her fireproof safe at home, but hadn't had time to get there yet. Her late-evening meeting came first, both in terms of time and priority. It presented risks—to her and to the cash. Best to remain in plain view, but unrecognized.

She browsed through the wares of a funky dress shop, then a crowded import store full of pretty but useless knickknacks. It reminded her that she needed to dump most of her belongings. She preferred to live and travel unburdened by things…and people. People often became the heaviest burden. She had a few more of those to shed, too.

One of them, very soon. Along with a big chunk of her on-hand cash. Luckily, the travel fund still carried a healthy balance.

She kept track of the time, and when her watch read five minutes before eight, she exited the store and turned up the street toward the tiny bar she'd chosen for her meeting. She took the only empty table, reserved for her in advance by way of a hundred dollar tip, set in the back corner where she could see the entire bar, except for the restrooms down the hall. A glass of pinot noir waited for her at the table. She sipped it. Ugh.

"Buenos noches, señorita."

She froze. The voice came from the hallway behind her—problem number one. Number two: it came from the wrong man.

Raul stepped to the side of her table and pulled out a chair.

"That seat is taken," she said. "And you shouldn't be here."

Raul paused, shrugged, and sat anyway. "I will be happy to make this brief. I have been looking for you."

"Congratulations. Now I'm it and it's your turn to hide. Go on, hide really well. I'll be right there."

"Very funny, señorita. But I would rather we conclude our business right now, rather than play childish games."

"We've had this conversation. Nothing has changed." She sipped her wine again. It tasted sour now.

"Oh, no, señorita. That is where you are wrong. Everything has changed."

She sipped the wine again, buying time. "Oh? Do you have news?"

Raul smiled and signaled someone with an overhead flick of his hand. A blond man appeared in the doorway of the bar. A man who looked a lot like Kyle Campbell, although she could tell them apart at a glance. He seemed unsurprised and unperturbed by Raul's presence. Pleased, even. He strolled to the table and pulled out a chair, then extended a hand to Raul, who shook it. The blond man sat, cutting off any escape path. "I thought it might save everyone some time if we held our meeting jointly," he said.

Christine's heart pounded. Heat rose in her ears. How dare they gang up on her!

But she knew the key to these types of situations. Keep cool. Never let them see her discomfort. She smiled. "So, Raul, I see you've met Kyle's brother, Earl."

Earl grinned and, after brief eye contact with Raul, signaled the bartender. "Met? Why, my dear Christine, we've much more than met. We're a team now, aren't we, Raul?"

"Si, señor," Raul said. "We have had many, how do you say, team-making experiences?"

"Team-building," Earl said. Their drinks arrived and they toasted her in unison, the blond with a shot of whiskey, Raul with a light lager.

"Well." The fabric of Christine's skirt stuck to her legs, and she adjusted it beneath the table. "This poses a bit of a problem, you see. I didn't bring enough cash to pay both of you." Not true, but believable enough. She hoped.

"Ah, that is a problem. If it is true." Raul sipped his beer. "We might all need to take a walk down to your bank. It is right up the street, after all."

So, he'd followed her all evening then, without her noticing. She needed to up her game. "That won't do any good," she said. "The money isn't in that bank, and even if it were, it's closed."

"They have an ATM," Raul said.

"With a five hundred dollar limit. Are you willing to take less in payment?" She sipped more wine. Despite its horrible taste, she'd nearly finished the glass. No matter. She wouldn't need a second. She needed, in fact, to get the hell out of there.

"Gee, maybe we need to take a detour," Earl said. "A nice long walk down one of those quiet side streets. Maybe we'll find another bank there."

"Some sort of bank," Raul said with an evil grin.

"A money bank, a river bank…any bank will do," Earl said.

"I prefer money banks," Raul said, "but we know how you love nature. Don't you still run on the banks of the Willamette River most evenings?"

Christine took a deep breath, toyed with her wine glass. She stole quick glances at each man, registered their anger and their impatience. She realized her only escape path: money. Which she had, and could afford to part with.

"Let me make a call," she said. "I'm sure we can—"

"Let me make the call." Raul snatched the phone from her hand. "Let's see, who might you want to call? Peter Robertson? No? The police, perhaps? Yes, let's try them, shall we?" He laughed. "What a nice chat we could have, all of us together."

"All right, fine. You win. I'll pay you both." She dug in her purse and opened the hidden compartment where she'd hidden the cash. She counted out six thousand, separated the bills into two envelopes below the table, out of their view. She dipped her head and held an envelope toward each man under the table. The men took the envelopes and each counted their money.

"It's all there," she said.

"Is it?" Raul said. He held up two fingers. Earl chuckled, help up four.

"Oh, señorita. I believe you have made a mistake. A, shall we say, accounting error?" His face grew dark, his expression menacing. "You are cheating me!"

Christine's lungs turned to stone, unable to draw air. "We agreed to two. What I pay him is none of—"

"You will pay me the same as him. Or shall we take that walk and see how much more is in that purse of yours? Hmm? How many secret compartments it has, full of cash?" He downed his beer. Earl signaled the barkeep for two more.

"Different pay for different jobs." She clutched her purse and hoped her voice did not betray the tension rising within her chest.

She hoped wrong. The two men slid their chairs around to the sides of the table, blocking her in.

Raul rested his hands on the table, palms up. He wiggled the tips of his fingers toward himself, the universal sign for "give me more." He smiled, but his eyes were all business. "We all took the same risk. If one goes down, all go down."

"I dunno," Earl said. "I took a little more risk, don't you think?"

"I would think so," Christine said. "You pulled the trigger, so to speak, while you, Raul—"

"Would die in the chair alongside both of you." Raul's voice dropped to a whisper. "Conspiracy to murder carries the same penalty—"

"Shush, you idiot!" Earl said, grabbing Raul by the front of his shirt. Raul grabbed his hand and yanked it away. The two men hand-wrestled a moment, than shook free, glaring at each other and breathing hard. After an eternity of macho glaring, the blond glanced down to his side. Raul nodded, awareness dawning.

And then Christine knew: they were wired. "You rotten, dirty, sons of bitches!"

Earl grabbed at her, caught the ends of her hair, tugged. Her head slammed onto the table, then across it, her body following.

She flailed her arms, found purchase on something soft, and dug in with her nails. The man attached to the injured body part screamed and pushed her away. Her head slammed into the wall and she fell to the floor, dazed, but at least she felt no hands on her body. She scooted backwards into the hallway. The two men crashed through the tiny bar to the door, knocking over drinks, tables, chairs, and a few customers en route. They disappeared out the door before she could regain her feet.

No point going after them. If anything, she needed to run in the opposite direction, far and fast. She reached for her purse on the chair next to hers, and clutched only air.

The bastards!

The purse, along with all of her cash, was gone.

Chapter Thirty-Eight

"You must be Mr. Robertson," said the young man behind the reception desk at Cascade Legal. "I'm Aiden. I'll let Sam know you're here. Can I get you a cup of coffee while you're waiting?"

"I'd love some," Peter said. Before he could ask for cream and sugar, Aiden disappeared behind an open doorway, leaving Peter to take in his surroundings. Abstract art in large metal frames hung on the walls in place of the usual array of certifications, licenses, and diplomas found in most law offices. Bright sunlight shone through gauzy curtains covering tall wood-frame windows filling almost an entire wall of the spacious room. It felt more like the living room of a wealthy art collector than the reception area of a law office.

Aiden reappeared, carrying a bowl-shaped white ceramic mug on a matching saucer. Steam rose from the black liquid sloshing around inside the mug. "Careful, it's hot," he said. "I just brewed this a few minutes ago. An Ethiopian blend, water-processed fair trade organics from a family farm outside Eritrea. It's Sam's favorite."

"Uh, cool. Thanks." He forced himself not to roll his eyes at the politically correct coffee babble. Christine would have engaged with him for hours about it, but for him, coffee was coffee. "Do you have cream and sugar, by any chance?"

"Taste it first." Aiden sat down at his desk and busied himself on his computer. Peter sighed. He hated black coffee.

One sip, though, changed his mind. "Wow. This is delicious."

"I know, right? I think using carbon-filtered water makes all the difference. And the French press, of course." This time Peter couldn't suppress the eye roll. Luckily, Aiden's desk phone lit up, distracting him. "Cascade Legal, can you hold please? Thanks." He pressed a button and his voice lost the impersonal officiousness he'd adopted for the previous caller. "Hi, Sam. Sure thing." He smiled at Peter. "Mr. Robertson, Ms. Pullen will see you now." He gestured toward the door he'd disappeared behind a few moments before and returned his attention to the computer display in front of him.

Peter sipped the coffee again, savoring its rich, sweet complexity, and pushed through the doorway, careful not to spill any onto the spotless white carpet. Sam Pullen greeted him a few steps beyond the door, hand outstretched. He shook it, a firmer grip than he remembered, and lost a few drops of the precious brew onto the floor.

"Don't worry, it happens all the time," she said, escorting him to a chair facing her desk. She adjusted the shades covering yet another towering window along the side wall. Peter, remembering how he'd chided Frankie for obsessing on her looks, had to admit to taking a second look at her legs. Her blonde hair flowed freely over her shoulders, and when she turned, her blue eyes shone like meteors on a clear night.

Don't. Stare.

They sat, and she got right down to business. "You said you had new information that could help clear Mr. Kowalczyk of the murder charge?" She wrote something at the top of a legal pad on her desk.

He nodded, swallowing a mouthful of coffee. "I know who did it."

She cocked her head, and her thin eyebrows curled high above her long lashes. "Do tell."

"It's Christine Nielsen. She essentially admitted it to me." His heart pounded. He'd believed it from the start, but had never said the words aloud in front of another person. Even at that moment, he wondered if she was somehow listening in.

"Essentially told you? Does that mean she confessed? Gave you a hint? What?" Sam's pen hovered over her legal pad. "I thought you and she had, shall we say, the same alibi…?"

"She told me she had it done."

"In so many words?"

He struggled to remember how she'd put it. "No. But she made it very clear."

Sam sat back in her chair. "Tell me what she said. In her own words, if you can."

Peter sipped his coffee. He'd drained half the cup already, and wondered if there would be more. "I can't remember her exact words, but—well, you see, Ms. Pullen—"

"Sam." She smiled.

Peter's apprehension faded. That smile. It was motherhood, apple pie, truth-beauty-and-justice and every girlfriend he ever knew, all rolled into one. It said she liked him. Trusted him. Wanted to hear what he had to say.

And, in that moment, he trusted her. Wanted to tell her everything. Confide in her.

He leaned forward, set down his coffee cup, and rested his elbows on her desk. "Christine blackmailed me. She had, or thought she had, incriminating evidence against me, and used it to force me to kill Kyle for her. When I refused—well, according to her, she had what she called Plan B."

"Did she elaborate?"

"Just that she had what she called 'better men than me.'"

Sam smiled, reached across the desk, and patted his hand. "I doubt that."

Warmth emanated from where she'd touched him, and he smiled at the compliment. "Thanks. But when it comes to murdering people, almost anyone's a better choice than me."

She laughed and jotted down a few notes. Looking up at him, she said, "You realize, I hope, that there's no attorney-client privilege protecting what you tell me here."

Peter took a deep breath. "Does what I'm telling you put me at risk, legally?"

She frowned and collected her thoughts. "It could. If you testify to what you've told me, you could, potentially, be charged with conspiracy, or aiding and abetting. If you don't, then you could potentially be charged later for withholding evidence of a felony."

"Unless I come forward now."

She shook her head. "The problem is, you don't have any solid evidence that she actually did anything. It's mostly hearsay, which probably wouldn't even be admitted."

"For God's sake, I'm screwed no matter what I do!"

Sam held up her hands. "Not necessarily. While I can't protect you with attorney-client privilege, I also don't have to disclose information if I don't plan to use it. At this point, I wouldn't. Not in court, anyway."

"So it's useless. I put myself at risk today for nothing." He pushed out of the chair and strode toward the door. Her voice stopped him.

"Peter."

He turned. She circled her desk and took deliberate steps toward him. "It's not hopeless, and definitely not useless. It helps me with strategy."

Peter sighed and crossed his arms. "Tell me honestly. What are Frankie's chances of beating this rap?"

She rested her hand on his elbow. "Good, actually. And if we can find hard evidence supporting Christine's guilt, then I'd upgrade that to a certainty."

Peter considered that a moment. "So, if I can somehow get her to admit what she's done…?"

"You'd need to get it in writing, or on tape, or convince one of her co-conspirators to come forward. Can you do that?"

"Not if I follow your directive to stay the hell out of it."

She smiled. "One of these days, I'll learn to keep my big, over-protective mouth shut."

Peter laughed. "Ms. Pullen, I don't know what I'll come up with. But I promise you, I'll do everything I can to help Frankie."

He extended his hand. She shook it. "Be careful out there, Mr. Robertson."

***

Hunched over his desk at Stark's late that night, Peter pushed his keyboard away in frustration and rubbed the blurriness from his eyes. He'd searched back through his email from the past several weeks, both business and personal, and listened to every saved voice mail message on his cell, work phone, and even his ancient answering machine at home. He'd gone through the piles of old mail, his knickknacks and memorabilia. In all of it, he'd come up blank. Not a single message from Christine betrayed any sign of her intentions or plans. No mention of Kyle, of being harassed, stalked, threatened, or injured. Not a single physical clue remained that she'd had the slightest inclination to conspire to rid herself of her dangerous ex-boyfriend.

But it went even deeper. Not only did he fail to find any incriminating messages, but he'd found none at all. The few voice mails he remembered, he must have deleted. As for email, she'd never sent even one. He had no pictures, no cards or love notes, no little gifts or mementos of their time together. No sign that they'd even been friends, much less lovers.

Forensically speaking, their relationship might never have existed.

This realization shook him. While at one level he'd known she'd been using him, a part of him had always believed that some part of her affection had been genuine. That she'd liked him, at least a little bit. That he'd been more to her than just a means to an end.

Instead, he realized that Frankie had been right all along. He'd been her sucker, start to finish. She was nothing but trouble. And plenty of it.

As a result, Frankie sat in a jail cell, facing murder charges. Frankie, of all people.

Of course, she'd meant for it to be Peter.

Anger rose in him, replacing the guilt and fatigue. His stupidity had put his best friend's life in peril, and perhaps ruined it outright. His stupidity, and her cruel manipulations, to which he'd fallen prey like a child. Like an idiot, he'd believed her protestations of fear and love, and mistaken her physical affection for real attraction.

He'd been victimized by her charms, but no more. He would

do everything he could to free Frankie. And he vowed that, from that moment forward, Christine Nielsen would pay for all of the suffering she'd caused. As would her co-conspirators. As Sam Pullen had pointed out, she hadn't worked alone. But who had helped her?

His computer dinged, a soft bell tone that indicated incoming email. Despite his exhaustion, he lifted his head and double-clicked on the new message. The message, while odd in its timing, contained no surprises.

The header showed the sender's name, Raul Vasquez. The subject: "Resignation, effective immediately."

Chapter Thirty-Nine

Multiple phone calls to Raul went straight to voice mail, so Peter scribbled down his home address and sped over to the high-rise apartment complex in southwest Portland. The superintendent, a thin, white-haired man wearing a blue short-sleeved shirt and paint-splotched work pants, refused at first to confirm or deny that Raul had ever existed, much less lived there. "It's company policy, and it's in our lease," he said. "We protect the privacy of all residents."

"So if he wasn't a resident, you could tell me?" Peter asked, leaning back in an uncomfortable black metal chair in the man's cramped, dingy office. The chair's almost nonexistent padding ensured that his visitors wouldn't sit for long.

"If he never lived here, I still couldn't tell you anything," the man said. But his weak tone told Peter everything.

"Well, if he does show up again," Peter said, "tell him to contact me for his paycheck." He held up a white envelope with Raul's name typed on it. An empty envelope, but only Peter knew that. The man reached for the envelope, but Peter snatched it away. "Sorry," he said. "I can't leave it here. Company policy. Privacy, security—of course you understand."

The superintendent's mouth fell in defeat. "Okay, okay. Raul lived here. But he moved out this morning. No forwarding address—and no payment of his final month's rent, either." He eyed the envelope, greed in his eyes. "I got the impression he was in kind of a hurry to leave town. He threw most of his belongings in the garbage. I don't expect him back here."

Peter stood and set a business card on the manager's cluttered desk. "If he does, ask him to call me." But he doubted

Raul would ever see the card.

After searching the neighborhood on foot, he camped out in front of the building again and asked other building residents if they'd seen Raul. None admitted to even knowing him. He realized that he didn't know much else about the man, in spite of having supervised him for two weeks and having sat in judgment of him in court for capital murder. Raul had slipped out of his life as suddenly as he'd re-entered it, and with him went Peter's best chance of tracking down evidence of Frankie's innocence.

He returned to his truck, parked on a neighborhood street a block or so from Raul's high-rise. As he approached the vehicle, he sensed movement near the tailgate. A heavy-set man with shaggy hair crouched near the right rear tire, his back to Peter, reaching under the chassis.

"Hey! Get away from my truck!" Peter ran toward the man, who bolted in the opposite direction, lost his balance, and landed face-first on the pavement. He staggered back to his feet, but not before Peter landed a kick to the back of his knees. The man crumpled to the ground again and rolled onto his back, hands up, protecting his face.

"Don't kill me! Don't kill me!" the man shouted. "I'm not trying to steal your truck, man! I promise!"

Peter, breathing heavily, lowered the fist cocked by his ear and relaxed his fighter's stance. "Don't try to get up," he said.

"Just don't kill me, man," the man said.

Peter peered down at him, recognition dawning. "What the hell? You're the guy I chased out of the bushes at my house the other day, aren't you?"

His face pale and eyes wide, the man nodded and started to crab-crawl away. Peter stomped on the man's ankle. The shaggy-haired man howled in pain. "Stay put!" Peter shouted. "If you move again, the next kick will make you a soprano."

"I'm not moving, I promise." He sat up halfway and rubbed his ankle. "Damn, man. You like to broke my damned leg."

"What were you doing to my truck? And why are you following me?" Peter leaned over the man, crowding him.

"I'm just getting my stuff back, man. It's expensive."

"What stuff?" Peter stole a glance back at his truck. So far as he could remember, the truck bed was empty.

"My gear, man. It's—it's a long story." The man cowered back to the ground.

"Tell me. I've got lots of time." Peter crossed his arms and gave him a little space.

He sat up. "Tracking gear, man. I put it there a few weeks ago. Once you started seeing the girl."

"You mean Christine? Is that who you're working for? Man, who doesn't she own in this town?"

The man sat up a bit more, rested on his elbows. "No, man. Not for her. She's the one I was watching. Then when she started seeing you, my, uh, client said to watch you, too."

Realization dawned. "You worked for Kyle?"

The man cringed, nodded. "And then he stiffed me. Well, it wasn't entirely his fault. He might have paid me…but then, well, you probably know what happened."

"No. What happened?"

The shaggy-haired man's face crinkled up in disbelief. "He's dead, man. Wait—aren't you the one who did him, man?"

"Of course not!"

"Man, I ain't telling nobody, trust me. But I'm broke, man. I need my stuff back if I'm gonna work."

Peter rubbed his chin, still skeptical. "Seems to me if he stiffed you, you've got motive."

"No way, man. I don't do wet work. I'm just a private eye, man. I watch and report. And sometimes I get paid. Sometimes it takes a while. But if I offed everyone who stiffed me, I'd be a serial killer. And forever broke. Who'd hire a guy who waxes all of his clients? Nobody, man. Look, you gotta believe me."

Peter couldn't suppress a smile at the man's torrent of words. "Okay, so let's say you didn't kill him. Who did?"

The man sat all the way up and dusted himself off. "Your boy Frankie sure gave him quite the lick in the head in the woods that day. I think maybe the cops got the right man."

"Frankie didn't—wait, you were there? On the hiking trail in

Forest Park?"

The man's mouth opened wide, as did his eyes, but he gave his head a tiny nod.

"And you're the one who ambushed me off the trail, aren't you?"

Another tiny nod, and the man shrank back onto his elbows. "I—I didn't mean nothing personal by it. It's just business."

Peter stepped into his punch, flattening him back to the ground. "Nothing personal," he said. "But I owed you one."

"Fair enough," the man said, touching his cheek. "Are we even now?"

"I guess." Peter held out a hand. The man took it, and Peter lifted him to his feet. "So, these devices. How good are they?"

The heavy-set, shaggy-haired man beamed with pride and crouched again near the rear of the truck. He reached under and when he pulled his hand out again, he held a small black rectangle in his palm. "They're awesome, man. See this one? It's how I followed you to eastern Washington, and followed your buddy back to Portland. Hey, can you pop your hood? I got another one up there, man."

Peter blinked. "So, you knew he'd followed you to the house?" He opened the car door and pulled the lever to release the hood latch.

The man lifted the hood and stuck his hand inside. "Totally, man. And to the murder scene."

Peter's jaw dropped. He slammed the truck door shut and clenched his fist. "So...you're the anonymous tipster?"

The man danced away to the truck's passenger side. "No, man! I don't truck with cops. But your girlfriend..." He shook his head. "You want to find the killer? Follow the money, as they say. And all of my money's on her."

"Yeah, easy for you to say. And rather self-serving."

The man shrugged. "I'm just saying. She had a lot of help. And everyone but you got paid in cash." A sly smile crossed his face. "We all know what you got, you dog."

Peter ignored the dig. "How much help? Besides Raul, who?"

"Oh, so that's the Mexican guy? I never knew his name. But there's also the little brother, man."

"The guy who looks like Kyle—he's real? He's his brother?"

Kyle spread his hands wide. "I guess she likes blond jocks. He's a bad dude, man. You find him, I think you've found yourself a killer."

Peter nodded. "I think you may be right. Now, do me a favor. Get yourself and your damned bugs away from my vehicle."

The man grinned. "Happy to, man. But first, could I ask you one little favor?"

Peter's eyes narrowed. "What?"

The man hedged. "You wouldn't happen to have found my keys, would ya?"

"I did," Peter said. "And you can have them any time. All you have to do is call this number." He reached into his wallet and handed his nemesis a card.

The one with the name and phone number of Officer Tennyson Howard.

***

The bastard!

Shaggy hung up his phone, crumpled the card into his fist and tossed it into a solar-powered trash can the city had so generously provided its citizens. So, Lumpy pulled a fast one there. But two could play that game.

He still had expensive gear to retrieve from Lumpy's place—and even one still somewhere in his truck. He'd planted three, only retrieved two. And Lumpy's house had more surveillance than the White House. All expensive gear. Stuff he couldn't afford to lose, or replace...or, let sit idle. The gear didn't make him any money sitting in a crate somewhere. It needed to be on, active, feeding someone's hunger for information.

Kyle was gone, but Kyle wasn't the only person in town who wanted to keep track of Lumpy's comings and goings.

How did the old saying go? *The enemy of my enemy is my friend.*
He dialed.

Chapter Forty

Christine woke with a start. Always a light sleeper, the slightest disturbance could shake her out of bed—a footstep on pavement, the flick of a light switch, a radio in a passing car. Lately, high stress had prevented her from sleeping more than a few hours at a stretch, not matter how still her environment.

But it also heightened her awareness, and she hadn't imagined the sound outside her bedroom window.

She opened the drawer of the nightstand and retrieved the pistol she'd moved there the morning before. Checked to make sure it was loaded. Slipped on a robe and slid the gun under its folds. Listened.

Yes. Someone was outside.

She crept to the hallway. A louder sound came from the guest room: the window being lifted open in its tracks. Damn. She'd never gotten that lock fixed after the night of the staged break-in. It hadn't occurred to her that she'd be vulnerable, with Kyle gone. Not so soon, anyway.

She planted herself in front of the closed door, feet shoulder-width apart, arms extended, both hands clutching the gun and shaking like willows in a windstorm. Whoever had just thumped onto the hardwood bedroom floor probably didn't know that she'd never shot anything other than a sheet of paper on a gun range. And had missed, every time. Only three people on the planet knew it: One, her shooting instructor, a man who, at the ripe old age of seventy-eight, couldn't lift himself onto a windowsill if the existence of the world depended on it. Two: Kyle, who lay on a cold slab in the county morgue. And three: Peter.

Peter, she would shoot. This time.

She steadied her breathing, if not her hands, and focused her aim on what she imagined to be chest height on a man, and leaned her weight against the wall behind her. Footsteps padded to the door. The doorknob turned at a glacial pace, then the door slid open away from her. The figure of a man emerged in the open doorway.

A man the spitting image of Kyle Campbell.

She gritted her teeth, squinted, squeezed—

The explosion of the gunshot echoed off the walls, hurting her ears. The gun kicked back hard, pushing her hands high and to her left side. For a moment, both she and the man stood frozen in place. She wondered how he could still be standing after having been shot point-blank in the chest. Why he hadn't cried out in pain, crumpled to the floor with a gushing chest wound. Why he still stood there, grinning, not a drop of blood on him.

"Wow," he said after an eternity. "You're an even worse shot than that guy at the gun range said. Well, that was two hundred bucks well spent."

She glanced to his left, then his right. Behind him, a small round hole, about a half inch in diameter, appeared in the drywall. Somehow, she'd missed by a foot.

"Still," he said, stepping back against the door jamb. "You fired. I never expected that. I'll give you credit for that."

"Earl?" She lowered the gun a bit, but kept it aimed at his midsection. "What the hell are you doing here?"

***

"You expected maybe my brother Kyle?" Earl said a few minutes later while rummaging for food in her kitchen. He grinned, a lopsided affair that looked nothing like his brother's charming expression of humor. "I'm afraid he won't be visiting any longer. You really need to keep up with the news, hon." Earl cocked his head and smirked. Just. Like. Kyle.

She sat at her dining table, something she rarely did unless Peter happened to be cooking for her. Which he would never do again, she guessed. "It didn't occur to you to knock on the front door? During, you know, the day?"

He lowered his hands a little. "I wanted to surprise you. Besides, wouldn't that have set off your alarm?" He blinked and waited.

She set her gun on the table, but kept her hand on it. "I didn't expect you back here, ever. Especially after you ripped me off!"

Earl shook his head. "*Au contraire, ma chère.* I'm actually here to return your belongings." He left the room for a moment and returned with a small leather object in his hands. Her purse! He set it on the table and gestured to it with a toss of his platinum blond hair. "Back home to momma."

She opened the purse. Sure enough, it still contained all of her belongings, down to the lipstick and spare tampons. Well, almost everything. "It's light about four thousand in cash."

He smirked again. "Well, you owed me. Still do, in fact."

"If all of that cash is still gone, you were way overpaid!" Her hands shook. She pointed the gun at his chest again.

He raised his hands. "You mean, Raul was way overpaid. He kept most of it. And I haven't seen hide nor hair of him since then. The man has flat out vanished."

"What do you mean, vanished?"

Earl shrugged. "I suspect he's returned to his native land, but I doubt he left behind any traces. He's pretty good at things like that. Now, come on. Put the gun down and let's talk about how to settle your debts, shall we?"

She steadied her aim. "How do I know you're not lying about Raul?"

He gestured around with his arms. "Do you see him anywhere? Have you heard from him since we met at the pub?"

She lowered the gun a bit. "That's a problem. I had another job for the two of you."

"Oh? You want another hit? Sorry. I was only too happy to take out my asshole brother, but I have no beef with Raul." He opened the refrigerator and peered inside. "Speaking of beef, I'm starved. What have you got to eat in this dump?"

"No, not a hit. But I have another job for you."

"No more jobs until I get paid for the last job," he said,

moving stuff around inside the fridge. "God, don't you eat anything except yogurt?"

"Not at home," she said. "Listen. I'll pay you for the last job and then some. But I need you to do something for me. One more iteration of Operation Mahogany."

Earl glanced back at her, irritation on his face. "You're kidding me." He found an overripe pear, examined its many bruises with a critical eye.

"I am not. I need another diversion. Something to keep our boy busy. He's getting too close. We need to slow him down, buy us some time." She sat in a chair at the kitchen table and pulled the robe tight around her.

Earl bit into the pear and closed the refrigerator door. "Alone? With Raul gone?"

She rolled her eyes. "That was the whole point of getting you that delivery job at Cal-Tex. So we wouldn't need him anymore. And we don't. You know enough now. God, man, do I have to lay it all out for you?"

"It's always been a two-man job. One to work the inside—"

"I don't need anything big or elaborate. Just something to set off some alarms and get my boy focused on something else besides me for a few days. I want him looking for Raul, rather than us."

Earl's face screwed up into a puzzled frown. "I don't get it. We get him all worked up so that he puts all those cameras and stuff in, and now we parade ourselves right in front of them? Why don't we just hit him at home?"

She waved him off. "His home is taken care of. I need to hit him again where it hurts. For Peter, that's work. It's his refuge, his safe place. I want his boss doubting him, riding his ass, keeping his attention on Raul rather than us."

Earl shook his head. "I dunno. It's too risky."

She rolled her eyes. "Everything about this is risky. But the cameras don't matter any more. We got what we wanted from them." A stretch, but he didn't need to know that. "And so what if they catch you on tape? Peter will think you're Kyle…and won't that blow his mind?" She laughed, hoping he'd play along.

Hoping he'd remain as stupid as ever. "Come on. You need the money."

Earl mulled it over, chewing, and wiped pear juice from his chin. "When do I get paid? For this job and the other ones?"

"Half now at the usual rate—"

"I get Raul's share too, then, if I'm working alone."

She considered this, nodded. A bargain. "Do it tomorrow and I'll pay you the other half, plus everything else I owe you, the day after." She dug in her purse, extended a handful of bills, and smiled. "Cash."

He took another bite of pear and considered it a moment. He swallowed, tossed the rest of the pear in the sink, and extended a handshake. "Deal."

She smiled, stuffed the bills into his sticky palm, and pointed the gun at his head. "Get out. And this time, Earl, for a change...use the front door."

Chapter Forty-One

Twenty-four hours later, "Taking Care of Business" blared from Peter's cell phone. His alarm read 1:38 a.m. He cursed his decision to make an exception in his phone's late-night "Do Not Disturb" setting for Gregg and rolled over to silence it before its tinny speaker split the late-night silence again.

"S'up, Boss?" He yawned and rubbed his eyes.

"You're not gonna believe it."

"Gregg, it's almost two in the morning. Don't make me guess."

Gregg emitted an exasperated sigh. "There's been another break-in. Can you come down?"

"Crap. Uh, yeah, I guess." He swung his legs over the side of the bed and let his toes search for his robe on the floor. "Any damage?"

"Not much. The cameras in front got whacked and the front door locks got torn up. Looks like the cops or alarms chased the perp away before they got inside."

"So we didn't get anything on video?" Peter trudged downstairs to reheat some coffee, turning on lights as he went. The journey toward his coffee salvation seemed to take forever.

"Not sure. That's what I'd like you to do—check the tapes, see if we can find anything."

"Okay. I'll be there as soon as I can get some coffee in me." He started the microwave and leaned his head against the kitchen cabinet for support. He'd had maybe an hour of sleep, and it felt like less.

"I'll make coffee here," Gregg said.

Peter made a face, glad that his boss couldn't see it. "That's all right. Already underway. Any idea as to who did it?"

"Same as before. A former employee is my guess. Except now I'd move Raul to the top of the list."

Peter pulled cream out of the fridge. He had apparently purchased the slowest microwave on the planet. "Maybe, maybe not. He seems to have skipped town."

"Seriously? Crap. Then I'd definitely put him at the top of the list. That dirty, rotten, no good—"

"Calm down, Gregg. You're not making any sense. If he's left town, how could he—"

The microwave beeped. Peter retrieved the magic elixir from within and stirred in some cream and sugar. Sipped. Forgot what he'd been saying.

"Yeah, well, we'll see," Gregg said. "Just get down here ASAP."

Peter slurped more coffee. He'd need more, but he'd emptied the pot. A stop at a 24-hour donut shop on the way would work wonders. "Will do, boss."

"Thanks. And, Pete?"

"Yeah?" He knocked back the rest of the coffee in one gulp.

"Thanks for not saying 'I told you so.' About Raul. I should listen to you more."

He thought of Frankie, still stuck behind bars because of Peter's stupidity. "Well, boss," he said, "there's a lot of that going around right now."

He hung up and pulled on a light jacket. Something nagged at him—a connection he'd missed, a cause-and-effect he couldn't see. Too many coincidences had piled up: Raul coming on scene and then disappearing, his ties to Christine, her plotting and scheming around getting rid of Kyle, the fake burglary at her place, break-ins at Stark's. They all had to be connected somehow. But how?

***

Peter stared at the screen in disbelief.

The video from the security cameras in front of the store showed precious little. Whoever broke in knew how to keep their faces, bodies, and vehicles out of viewable range until they disabled them, and the audio captured no voices. For all the money he'd spent on buying and installing those cameras high up in the eaves, Gregg would get little in return.

But the would-be thief hadn't prepared for Gregg's thoroughness—nor Peter's. On a whim he'd checked video from the inside cameras. Two provided rotating glimpses of the front door and various areas of the interior of the store. In the last few seconds of video from the second camera, the camera caught movement by the door. Movement of a man stumbling as the lock broke, exposing his face for a few seconds on camera.

The face of Kyle Campbell.

He blinked, rubbed his eyes, and zoomed in on the video image. Increased the brightness and contrast. Hit pause.

No. Not Kyle. But a man who looked an awful lot like Kyle. The same short blond hair and athletic build, the same clean-cut face, the same clear blue eyes, same disdainful expression. But not exactly alike. This face carried a little more weight, had a rounder shape, and had a few laugh lines missing from Kyle's sterile, serene face.

But, damn. Otherwise, a dead ringer.

Just like the guy he'd seen breaking into Christine's house that night.

"What does this guy have against us?" Gregg said when Peter briefed him a few minutes later in Peter's office. "What have we ever done to hurt him?"

Peter shook his head. "Not you. Me. And it's not him that carries a grudge. I think I know who he works for." He sighed, wishing he didn't have to tell Gregg any of this. "He and Raul both work with a woman that I was involved with briefly. I'm their target, not you."

"You think he's working with Raul on this? The whole time?" Gregg fidgeted with the cigarette tucked behind his ear. The paper ripped, and tobacco shreds drifted to the floor.

"I can't be sure, but the police will sort—hold on. Holy cow! Gregg, you're a genius!" Peter clicked on the "Search" button in the video database. "Our cameras cover the whole store, don't they?"

"Video, audio, phones, the works," Gregg said. "Every square inch of this place is taped and bugged. It's all motion- and audio-activated. You can't fart in your office without me knowing about it. Hell, we're being recorded right now."

"How far back do those tapes go?" Peter filled in the form that narrowed the search to his own office and clicked on the date field, ready to enter a value.

"Since the last break-in," Gregg said, tossing his broken cigarette into the trash. He circled around behind Peter so he could see the screen. "You're going to look now? This search could take hours, and it's almost four a.m."

"What the hell," Peter said. "I'm not getting any sleep tonight anyway."

Gregg started to protest, then shrugged. "You're probably right. Okay, we'll work in shifts. You keep going now. I'll bring in a couple of fresh bodies from the security firm tomorrow. They know the system best. I'm sure with all of us working together, we'll find the culprit in no time."

Peter shooed him out of his office and finished entering his query. In less than two hours, he found what he needed: incriminating conversations, with plenty enough evidence to convict Raul and his co-conspirators—and not only for the break-ins. The evidence he found would convict them all of a much more serious crime.

He copied the video files to his hard drive, then to a thumb drive, and finally, just to be safe, he burned them to DVD. Then he made duplicates and slipped a copy of each into a manila envelope, sealed it, and stuffed it into his bottom desk drawer. He tucked another pair of envelopes, each with identical contents, under his arm and headed out to his truck. Once inside the cab, he pulled a business card from his wallet and dialed the number.

After a few transfers, a familiar voice answered. "This is Sam."

"Miss Pullen? Peter Robertson. I hope it's okay to call so late."

"You mean early. I assume it's important, if you're calling at six a.m. What's up?"

Peter held one of the envelopes between his thumb and forefinger. "I have evidence," he said, "that will set Frankie free."

"Physical evidence?"

Peter swung the envelope like a pendulum in his fingers. "I guess you'd say so. But I need your help in dealing with the police. I—I can't just bring it to them. It's...hard to explain. It involves another murder case, and a series of break-ins at my store, and, well, I might need some legal advice, because—"

"Is this call being recorded?" she asked.

He froze. Of course! "Yes," he said. "That's how I—"

"Meet me at my office," she said. "We need to talk."

Chapter Forty-Two

Hours later, Peter fidgeted in the comfortable guest chair in the waiting area of Cascade Legal. His initial, marathon conversation with Samantha Pullen when he'd arrived had not gone well, and her frustration made him doubt his strategy altogether. "I warned you about playing amateur sleuth," she'd said. "An objective third party is always preferred in these situations." Her voice portrayed calm on the surface, but betrayed condescending fury beneath. She'd listened to his story, then taken the files from him and told him in a no-nonsense manner to wait in her lobby. Her tone suggested what she really meant: don't do anything else stupid.

In retrospect, he agreed with her. He could have, and perhaps should have, waited to let the security company copy the recordings. The police might suspect him of doctoring them, hiding evidence, or worse. Out of exhaustion and in his haste to free Frankie, he'd rushed in, not fully prepared for the potential ramifications of his actions on his own fate.

The phone on the receptionist's desk rang, and Aiden, the chipper young man in the black headset, answered with a smile. "Yes, Sam? Okay, I'll send him in." He pushed a button and waved Peter over. "Ms. Pullen will see you again now."

Peter stood, his body heavy on his feet. "Should I notify my next of kin?" he asked with a wry smile. Aiden's expression went blank. No frigging sense of humor, these kids.

He slid into Sam's office, closing the door behind him.

Sam looked up from her desk and pointed with an open palm to a chair. "Come in, Peter." No smile, no jury-wowing charm. Just business. "You took an enormous, unnecessary, and foolhardy risk last night," she said without preamble. "The evidence you provided exonerates Frankie, but could implicate you in both the Alvin Dark and Kyle Campbell murders."

"How deep did I step in it?" he asked. He didn't really want to know, but couldn't stop himself from asking.

She raised both arms, palms up, and shrugged. "We'll know in a few minutes. I'm fairly confident Frankie will be released sometime today. For you, worst case? On Alvin Dark, aggravated assault, maybe attempted murder. Best case, definitely a charge of withholding evidence. On Kyle Campbell?" She paused, started at him with a grim expression. "Worst case, conspiracy to commit murder. Best case, again, withholding evidence. You could go to prison for a long, long time, my friend."

He sank deeper into his chair, his insides turning to jelly. He felt like an idiot. What he'd worked so hard to avoid since that awful night the previous November—the prospect of enduring the hell of prison for years to come—felt imminent now. Worse, his long battle with his siblings to keep his mother under the comforting care of the doctors, specialists, and the other kind souls at Sunset Hospice would be lost. His brother would take over and move her into the facility in Oakland run by nutty faith-healing cultists. She'd be dead before they finished packing her toothbrush.

"I'm going to do what I can to prevent any of that from happening," Sam said. Her tone and face finally reflected compassion rather than frustration. "That is, if you would like me to represent you. Unless you'd rather find someone else? I'd understand if you preferred another attorney."

"I'd love it if you would represent me." He pulled himself back to an upright sitting position. "I promise, no more screw-ups like last night."

She laughed. "Have I scared you? I'm sorry. I didn't mean to. I just want what's best for you and Frankie."

Peter sank into his chair, numbness washing over him. "Will they press charges?"

She sighed. "I can try to cut a deal. I'll need your permission."

He swallowed, or tried to. The cement block in his throat wouldn't go down. "I promised Frankie. And he's innocent. So—do whatever it takes." He leaned over, placing his head almost to his knees. His stomach churned. Honor and loyalty sucked sometimes.

"Sign here," she said, pushing some forms across her desk with a black ball point pen. He scribbled on the page. She gathered them up and frowned at him. "Now," she said, "I suggest you get your affairs in order...just in case."

Peter swallowed, or tried to. The cannonball in his throat wouldn't go down. "In case of what?"

She grimaced. "In case they don't go for the deal."

He tried to leave the office, but his feet would not move.

***

Once he willed his body into action, he drove straight to Sunset Hospice and hustled to Thelma's room. He tried to explain his situation, but she mostly ignored him, instead paying more attention to an all-day marathon of old Celebrity Jeopardy shows and singing along with ad jingles for products she'd never understand, much less buy. After a frustrating hour, he kissed her good-bye, and hoped it wasn't for the last time.

Angela Wegman met him outside the door.

"More moonlighting?" he said, accepting her warm hug. Her lips brushed his neck as they broke the embrace.

"Yup." She grinned. "I'm almost halfway to my savings target for my Europe trip. I'm thinking about extending another week. Have you ever been?"

"To Europe? Once, after college. Loved it."

She hooked his arm with hers and walked him down the hall. "Ever thought about going back?"

His heart pounded. They hadn't even gone on a date, and here she was, hinting at traveling Europe together. "Someday," he said. "But no time soon. I'm a bit low on savings myself right now. I've had some unexpected expenses lately." And if Sam couldn't negotiate a good deal, he'd have no freedom to travel. He shook that thought out of his mind.

She gave a slow nod. "I keep forgetting that you are recently divorced. Well, maybe you could share a few travel tips over breakfast tomorrow. We're still on for our nine a.m. brunch on Saturday, aren't we?"

Peter stared at her. He'd clean forgotten. "Uh, yeah, for sure. Yes. Definitely."

She laughed. "You're a horrible liar. Well, look, I'm flexible. My shift is about to end, and if you haven't eaten lunch yet…?" She squeezed his arm closer to her warm body.

"Um…well…" Dammit. It felt good, what she was doing. Really good. Angela was a genuine and kind human being, exactly the kind of woman he'd hoped to meet after his divorce.

But his divorce, and everything that had happened around that, was part of the problem. The night that his marriage—and his whole life—fell apart also resulted in the tragedy that also tore at Angela's heart. Whenever he looked into her eyes, as he did in that moment, he saw the pain of her losing Alvin Dark. Felt the guilt of never having told her of his role in her friend's death. Of the secrets and the lies.

Not a good way to start a relationship.

He stopped walking, and with some effort, pulled his arm from her. "Angela, I have a confession to make."

Her eyes widened and her expression fell. "Uh, oh. This feels like I'm about to be let down."

He met her gaze, sadness and disappointment filling her moist eyes. He held her hands in his, their arms forming a steep "V" between them.

"I suppose I am letting you down, but not because of anything you've done. I—I'm just not ready. Do you understand?"

She searched his face for a few moments. "The old 'it's not you, it's me' thing? Too soon after the divorce?"

The divorce. Yes. Perfect. No need to inflict pain on her and reopen those old wounds. Relief flooded over him. "Yeah. I jumped back into dating too soon with Christine, and I just need some time alone for a while. Does that make sense?"

She nodded, fighting tears, and smiled. "Of course. I'm sorry for being so pushy."

"No, no. You've been wonderful." He squeezed her hands. "I've not been so wonderful, and I apologize."

He held her hands several moments longer, hoping she could not read his mind, which would reveal the real reasons he could never date her. If she ever discovered his role in the death of her friend, she would hate him. And how could she not, if their relationship caught fire? Or if the police refused immunity in exchange for his testimony? Sooner or later, she would know.

"When you said you had a confession to make," she said, "I thought it had something to do with Alvin."

His blood froze. How could she—

"When you said the defendant really was innocent, something seemed, I don't know, strange," she said. "Like maybe you weren't really convinced of it. Was he really innocent? I mean, I know you can't really talk about it, but—"

"No," Peter said. The words flooded out of him, along with all of the air in his lungs. "No, Angela, he wasn't. Don't ask me how I know, but—I do. And he'll pay, someday, Angela. I promise you that."

She smiled, a sad smile of acceptance. "Thank you for your honesty," she said. "And now I understand why you can't date me." She kissed his cheek, gave him one final glance, and strode back into the long hallways of Sunset Hospice.

He stared after her. He felt like crap. Honesty, she said. The one thing he'd never be able to claim. Not with her.

Sadly, he exited the hospice, letting the warm summer air greet him, and he walked into the dark gloom of nightfall.

Chapter Forty-Three

Aiden signaled Peter back into Sam's office a few hours later, and he settled back into the guest chair in front of her desk. Dread weighed him down, and he found he couldn't move once he'd taken his seat.

"I shared some of your recordings with Detective Collins and Officer Howard," she said. "Selectively, of course. I told them that concrete evidence on the Alvin Dark murder would require a deal. They were noncommittal at first, of course. Nothing's official until the D.A. signs off on it."

"What do you know about him?" Peter asked, expecting the worst.

"Her," she said. "I know her well. I clerked at the D.A.'s office when I got out of law school."

Peter's spirits lifted. Maybe she could work some behind-the-scenes magic.

The phone on her desk buzzed, indicating an internal call. She picked up. "Yes, Aiden? Oh, perfect. Patch him through." She mouthed to Peter, "Officer Howard." She waited a moment, then her face brightened. "Tens? Nice to hear from you. Yes, I heard. Is there a decision? Oh, perfect. Thank you…Yes, Mr. Robertson is with me now. Is there—I see. Uh huh. Okay. Fair enough. I'll tell him…Oh, sure. I don't see why not." She frowned at Peter. "The police would like a word with you. Would you care to speak to them?"

He sat forward in his chair. "If you think it's wise."

She shrugged and handed him the receiver. Her gaze settled on him a moment. Something in her eyes told him he should take the call. He reached for the phone and brought it up to his ear. "This is Peter."

"Mr. Robertson? Tens here. I have some good news and some bad news."

Dread washed over him. The good news he could guess. The bad... "What's the verdict on Frankie?"

"Mr. Kowalczyk is being released and cleared of all charges," Tens said. "He can go home today."

"That's great!" Peter's voice cracked. His joy over his friend's exoneration suffered only in anticipation of what he expected to hear next regarding his own fate. "And the bad news?"

Moments passed. Static crackled on the line, then a sigh. "You need to come down to the Justice Center, I'm afraid."

He collapsed back into his chair. "Oh my God. What am I being charged with? What's the—how long will I—" He glanced at Sam, who busied herself in the drawers of her desk.

"There's no free ride, Mr. Robertson. You'll have to pay. About three to five, I'm afraid." Tens coughed. "You're going to be inside for a while. The wheels of justice turn slowly."

His insides turned to mush. Three to five years! He'd never last in prison. Nor would Thelma survive that long under Jimmy's supervision. "For what, exactly? I mean, I thought we had a deal." He wrapped his arms around himself, trying to suppress the nausea building inside of him.

Sam glanced over the desk at him. Her eyes danced, and a smile played on her lips. Damn her—she was enjoying this! Fury built within him. How vindictive could a person be? She had a right to be frustrated with him, but to get this much joy out of his misfortune went beyond the pale. He gritted his teeth, wondering how to say what he felt without further poisoning their relationship, when laughter erupted over the phone.

"I'm sorry, I can't keep this up," Tens said between giggles.

He sat, bewildered. How could he find this funny? And Sam, too—how could she? "What the hell?"

Laughter filled the receiver again. "I'm sorry," Tens said. "I'm playing with you a little. Three to five is what it'll cost you to park downtown. Dollars, I mean!"

His jaw dropped, and he shook his head. He gripped the

armrest of his chair with his free hand to hold his body upright. "Please, explain."

Tens' laughter subsided and his voice grew serious. "The district attorney agreed not to charge you, provided you cooperate in the investigation of Christine Nielsen and Earl Campbell. You'll need to testify—"

Uncontrolled whoops of joy escaped Peter's mouth, and he jumped out of his chair, fists punching the air. Sam laughed as he danced around the room, still cheering. "That's amazing!" he shouted. He ran around her desk and pulled Sam to her feet, burying her in a massive bear hug. "Thank you, thank you, thank you!"

She laughed and mussed his hair. "I wish I could take credit for it, but you did most of the work. What you gave them is enough to indict, and they expect your testimony and cooperation will be enough to convict. Congratulations, Peter. Because of you, Frankie is a free man, and the real killers will be brought to justice."

"Incredible! That's...wow!" He danced a bit more around her desk, then stopped when he remembered something. The phone! "I still don't get the three dollar parking thing," he said to Tens. "Why do I have to go down to the jail?"

"It means," he said, "that you have to come down here to pick up Frankie. He's waiting for you." He laughed again. "He insisted that you be the one to pick him up."

With three more whoops of joy, Peter grabbed his keys and dashed out of Sam's office.

***

"Dude!"

Frankie blindsided Peter with a crushing bear hug moments after he stepped inside the lobby of police headquarters in the Portland Justice Center, emptying his lungs of air. "I knew you wouldn't let me down!" Frankie lifted him off of his feet and swung him around like a soldier might embrace a spouse upon returning from overseas duty. Except that Frankie also, somehow, managed to pound his back at the same time.

"All right, all right, get a room, you two." A laughing Officer

Tennyson Howard extended an open hand. Peter shook it after breaking free of Frankie's embrace, only to discover that Howard's true intention was to hand him a business card. "When can you talk?" Tens asked. "We need to know everything you do—the details this time, not just the nickel tour your lawyer gave us."

"Tomorrow," Frankie said before Peter could reply. ""He's taking me out to get drunk right now."

"Fair enough," Tens said. "But don't go anywhere I can't find you, like your pals Raul and Christine did."

"You can't find them either, eh?" Peter asked. Frankie pulled him toward the exit, his free hand ready to push the door open.

"I was hoping you'd have some way of reaching them that we hadn't thought of," Tens said. "Did either of them mention travel plans to you?"

Peter searched his memory. "Not in so many words. I should have known Raul would run—he had one foot out the door the last time we talked. But I haven't spoken to Christine all week. She could be anywhere."

"We have the FBI tracking her passport now, and flight records," Tens said. "But my guess is, she's ten steps ahead of us."

"I doubt I'll hear from her," Peter said, "but if I do, you'll be the first to know."

"Thanks. That goes for Raul, too."

"Are we done here, then?" Frankie pushed the door open and swept Peter into the hallway. "There's alcohol to be had."

Tens followed them into the hallway, chuckling, and checked his watch. "It's five o'clock somewhere. Ireland, I think."

"Excellent," Frankie said. "In that case, let's start with a Guinness and some Jameson's."

Chapter Forty-Four

The grilling at the hands of Detective Collins and Officer Howard lasted most of the next day, and included a couple of lawyers from the district attorney's office, lots of taping and signing of documents, and more than a few tense, private conversations between the assistant D.A. and Sam Pullen. Each time, however, Sam emerged triumphant. In the end, she negotiated a deal that netted Peter no jail time, although he'd serve two years' probation with a suspended sentence that would disappear off his record when complete, and travel restrictions that would keep him in the U.S. for the foreseeable future.

"That's okay," he confessed to Sam when she recommended the final deal to him. "Paying my legal bills is going to wipe out my vacation fund anyway."

She patted his hand and smiled, sending electricity up his arm and straight to all pleasure centers. "We'll make payment arrangements for both you and Frankie. I understand he's going to room with you for a while?"

Peter nodded and surrendered a nervous smile. "To save money, for both of us. Although he's not the best influence at times. I may regret this drunken decision."

He swung by Stark's to bring Jessica and Gregg up to date on the developments and to review a new stack of resumés Jess had collected already in the search to replace Raul. The applicant pool looked strong, despite the limited time Jess had to pull it together. "I made a lot of phone calls, and got almost all of the applicants from last time to come back," she said, chomping on what appeared to be a football-sized wad of pink gum. "You might need a full day for interviews."

"Time well spent," he said. "At least Gregg committed to letting me make the selection this time."

"General Gregg Patton did what? What'd ya do, promise to wash his car for a year?" She laughed, a rambunctious braying that Peter feared might shatter the surveillance microphones.

"No," Gregg said, ducking his head into her office door, "although I wish I'd thought of it. Instead I simply made him promise to make a diversity hire...and he offered to work through his vacation. How could I say no?"

It took until nine p.m. to cull the pool down to a manageable dozen, which he dropped onto Jess's desk on his way out. He closed and locked the double doors leading outside, then ambled toward his truck. A beeping sound halted him in his tracks. Lights flared on, flooding the parking lot in a hot white glare. A loud horn nearly knocked him off his feet.

After all he'd been through, he'd forgotten to set the stupid alarm.

It took until well past ten to reopen the store, call off the security dogs, and wolf down a terrible fast-food hamburger on the drive home. Leaving his own house unlocked, he crashed into bed, exhausted.

***

The familiar, scratchy tune of Carlos Santana's "Black Magic Woman" split the darkness, startling Peter out of a deep slumber. He sat up in bed, shaking off his deep REM sleep and a vague dream memory of traveling through ancient cathedrals of western Europe with a smiling Angela Wegman. A pleasant dream. One he'd never realize in waking hours.

The ringtone echoed again off the bungalow's walls and he fumbled for the phone resting by his alarm clock. 3:05 a.m. Crap. Even worse, caller ID confirmed the ringtone's warning. He answered and leaned back in his bed. "I did not expect to ever get a call from you again."

"Oh, really?" Christine sounded as chipper and confident as ever. "And why is that? Are you saying you don't miss the sound of my voice?"

He rubbed his temples. "Yes, that is exactly what I'm saying.

And I can't say that I welcome the surprise, either. By the way, do you know what time it is?"

"Let's see, it's a little after one p.m. here, so, about three a.m. your time?"

"So your timing is not accidental."

"Peter, nothing I do is accidental. You know that."

Indeed he did. "So, to what do I owe the very limited pleasure of this call? Are you calling to tell me you're turning yourself in?"

She erupted into laughter. "Don't be ridiculous. I have nothing to confess."

"The police feel otherwise."

"Yes, Peter, I know all about what you've been up to, and the stories you've been spinning. Oh, what a lovely view! Have you ever been to Switzerland?"

Why, he wondered, were all of the women in his life suddenly invading Europe? Another reason not to go. "You tell me, if you know so much."

"Don't snap at me. I'm just making polite conversation."

"I don't do polite conversation with you, and certainly not at three a.m. If you have something to tell me, say it, because in ten seconds, I'm hanging up. Unless you want to hear me pee." He threw off the covers and swung his feet over the side of the bed.

"Don't be crass. Besides, I can listen to you pee anytime."

His breathing stopped. "What is that supposed to mean?"

She sighed. "Is your computer on?"

"Why?" He slid his feet into slippers, padded down the stairs to his den, and woke up his laptop from hibernation.

"Check your email." She hummed off-key, some classical melody he recognized from somewhere. He double-clicked on the email icon. Moments later, a message from Christine appeared in his inbox. A paper clip icon indicated an attachment. He opened it. A video montage filled his screen.

Of him. In his car. At his desk at work. In his back yard. In his bedroom. Yes, even in the bathroom.

"What the hell—?"

She laughed. "You're very photogenic, Peter. Even through

such awful lenses."

"How did you do this? More important, *why* did you do this?"

After a few moments of silence, she spoke in a low, measured tone. "You thought you were done with me, didn't you? That you could just pin everything on me and walk away. Didn't you?"

"It was you, all along—"

"But I couldn't have done it without your help, Peter. And for that, I'm ever so grateful."

"I did nothing to help you!"

"Oh. Smart move. You know your phone is tapped, don't you? But it doesn't matter. You've cut your deal and left me as your sacrificial lamb. Well, it won't work, Peter. You'll see."

"I'm hanging up."

"Oh, yes, that's right. You have to pee. Don't worry, I won't watch you this time. But, Peter…"

A long pause. He couldn't help it—he bit. "Yes?"

"This isn't over. No, sir. Far from it."

The phone went silent.

Peter lowered the phone and turned it off. He considered returning to bed, decided against it.

There was no point. He would not sleep that night.

ACKNOWLEDGMENTS

Lying in Vengeance came about for one simple reason: you. All of you, that is, that read *Lying in Judgment* and immediately asked, "Where's the sequel?" At the time the first book went to print, I had no answer, because I had no sequel. How, I wondered, could I continue a story about an unlikely trial that ended in the first novel? But, as many readers pointed out, the story about Peter and Christine wasn't over. And so, thanks to you readers, *Lying in Vengeance* was born. I thank you all.

But special thanks goes out to those whose support really pushed me when I needed it to get this story published. They include:

Randall Houle, Kelly Garrett, and Suzie Harvey, all members of the "Bar Noir" Critique Group, whose chapter-by-chapter critiques made this story better on a weekly basis.

Beta readers Richard Gray, Kate Kort, and Patsy Silk, who pointed out numerous errors and oversights in the original draft so that you wouldn't have to suffer through those;

The Willamette Writers Group, the best bunch of writers, editors, and storytellers around;

My editor, Laurie MacPherson, whose sharp eye and quick mind honed in on my writing tics and errors, which were far more legion than I would care to admit (and if any remain, they are my fault, not hers);

Patsy Silk, whose final proofread caught many errors my eyes could not;

Steven Novak, for an amazing cover design;

Patricia and Donald Corbin, my mother and father, who made me love books, and who always encouraged my love of writing; and

Renee…for the love, the support, the day to day cheering up when the words don't flow, the amazing smiles, and…everything. To thank you enough, I'd have to write another book, just about that.

Thank You

Thank you for reading *Lying in Vengeance*. If you enjoyed reading it, won't you please take a moment to post a review on Goodreads, Amazon, or your favorite online review site?

Please also check out the information about my other books on the following pages, including an excerpt from my forthcoming third novel in the *Mountain Man Mysteries* series, *The Mountain Man's Badge*.

And please, tell your friends!

About The Author

Gary Corbin is a writer, actor, and playwright in Camas, WA, a suburb of Portland, OR. His creative and journalistic work has been published in BrainstormNW, the Portland Tribune, The Oregonian, and Global Envision, among others. Several of his plays have enjoyed critical acclaim in Portland-area productions.

Gary is a member of PDX Playwrights, the Portland Area Theater Alliance, the Willamette Writers Group, Nine Bridges Writers, The Northwest Editors Guild, and the Bar Noir Critique Group, and participates in workshops and conferences in the Portland, Oregon area.

A homebrewer as well as a maker of wine, mead, cider, and soft drinks, Gary is a member of the Oregon Brew Crew and a BJCP National Beer Judge. He loves to ski, cook, and garden, and hopes someday to train his dogs to obey. And when that doesn't work, he escapes to the Oregon coast with his sweetheart.

Connect with Gary Corbin

Keep up to date with the latest at
http://www.garycorbinwriting.com.

Follow me on Twitter: http://twitter.com/@garycorbin

Follow me on Facebook:
https://www.facebook.com/garycorbinwriting

Follow my Amazon Author Page:
http://smarturl.it/GaryCorbinAuthor

Favorite me at Smashwords:
https://www.smashwords.com/profile/view/GaryCorbin

Also by Gary Corbin

Lying in Judgment

A man serves on the jury trying a man for murder—
the murder that he committed!

Peter Robertson, 33, discovers his wife is cheating on him. Following her suspected boyfriend one night, he erupts into a rage, beats him and leaves him to die…or so he thought. Soon he discovers that he has killed the wrong man - a perfect stranger.

Six months later, impaneled on a jury, he realizes that the murder being tried is the one he committed. After wrestling with his conscience, he works hard to convince the jury to acquit the accused man. But the prosecution's case is strong as the accused man had both motive and opportunity to commit the murder. The pressure builds, and Peter begins to slip up and reveal things that only the murderer would know – and Christine, a flirty and intelligent alternate juror, suspects something is amiss.

As jurors one by one declare their intention to convict, Peter's conscience eats away at him and he careens toward nervous breakdown.

Lying in Judgment is a courtroom thriller about a good man's search for redemption for his tragic, fatal mistake, pitted against society's search for justice.

ISBN: 978-0692642689
Available on Amazon.com, Smashwords.com, CreateSpace.com,
garycorbinwriting.com, and at your favorite local retailers.

Valorie Dawes Thrillers

In Search of Valor

Valorie Dawes fights an international kidnapping syndicate on behalf of a new college friend--and harbors serious doubts about her future as a police officer.

At a young age, Valorie Dawes vowed to avenge the death of her uncle, a policeman killed in the line of duty, by following in his footsteps. During her first month at college, the mysterious disappearance of a close friend's child drags her into the role of crimefighter much earlier than planned.

But Val's initial attempts to help lead to mistrust and recrimination. Self-doubts escalate, not only about Val's future as a cop, but over her ability to make and sustain the trust of a friend. Anxious to prove herself worthy on both counts, Val puts her own life on the line--and discovers that the kidnappers will stop at nothing to get rid of obstacles like her.

ISBN: 978-0-9974967-9-6
Available in hardcover, paperback, audiobook, and all eBook formats at garycorbinwriting.com, and at your favorite local retailers.

*Read the free excerpt of **In Search of Valor** at the end of this book!*

A Woman of Valor

A rookie policewoman, who had been molested as a young girl, pursues a serial child molester–and struggles to control the anger his misdeeds awake in her. Can Valorie overcome the trauma she suffered as a child and stop this dangerous criminal from hurting others like her—or will her bottled-up anger lead her to take reckless risks that put the people she loves in greater danger?

ISBN: 978-0-9974967-9-6
Available in hardcover, paperback, audiobook, and all eBook formats at garycorbinwriting.com, and at your favorite local retailers.

A Better Part of Valor

When Valorie Dawes discovers the body of a young girl who had also been sexually molested, Lt. Gibson assigns her to assist the detectives investigating the case. Then Clayton Mayor Megan Iverson, candidate for governor of Connecticut, ties her political fortunes to the case, vaulting herself into the lead in all of the major polls with her law-and-order campaign.

Iverson's meddling in the case costs them dearly when key evidence disappears and other evidence, withheld for strategic reasons, gets leaked to the press. The pressure intensifies when a former campaign aide, Val's childhood friend Amy, becomes the next victim.

Can Val find and stop the killer before he strikes again?

Expected release: Summer, 2020

The Mountain Man Mysteries

The Mountain Man's Dog

In the small town of Clarkesville, in the heart of the Oregon Cascade Mountains, Lehigh Carter, a humble forester, stumbles into the complex world of crooked cops and power-hungry politicians…all because he rescues a stray, injured dog on the highway.

The *Mountain Man's Dog* is a briskly told crime thriller loaded with equal parts suspense, romance, and light-hearted humor, pitting honor and loyalty against ruthless ambition and runaway greed in a town too small for anyone to get away with anything.

ISBN: 978-0-9974967-1-0
Available in hardcover, paperback, audiobook, and all eBook formats at garycorbinwriting.com, and at your favorite local retailers.

The Mountain Man's Bride

In this thrilling sequel to *The Mountain Man's Dog*, the murder of popular Acting Sheriff Jared Barkley. The murder puts Lehigh and Stacy's plans to marry on hold when Stacy is arrested for committing the crime.

But evidence of a secret affair makes even Lehigh wonder if he should fight for her freedom against the corrupt local machine that accused her.

ISBN: 978-0-9974967-3-4
Available in hardcover, paperback, audiobook, and all eBook formats at garycorbinwriting.com, and at your favorite local retailers.

The Mountain Man's Badge

Appointed to fill out the unexpired term of disgraced sheriff Buck Summers, mountain man Lehigh Carter investigates the murder of sleazy businessman Everett Downey, murdered in a forested area frequented by off-season hunters and poachers.

As the evidence mounts, pointing to Stacy's father, George McBride, Lehigh battles the mistrust of the entire sheriff's department as well as the District Attorney, the County Commission Chair and his own wife—until he finds shocking evidence of the killer's true identity.

ISBN: 978-0-9974967-7-2
Available in hardcover, paperback, and all eBook formats at
garycorbinwriting.com, and at your favorite local retailers.

Excerpt from

In Search of Valor

by Gary Corbin

Chapter One

The short, squat man shaded his eyes, as much to hide his face as to shield his vision against the intense late-summer sun. "Built like a fireplug, sweats like a pig," his football coach used to say. Mostly to get under his skin, but also to make an excuse for not letting him play quarterback. Never mind that he had the best arm on the team and could read defenses better than anyone. That he could outrun all but the fleetest of wide receivers and running backs, and every last defensive lineman who lumbered after him in parks-and-rec league. That he'd broken records for touchdowns and passing yardage in junior high ball. And—

Dammit! Focus! He cursed himself and shook his head to force the distracting thoughts away. Look for the girl. Ensure she's a safe distance from Ground Zero. And that she didn't return to her car and drive to where her kid played under adult supervision...for now.

He smiled. Such a great plan. If he didn't have such an important job to do at the moment, he'd pat himself on the back, literally. Something his coach would never do.

Movement caught his eye to the left. A tall, curvy woman with light brown skin and thick black curls emerged from the parking structure. Even wearing those stupid oversized sunglasses, he recognized her. The bitch. He'd never forget that face. That condescending stare, telling him he wasn't good enough for her.

She'd regret that decision. He'd make sure of it.

He watched her walk for a moment, striding toward the center of campus, checking her cell phone. Oblivious. Unsuspecting.

Perfect.

He tapped a message into the burner phone in his hand. "Move. Now." Hit Send. Then he walked in the opposite direction from her, tossing the burner into a garbage can on the way to his car, never looking back.

Chapter Two

Valorie Dawes averted her hazel eyes from the intense morning sun, an unseasonably warm mid-September day on the campus of the University of Connecticut. She'd dressed for the heat: shorts, running shoes, and a "Property of UConn Huskies" t-shirt. Nevertheless, sweat dripped down her back, soaking not only her skin, but also the sturdy backpack holding her books and laptop. She brushed damp, light-brown hair away from her face and stretched her wiry, five-foot-six frame onto her tiptoes to see over the heads of a few oncoming upperclassmen. Still no sign of her.

She checked the time on her cell phone. She'd arrived at 9:25, five minutes early, but that was fifteen minutes ago. Maybe she'd gotten the location wrong.

Val searched the busy sidewalks, crowded with students hurrying to their next air-conditioned classroom. Still no sign of Rhonda LeMieux's tall, curvy frame. Despite having moved to the mainland in her teens, Rhonda continued to operate on what she called "Jamaica time." Her habitual lateness had made her a favorite whipping post of their cantankerous professor of Criminology, Warren Hirsch. Doubts crept into Val's mind once again over her choice of a research partner for the Crim 101 term paper, the first class in her chosen major.

She scolded herself a moment later. Rhonda had mentioned when they'd first met that she had a daughter, and as a young single mother, she worried constantly about the girl's well-being. No doubt something had come up with the girl's care, and—

"Well, well, what have we here?" said a familiar male voice. She turned toward the glass doors of the Student Union entrance. A thin-shouldered, blond-haired man wearing khaki shorts, a Polo shirt, and deck shoes stared back at her behind expensive Oakley sunglasses. He uncrossed his arms and pushed off of his shaded perch, ambling toward her with a silly grin on his face. "If it isn't the famous Val Dawes, all by her lonesome."

"Hoping to stay that way, too, Robb," she said, sighing. If anyone on the UConn campus represented privilege and arrogance, it was Robbin J. McFarland. "Esquire," as he'd emphasized when introducing himself on the first day of classes a few weeks before. She'd joined the few women and most of the men in the classroom in a group eye roll, but Robb remained oblivious.

"What are you waiting for, the press to show up and interview you *again*?" he said with a sneer. "Oh, right. *That* hasn't happened yet. That must be *absolutely* killing you, am I right, *Val*?"

"My name's Valorie," she said, then smirked. "Only my friends call me Val."

"Well, *excuu-uuse* me." Robb stepped closer to her. "I wouldn't want to presume. I only wondered if you'd reconsidered my offer."

"Which one?" She eased away from him, squeamishness rising in her abdomen, and scanned the sidewalks again for Rhonda. "The four awkward invitations to go out with you, or the even more absurd notion of partnering with you on the Criminology paper?"

"Oh, so you do remember." He smiled, which made his face resemble a snake's, or a fully shaved weasel. He wiped sweat from his brow with a handkerchief and edged closer. His six-foot-plus frame towered over her. "Well, I thought we could kill two birds with one stone and discuss our project over dinner tonight." He reached out to touch her. Val batted it away, hard.

"Ow!" he said, rubbing his arm. "Geez Louise, Dawes. Such a slender little thing, but you sure pack a punch."

"Sorry," she said, not sounding sorry. "Martial-arts reflex. Happens every time someone misunderstands the word 'no.' Now, if you'll excuse me, I think I see my real research partner."

Sure enough, a tall, dark-haired woman sashayed up the walk with an enviable air of confidence. She appeared to be in her early 20s, with smooth, light-brown skin and a toothy smile. A bright yellow sundress hugged her curvy figure, and three-inch heels brought her eyes almost even with Robb's. Unlike Val and Robb, Rhonda seemed unaffected by the late August heat.

"Is this boy bothering you?" she asked in her island lilt. "You let me know, and I'll have my Jamaican boyfriends take care of him, eh?"

Robb blanched, edging away as Rhonda approached. "Miss Dawes and I were just discussing the potential of teaming up on—"

"*Ms.* Dawes and I," Rhonda said, her eyes hardening, "are already a team. No room for you, boyo."

"Oh, really?" Robb said. "And what do you bring to the table, *Miz LeMoose?*"

"De name's LeMieux. That means, de best." Her accent became more pronounced—intentional, Val guessed. Rhonda's grin widened as she went on. "And I live up to my name. Now go play on yo sailboat, or whatever you do in Martha's Vineyard." *Maw-taw's* Vin-*yawd*, to Val's ears.

"Narra-*gan*-set, please," Robb scoffed. "For Gawd's sake. Don't lump me in with the freaking Kennedys." He turned away, his nose high in the air, and strode off, muttering and shaking his head in disgust.

Val expelled a loud breath and glanced at Rhonda. "What a character," she said.

"Get used to it, my friend," Rhonda said. "These rich UConn boys think themselves to be king. And we are their pawns, no?"

"Not in my world," Val said. "So, are we a team for real, then? We have to confirm with Dr. Hirsch by Thursday afternoon."

"It would be my honor to partner with the niece of the great Valentin Dawes," Rhonda said, tugging her toward the building's entrance.

Val jerked to a stop, forcing Rhonda to halt her progress as well. "None of that, okay?" Val said. "Yeah, my uncle died a hero, and he means much more to me than anyone will ever know. But I'm not trading on his fame, and I don't expect you to, either."

Rhonda hung her head and took a deep breath. "I'm sorry,

Valorie. I meant it as a joke, only. Forgive my bad taste."

Val sighed. She envied Rhonda's unpretentious, laid-back style, one that contrasted so much from hers. She needed to learn how to be like that, somehow. "Of course. Apology accepted. So, why don't we get a cup of coffee and plan our project? I'll buy."

Rhonda grinned and extended her hand. "You got it, partner!"

***

Ten minutes later, Val and Rhonda squeezed into adjacent seats at a tiny table in the crowded Student Union café. "I insist," Val said when Rhonda protested Val paying for their coffee. "I offered. Besides, don't you have a baby to feed?"

Rhonda laughed, a sound Val found infectious and charming. "Jada is only eighteen months old. She hardly eats anything." She showed Val a photo of a curly-haired girl in a pink dress whose smile seemed a miniature carbon copy of Rhonda's.

Val's heart melted at the sight of the little girl. "That's the same age as my niece, Alison," she said. "I love that little imp so much! And what a pretty name!"

"I knew I liked you for a reason," Rhonda said, grinning. "It's Jamaican, like my father, and it means 'God's gift.' And she is, to me. In fact, she is part of the reason I was late this morning. I drove almost the whole way to her day care center before I remembered we were meeting today." She checked her watch, a cheap Rolex knock-off. "I need to pick her up at day care in a half hour, so we'd better work fast. What topic should we choose?"

They opened their laptops and discussed the approved topics listed on Professor Hirsch's faculty page. "I like 'Women in Crime: Victims and Perpetrators,' but is that too predictable for us?" Val said.

"Maybe," Rhonda said. "What about 'The Rise of Hate Crimes' or 'Police Use of Force'? Same problem?"

"Those sound great to me—I love doing statistical research," Val said. "But what about you? As a future social worker, maybe we should choose a topic focused on families. 'Intergenerational Recidivism,' maybe, or the 'The Contributions of Poverty and Class to Urban Crime.' Are those better?"

Rhonda frowned. "Those don't sound like good fits for a future policewoman."

Val waved her off. "They're all relevant. Besides, I'm not a hundred percent decided on my major," she said. "You know, I've always thought I'd become a cop, since I was a kid. But over the last few months I've had second thoughts. I might be happier doing social work, too—helping troubled families in a more constructive way, before they get swept up by crime—as victims or perpetrators.. Locking them up after they commit crimes seems kind of a negative approach."

"If you grew up like I did, you'd definitely look at cops as a negative approach," Rhonda said. "My brother spent a week in jail for a crime he didn't commit. 'Mistaken identity,' they said. Yeah, it was a mistake all right. They arrested him for being young and black."

"That's terrible," Val said. "To be honest, though, my focus would be on supporting young women and girls—victims of abuse and such." She went quiet, her heart pounding.

A silhouette filled the open doorway…the shadow of a large, overweight man, tufts of black and silver hair shining in the reflected light of the hallway. His heavy breathing filled her tiny bedroom with aromas of whiskey and sweat—

Rhonda cocked her head. "Is that motivated by personal experience, or—"

"Just something I'm interested in," Val said in a rush of words, pushing the memory out of her mind. "We'd best not get sidetracked here. You said time was short, right?"

They kicked the options around and chose the "Women in Crime" topic. "If we don't, it'll be left to the Neanderthal men like Robb McFarland," Rhonda said. "I hate to think what that paper would look like."

After dividing up the initial research responsibilities, Rhonda gulped down her coffee. "I need to get to the day care center," she said. "It's over on the west side, just off campus. Can I give you a ride somewhere?"

"I'd love that," Val said. "The surplus store is out that way, and I need a more comfortable desk chair."

"I can drop you off after we pick up Jada," Rhonda said. "It'll give us a chance to chat more about the paper."

Instead, however, their conversation shifted to more personal topics during the traffic-jammed ride across Storrs, a campus-focused village in the city of Mansfield. "Is your uncle the reason you want to go into law enforcement?" Rhonda asked.

"He definitely inspired me," Val said. "I saw how he made a difference in the community through police work. That's my real goal. I'm just not sure anymore if that's the right path for me. What about you? What motivated you to pursue social work?"

"When I first started, I wanted to make a difference in the community, like you," Rhonda said. "Now I just want to help women avoid the mistakes I made, try to keep them out of trouble." She fell silent a moment.

Val considered asking her to elaborate, then decided to steer the conversation toward less troubling topics. "You mentioned spending a year in college before you had Jada. Was that here, at UConn?"

Rhonda shook her head. "I had a full athletic scholarship to Yale," she said. "Volleyball and track. But I had to give it all up when I came back to Mansfield to take care of my mom."

"Wow!" Val said. "I have a partial scholarship—track and soccer. I didn't know women could even get a full ride for sports."

"Ah," Rhonda said. "That may be the only advantage of being a black woman in America. They assumed, correctly as it turns out, that I also had financial hardship. And finding female athletes of color with good grades is a very competitive market, it seems."

"That's awesome," Val said. "The scholarship, I mean. Will you be running track at UConn?"

Rhonda scoffed. "Not while raising a baby and working full time. Besides, it's best if I keep a low profile. Rizzo, my baby's daddy, has threatened more than once to sue for custody...or just take matters into his own hands. I haven't even told him about returning to school. I'd rather he doesn't find out."

"He threatened to take the baby from you?" Val said, her voice hoarse. "That's outrageous!"

"You don't know the half of it," Rhonda said, pulling into the parking lot of the day care center. "A few months ago he saw me out to dinner with a man. He tried to pick a fight with the guy...until my date stood up. He was six-five and built like a steamroller. Rizzo suddenly realized that he was double-parked. I haven't seen him since."

Val laughed out loud. "You have a great way of putting things, Rhonda. Hey, is it okay if I come in with you? I'd love to meet Jada."

Rhonda enveloped Val in a bone-crushing hug. "Girl, I think I already love you like a sister," she said. "Come on! Shoot, I'm already five minutes late."

They hustled inside, and a mousy, brown-haired white woman with horn-rimmed glasses greeted them. "Are you picking up, or dropping off?" she asked with a saccharine smile.

Val and Rhonda exchanged puzzled glances. "You don't honestly think I'm her daughter?" Val said.

"Name?" the brown-haired woman responded without hesitation, fingers resting on her computer keyboard.

"LeMieux. My baby's name is Jada." Rhonda showed no surprise or impatience at the receptionist's cluelessness.

The receptionist smiled again and tapped at her keyboard. Puzzlement spread over her face. "Jada? J-A-Y-D-A?"

"No 'Y'," Rhonda said, sing-song. "LeMieux is L-E—"

"Ah, here she is," the receptionist said, but her smile evaporated. "There seems to be some confusion."

"What sort of confusion?" Rhonda said, her face forming a worried frown.

"She's already been picked up," the receptionist said. "About twenty minutes ago, by her grandmother."

"Her grandmother?" Rhonda's frown deepened. "That's impossible. Could you please check again?"

The receptionist clicked a few keys, frowning, but said nothing.

Val edged closer to Rhonda. "Are you sure your mother didn't come by and get her?" she asked.

Rhonda's eyes teared up, and she glanced at Val, her lips trembling. "I'm sure," she said. "My mother died six months ago." She paused a moment to regain her composure. "Her life insurance policy is paying my tuition."

"I'm sorry," the receptionist said. "We show that Jada left under the care of an approved guardian. The woman identified herself as Karina LeMieux."

Rhonda burst into tears and slumped into a chair, moaning. "He did it. That son of a bitch took her!"

Val drew a steadying breath and turned to the receptionist. "Miss, about the woman who took Jada. Did you get a signature, an I.D., anything?"

The woman pecked at her keyboard and stared at the screen. "I wasn't here—somebody else checked Jada out," she said. "But her grandmother is in our system as an approved guardian."

"How is that possible? She's deceased, as Rhonda just told you!" Val said.

Rhonda groaned. "I never got around to updating my records here after Ma died," she said. "Oh, my God. Oh, my God!"

Val leaned across the desk, her face inches from the receptionist's. "You need to go check to make sure that little girl isn't here," she said. "*Now!*"

The receptionist froze for a moment, then disappeared through a door behind her.

Available now in print and all ebook formats from your favorite retailer.